Born in 1960, Ken began writing seriously in 2008 after joining a local writer's group. Following a short story publication, he created detective D.I Ray Keane. *Straw, Blood, and Bones* continues the popular series set in Norfolk, with ample ideas for Ray Keane's crime-solving adventures to continue. Writing is a solitary experience for Ken: just himself sitting at the computer, forming the story as the words gather pace. Yet the characters soon join on the journey, and as the storyline progresses, conversing with others brings helpful insights, inadvertently aiding the writing process.

When not crafting the next mystery, Ken lives in Norfolk with his supportive wife Jan, and two beloved poodles who enjoy accompanying him on the writing journey.

For my wife, Jan, a very special lady.

Ken Ward

STRAW, BLOOD AND BONES

AUSTIN MACAULEY PUBLISHERS™

LONDON • CAMBRIDGE • NEW YORK • SHARJAH

A CIP catalogue record for this title is available from the British Library.

ISBN 9781035845491 (Paperback)
ISBN 9781035845507 (ePub e-book)

www.austinmacauley.com

First Published 2024
Austin Macauley Publishers Ltd®
1 Canada Square
Canary Wharf
London
E14 5AA

Friends may not realise the help that is given by listening to me discussing the latest piece. Thanks go to Rib and Marina who as always come up with a good book cover, also to Carole who does the first read through to correct mistakes or change the order of things. Any mistakes left are my fault.

With this book, the support I have received from Facebook groups have made it an enjoyable project. There are too many to mention individually though I must say thank you to all at UKCBC, Crime Fiction Addict. Donna Morfett, and Sean Campbell, who all help when having doubts.

Thank you goes to Adrian and Anna at By the Book, a bookshop in Hunstanton Norfolk, who have given a lot of support with the last book *Time for Revenge* and towards this one.

Thank you to Austin Macauley for the work to get the book out, for all the people who enjoy a good story.

Chapter One

Ray had a feeling of déjà vu; it seemed that each case commenced in a similar way. Police cars are screaming along the road with the accompaniment of sirens and flashing lights. As late evening approached, the light bars on the roofs played out a pattern around the surrounding fields. He had completed several advanced driving courses over his career, though he still felt the anticipation throughout his body as he drove at speed. He felt totally in control of the car but was aware it could alter in a heartbeat; he knew of several emergency drivers who had accidents caused by something from outside entering the situation unexpectedly. As always, he was pleased to see that his team had reacted very quickly.

Within moments of reaching the A17, a road he had grown to know very well after his last case involving the murder of Steve Edwards. The noise of his unmarked car siren was drowned out by 2 marked police cars; as his car only had flashing blue lights on the front grill, he slowed down enough to allow one of the others to take over at the front of what was now a small convoy.

After 5 minutes of frantic driving, he could see the outline of the building, which was Sutton Bridge, which allowed the A17 to pass over the River Nene. Everyone was always amazed at how quickly traffic queues built up whenever the bridge was opened to allow ships through. The turning that would take them to the farm and the field they would be looking at was just before the bridge and led to an old lighthouse at the estuary with the Wash. The cars made their way along the road, and now the patterns of light took on another form as they reflected off the river that ran alongside the road. Ray was concentrating on the road but had time to glance around and was surprised by the landscape, which was a mixture of the river and fields.

To the left, he saw a tanker moored up waiting to be dealt with. He had always enjoyed the changing views of the area, and this was true again now. The area itself had a series of ports that made their way out to the North Sea. Then, on the opposite side of the road, was a mass of farmers' fields. He had a chance to see some of these as they slowed down as they approached the area they had been directed to. The fields were a mix of the remains of the crops that had been harvested, and blowing gently in the evening breeze were the tops of crops that were still waiting for the combine.

Ray followed the lead car into the yard as directed by a worker standing at the gate. During his time living in the area, he had gotten used to seeing farm machinery in the fields at all times of the day. As he parked his car, seeing the combine harvester on the edge of the field, his first thought was that the forensics team would not need any lights, as the headlights of the combine made it almost appear like daylight as it cast a glow of white lights. Getting out of the car and being this close to a combine, he realised they were beasts of machinery.

Ray walked over to a person standing by the wheel of the machine. Ray thought, well, at least if it rains, we can possibly stand inside the wheel and shelter. He took out his warrant card as he spoke.

'Good evening, sir, I am D.I. Ray Keane. I understand you have found a body.'

As expected, the reply was shaky, to say the least.

'I am Chris Small; this is my farm. I am afraid to say we have found bits of the body.'

By now, Tim and Sheila had made their way to stand by Ray. It was obvious to him that, looking around, they had been busy before events took over; he could see that there was shock registering on their faces.

'Sir, if you can give us an idea of where you made the discovery, our forensic team can start work. If you can all move away and give your details to DS Jarvis, we'll speak to you soon.'

Chris Small may have been initially shocked by the discovery, but he seemed even more put out by the thought of people trampling over his remaining crops. Even Ray was slightly surprised by his next comment.

'When can we continue the harvest?'

'At present, sir, this area is now a crime scene, until the forensic team finishes searching the area and allows us to establish what has happened.'

'Surely, it is just some bloody idiot who was possibly drunk and fell asleep in the field.'

Ray's thought was if only it could be that simple; instead, he added, 'We will know more once the doctor has had a look at things. Please just let us get on.'

The authority in his voice was enough to calm the situation. He was fully aware of the pressures a farmer was under, as his dad had owned a farm, until he was killed in an operation regarding some local drug dealers. He was also acutely aware of the need to discover exactly what the body in the field could tell them. Graham had now arrived at the scene; he was the police doctor, and Ray had a good working relationship with him. His car was closely followed by Lisa and her forensic team. When they arrived, Chris pointed out to them where a tractor and trailer were parked.

'That was where we first noticed something was wrong, though it had been a bit before that, that I felt the combine shudder as I obviously hit something unusual; it takes a time to stop the combine.'

'That is fine, thanks; we can take it from here.'

Chris pointed across the yard, 'We can take people into the house for one of you to talk to. I will wait for you to come and see me.'

Ray was polite as he answered, 'Someone will speak to you later.'

He gave no chance for any more chat by turning to face Sheila, who was waiting with the others.

'Shall we go and see what we have?'

The group, which now consisted of 8 people, started to walk across the field towards the tractor, and Ray was already taking notice of the ground to see what he could spot. The first part of the field had already been harvested, so it was easy to walk through. As they approached the tractor, they encountered crops that were almost waist high, waiting for the combine. Lisa was the first to speak.

'I know it is still bright due to the headlights, but looking at this area, we will need to set up our arc lights so we can conduct a proper search.'

'We can get the lights set up for you all as soon as we see if they are needed.'

Ray stopped speaking abruptly as he felt his foot catch on something, thinking it would be a root of some sort. He looked down to be greeted by the sight of a lower arm.

'Here is your starter for 10 Lisa.'

Ray moved to one side to allow Lisa to get a proper look at the limb.

'Well, no problem getting you a set of fingerprints.'

The "gallows humour" passed through the team quite naturally. It was a defence mechanism that allowed them to deal with the horrors they came across in their jobs. One of the forensic team called over.

'I have another piece of the jigsaw.'

It was the other arm; Ray took charge of the conversation easily.

'We need someone in the trailer to see if any pieces have passed through the combine. It will not be pretty, if they have.'

Jeff Davis, one of the forensic team members, climbed up the ladder at the rear of the trailer without saying a word. Ray had always been impressed by the people he met in this line of work, who dealt with dead bodies and sometimes gruesome sights as easily as someone who may have had an office job. He had once asked Lisa what had led her to her profession, as she was not only dealing with DNA and fibres but also dead bodies. She told him that even though she had wanted to be a doctor, she found that dead bodies did not talk back or argue as live ones did. She also enjoyed the challenge of learning the story from a body. Jeff called down from where he had been moving crops to one side.

'It looks as though we have some smaller pieces in here.'

Ray had realised that if anything had passed through the combine, it would be broken down.

'Is there anything recognisable?'

'Sorry, no, it just looks like some bones and skin.'

'Right, everyone, be careful now. The rest of the body must be nearby.'

They soon found what they were searching for, from their point of view; luckily, the majority of the body was still intact despite being a bit messy. One foot was missing which suggested this was what Jeff had discovered in the trailer. Though it was a mess, Graham said, 'I should be able to work with this; I have seen worse.'

Ray did not even want to imagine worse sights, so he pushed the thought away. With the light now fading and even allowing for the arc lights, Ray knew the best thing to do was get the body parts removed to the mortuary. This would make it easier for Graham to work on things and piece them together. They would need a more detailed search of the area to see if they could uncover any clues to help. It would be better to do this in daylight. Working out a rough area from where the body had been found, they commenced taping out the crime scene. Every senior officer had their own way of dealing with crimes. Ray had always felt it best to treat an area as a crime scene until they knew more. This way, if there was evidence to prove it would be easier. This is now the start of his investigation.

Graham was assisting the team in the removal of the body when Ray suddenly heard a voice curse.

'Don't you just hate it when that happens?'

When he looked up, he could see that, as they had picked up the body to put on a stretcher, a part of a leg had obviously been caught by the blades, and this meant that as they moved it, it had fallen off. Graham knew they were all good at their jobs but felt the need to say, 'Be careful; show some respect.'

The team acknowledged him with polite nods. Ray moved to one side and motioned his team towards him, as he said, 'There is not a lot more that can be done this evening, so we will all meet at 8 in the morning.'

He called over, 'Graham, would you be willing to do a brief examination when the body is at the morgue, really just to see if there is anything for us to work on?'

'Not a problem, Ray; I will ring you as soon as I can.'

'Thanks. I will let the farmer know we will be back in the morning and to avoid this area.'

Once Ray had explained the situation to Chris Small, who was not best pleased to hear that part of his land was off limits at least until the following lunchtime. Ray left and made his way back to King's Lynn.

'Just 1 other thing before I leave—is the person we have found likely to be 1 of your workers?'

'No, all my staff were out in the field just now and have all given details to your officer.'

Ray felt as though he still had questions to ask but could see by the body language that he had gotten as much information as he was likely to at this time of night.

'I will be back in the morning and may have some news for you. Hopefully, we will not hold up your harvest for too long.'

Chris seemed to accept that there was nothing else to say or do, and Ray took his leave. On his way back, at a more sedate pace than earlier, he made some necessary calls. The first was to Jenny, who by now was at the hotel; he told her he would get there as soon as possible. He then rang the CID office and spoke to D.I. Dave Hulme, regular night shift D.I. They had worked together for several years and on several cases. Ray had always admired how easily Dave settled into the routine of night shifts. As a young PC, he had no option but to work various shift patterns, which included nights. Being unable to adjust to sleeping properly during the day, he always found that by the end of a week of nights, he was shattered.

One benefit, as he progressed through the ranks, was having more say in his working hours, and he certainly always followed the assumption of the public, and in particular criminals, that a police officer was never off duty. Even more so now that he was settled into life with Jenny, he tried to keep regular hours, obviously a major case played a part in determining his hours. Dave was the total opposite in that he would always tell people that he slept the same during the day as at night, and with no family to think about, it suited him to do nights.

Another factor for Dave was that once he made the D.I., the only options were nights or a transfer. Dave had made it clear he had no thoughts of wanting to leave the area, and he liked the fact there was a different feel to a night shift. All PC's had been in the position of dealing with groups of drunks during the night; nowadays, Dave spent his shift in the office but was always on hand if anything major occurred. Working alongside a smaller team for the CID, they were the ones who would sort through paperwork that could always help unravel a case. Ray kept the conversation brief with Dave, just giving him the basic details and explaining they would hope to know more after the postmortem.

'So, with no need for you to inform Adam now, are you heading home?'

This brought a smile to Ray, along with many others, as they had been attending a leaving party for Superintendent Adam Church, who was taking on a new role at headquarters. The phone call alerting Ray to the body had come during the party, and Ray had seen it as a last chance to annoy Adam, which he had been doing for several years. It also just so happened that when Ray got up to leave, Adam was mid-speech. Over the years, Ray had always felt that Adam was a paperwork police officer, so this was going to be even more true in his new role. His job was to involve him in collating figures from all forces in the area. The station was still waiting to hear about an appointment for a replacement. No one even knew if Adam would be replaced, as the use of computers meant a lot more work could be done remotely. Ray ended by telling Dave he would see him in the morning, and he made his way to the hotel. When he hung up, his phone rang immediately with a call from Graham.

'Ray, I will do a full postmortem in the morning, but I already have an interesting fact for you.'

'Is this good news or not?'

'Our friend from the field had been strangled.'

'So, is that the cause of death?'

'I am not totally sure yet, but certainly I would hope for his sake he was strangled and then left in the field already dead.'

Ray found he was already starting to process the information as he pulled into the car park of the hotel.

Obviously, the hope of whoever killed the victim was that, by leaving the body in the field, any evidence would be destroyed by the Combine.

'Thanks, Graham. What time tomorrow?'

'I have a couple of pending matters first thing, so say lunchtime.'

Chapter Two

Jenny had been waiting up to see Ray when he returned from the farm, also to tease him for leaving her to suffer the rest of the party. She could tell as soon as he came in that he was at the start of a new case. The idea of staying over at the hotel was to allow them both to have a drink and, without having to be at work early, to enjoy the pleasure of a relaxing breakfast. As Ray explained the details as they knew them so far, Jenny quickly realised that breakfast would be a quick affair, then Ray would be off to the station while she made her way home, then onto her shift. After a few hours' sleep, they were saying goodbye, and Jenny could not help but feel she was missing the buzz of a busy CID office.

'I will see you when I do.'

'Yes, I will ring you later. Drive carefully, and remember, I love you.'

As always, this brought a smile to Jenny's face. Ray thought back to when he had first seen that smile, which always appeared to light up her face. He could do nothing to stop the grin spreading across his face at the same time.

'I love you too.'

Jenny gave him a kiss and got in her car. Ray had arranged with the hotel that he would collect his car later; when he needed to go out, he was going to take the opportunity to walk to the station. It was only a short walk through the town; it was something he did miss, as he had always tried to walk to work, though this had stopped once they had moved into the new house. The main reason for moving was to allow Jenny to transfer due to how Adam felt about relationships at work. Several of his colleagues had said how old-fashioned this was, but neither of them wanted to cause problems.

Both of them were very happy in the house, and despite Jenny still finding her feet in a new CID team, they would agree it was a good move. With the help of her parents, they decorated where needed and even spent some time arranging the small garden. Fortunately, the weather had played its part, and Ray found that as much as he enjoyed the garden space to work in, he had enjoyed several evenings sat with a drink, making the most of the surroundings. His dad had run the farm, but it was mainly cattle, and Ray had not thought about planting things, but talking to Jenny and her dad, he had plans for planting vegetables they would be able to enjoy the following year.

With the help of Jenny, he was pleased that, despite several high-profile cases that had been mentally draining, he felt that he had got the balance right between work and home. His memories since he joined the force and discovered it was the job he wanted to do involved him being totally focused on his career. Everyone who had worked with him over the years said that his nickname of "mustard" in being "as Keane as" was well suited. Once a case started, he would not be satisfied until it reached a conclusion. He had found it hard to accept that, even though the last case of the murder of a former colleague was not satisfactory, the outcome did have a feeling of karma about it. He smiled to himself as he thought about how much of this was down to Jenny; she had pointed out early in their relationship that, as much as she admired his work ethic, if they were to enjoy a life together, they had to take control of it rather than it controlling them. It now meant that he was as happy at work as he was at home.

'Ray realised that he was nearly at work, so he switched into officer mode and started by trying to put what they knew so far in order. He knew the morning briefing would be very basic, and they would need to wait to hear more from Graham after the P.M. also hopefully Lisa would have more information to pass on once they had been back to the farm. As he approached the steps at the front of the station, his mobile rang. Ray answered as he answered all the calls and said.'

'D.I. Keane's speaking.'

It was Chris Small, who with no opening conversation asked, 'Inspector, can I start work this morning?'

Ray felt himself inhale a deep breath before answering, 'Good morning. I have no problem with you working, but the area we cordoned off last night needs to be avoided.'

He knew by the sigh that this was not the answer Chris wanted, but until they knew a lot more, Ray was treating the area as a crime scene. If nothing else, it was the site of a vicious assault. He continued the conversation.

'The forensic team will be there again this morning to continue their work. Hopefully, they will find everything they need as quickly as possible, though we need to be sure it has been searched thoroughly.'

Chris accepted the explanation, even though it was begrudgingly. Ray ended the call by telling Chris he would be in contact later that day. The time on the phone meant that when Ray hung up, he was already in the CID office. He had always felt lucky that the size of the building that was home to King's Lynn police meant that the CID had a spacious area to work in. Ray had a separate office at the far end of the room, and despite there being a heavy oak door, it was rarely closed. There had been murmurs in the past that this was so he could keep an eye on what work was being done; everyone who worked in the team knew it was more to allow him to be in touch with the rest of the office.

DS Tim Jarvis was already sitting at his computer, and Ray could see that they had already made a start on an information board for the case. Currently, there were just a couple of pictures on it; one showed the scene at the farm last night; the other, a more gruesome image, was of the remains of the body as they had discovered it. If, as they all felt, this was to be a murder inquiry, the board would soon fill in a timeline of events. In the past, it was from an officer looking through the information on the board that could lead to a breakthrough in a case. Ray had been impressed by Tim and his work on previous cases; also, from the moment he joined the team, he showed potential and the signs he wanted to progress.

He had managed to study for and pass his sergeant exam while working on a case and was always looking to attend courses as work allowed. It did seem to be the case that every time he was studying or due to attend a meeting, a major case broke. Tim took it all in his stride, and his work was noticed and commented on by other superior officers. Ray knew that Tim had made inquiries about inspector exams, and despite meaning the possibility of him moving on, Ray would always encourage him. By the time Ray had finished saying good morning, the other members of the team were at their desks.

The CID team was relatively small, and as the case progressed, other uniformed officers would be seconded to help out. Ray was always trying his best to increase his core team by watching how these extra officers worked during a case. This had been the cause of many conversations with Adam Church, the superintendent, who had just moved to a new role at headquarters. He had always felt it was more important to have uniform officers on the streets; his favourite point to make to Ray was that each time he took another uniform into CID, it meant the force was recruiting and paying for another uniform. Ray had learned over the years how to put his point across, usually by telling Adam that with a good CID team, the clear-up rate on cases would improve. This figure was something Adam always liked to be able to report to his superiors, even being able to make it sound like the success of a conviction was partly down to him.

Ray moved to the front of the room, and due to it being the first full day of an investigation, he did not need to wait for any chatter to subside before speaking.

'Good morning, everyone; you are all up to date with events from last night, I presume.'

To show how comfortable Tim Jarvis was with the team, he spoke up, 'Do you mean how successful the superintendent's party was, sir.'

Ray allowed the laughter to last a few moments, 'Apart from that, Tim, you know full well what I meant. We have, at the moment, a suspicious death, to say the least. I expect us to know more about what we are dealing with after the postmortem.'

He was fully aware that the day's work would involve a lot of information gathering, as the start of piecing together any case there may be. The phone call from Graham the previous evening to inform him that the victim had been strangled suggested that the death was not accidental; he had his fingers crossed that they would get more from the P.M. The rest of the briefing was straightforward, as all the team members were used to the things required in the early stages of an investigation. Ray finished up by adding, 'I will make my way over to the farm this morning, then attend the postmortem. We will reconvene here at 17.00 hours.'

Ray left them all to get started on the initial items needed and took the walk back to the hotel to collect his car. The journey to the farm was at a much more sedate pace than the previous evening, but this did give him a chance to enjoy the scenery of the area as he left the town centre.

His dad had owned a farm for as long as Ray could remember; the farm was now run by his brother after the death of his dad. The death of his dad was never far from his mind, due to the fact that his dad had been killed in a shootout involving a local drug gang. An investigation into the death had shown several things had been mismanaged by the team investigating the drug gang. Even though he found the events influenced his feelings when dealing with drug-related crime, he always did his best to remain objective. He soon learned early in his career that usually any arrests or convictions would always be small fry. The chances of getting to the bigger players were always remote. As he drove, he had no idea how these feelings would be pushed to the limit over the next few weeks.

For now, he put the memories of his dad to the back of his mind and took a moment while in a queue of traffic to look around. Once onto the A17, it became very rural, and fields stretched away on both sides of the road. There had been a lot of building work over the recent years in both the town and surrounding villages, the biggest of which had been the paper processing plant on the edge of the river. Houses seemed to spring up out of nowhere with regularity. He was pleased to see that some of the fields here had remained the same for years. He spotted several types of birds, and even though he could not identify them all, he did enjoy watching them in flight. As he reached the junction for the farm, he admired the old swing bridge across the river.

This was the cause of many holdups for traffic, but despite many grumblings from road users, it remained the same as always. Once alongside the river, the scene changed again with the sight of a busy port. A large container ship was in the dock, loaded with grain that would be taken abroad. Along the edge of the river, a herd of cattle were grazing; it seemed as though if they moved too far down, they would end up in the water.

As he pulled into the farm, 2 tractors came out pulling fully loaded trailers; his first thought was that hopefully this meant Chris Small would be happy, as it appeared, that he had been able to continue working. Ray parked beside a car he recognised as being Lisa from forensics, and he could see the white-suited forms making their way slowly across an area of the field. Upon getting out of his car, he went through the performance of putting on an oversuit and shoe coverings before making any attempt to approach the others. He knew it was all necessary but still thought back to his early days, when officers would walk into a crime scene with no thought about contaminating the area. Lisa looked up and waved as he made his way across the furrows of the ploughed field. It made walking feel very awkward.

'Morning Lisa, found anything useful to help us?'

'Morning Ray, not yet. I have a feeling that the bulk of our finds were last night. Which I am sure the farmer will be glad to hear as we get out of his way.'

She went on to explain that the team had come across some small items, though they felt that the majority of them were just rubbish, either blown into the field or, more likely, thrown there by passing vehicles. Despite this, all of it would have been checked at the lab before being discounted. She did have one thing to say, which brought some small hope, 'We did find 2 cigarette butts, which could give us DNA to match with. I have already spoken to the farmer, and none of his workers' smoke.'

Even allowing for the fact they could have come from anywhere at this early stage in an investigation was a positive point.

'I will leave you to get on then. Can you just let me know if anything else helpful comes up by this afternoon?'

Before Lisa had a chance to get irritated, he added, 'If that is possible, thanks.'

Lisa looked up at him and rolled her eyes, and he quickly realised this was a good moment to leave her to get on. As he walked away, he saw Chris Small walking towards him, 'Morning, Mr Small, I was now on my way to find you.'

'Good, do you have any news for me?'

'As I am sure you are aware, sir; it is very early days, and I would think it will be a while before we have anything useful.'

'That is a shame; I have already had a reporter from the local paper here asking questions about what happened.'

Ray was always amazed at how quickly the news spread and when reporters all wanted their story.

'I hope you did not feel the need to tell them too much. We will be giving a press conference later.'

'What could I tell them, as it appears nobody knows very much, do they?'

'I can fully understand the inconvenience of all this; we just need some time to start piecing things together.'

Ray could see how frustrated Chris was and knew he had to do his best to keep him happy to allow them to work well. Despite knowing the work load he had, Ray suggested a coffee and chat if Chris had the time. As they made their way into exactly the room Ray would have expected, the farm kitchen, there was a pot of soup bubbling away on the stove. Once coffee had been made, a tin of cakes appeared on the table. Ray could not help but be transported back in time to his parent's kitchen on the farm. As he thought about it, he realised how modern this room was, but the working idea of a busy farm and staff being fed and watered remained etched in his memory.

'This takes me back to my childhood.'

Ray went on to explain to Chris how his parents had run a farm on the other side of King's Lynn and that his brother was now in charge.

'I thought your surname was familiar when you introduced yourself last night. I don't know your family well, but I do know of the farm.'

Chris told Ray how long the farm had been in his family and how things had changed. It could have sounded like a publicity broadcast about how farming had suffered over the years, but Chris spoke sensibly. Ray quickly realised how much had changed since his time helping on the farm, and some of the problem was that things had changed quickly and over a short period of time. As they talked, Ray could understand why Chris wanted to constantly know when he would be able to start working in the field again. He said, 'I have 2 tractor drivers who I employ when needed. At the moment, I would guarantee they will be working for the next 3 weeks. I am liable for their wages at present, but if I know how long it will be, they could go elsewhere. This would help me out.'

Ray knew how important finances were in the farming industry.

'I hope that the forensic team will be finished by the end of today.'

'That is good news. I should have already asked you; do you have any idea who the victim is?'

Ray was still on his guard as to how much information to give people, as it was very easy for rumours to start, so even though he was relaxed in the environment, he kept his answer vague, 'Not yet, no, the postmortem is later today. It might help us a bit.'

As they sat and talked, Ray took the opportunity to get some background from Chris on the local farms in the area. Also, if he knew how many of them would be employing foreign labour. He was aware that recently there had been a problem with travel restrictions in place due to the global pandemic that had broken out.

'I personally don't use much outside labour. I have 4 or 5 local people who are friends as well; they are happy to work for me as I need them to. It works well for us. You will find some of the others, especially the big vegetable growers, use them more when harvesting.'

The statement convinced Ray that the body had been brought to the field and dumped. He finished his coffee and added, 'Thank you for the coffee and chat. I will let you know more as soon as I can.'

After leaving the house and telling Lisa he would speak to her later, he left the farm to make the journey to the far side of King's Lynn and the mortuary for the postmortem.

Chapter Three

As Ray manoeuvred the car into the 1 available parking bay at the mortuary, his phone rang. He glanced at the screen and saw that the caller was DS Tim Jarvis. He hoped that as they were aware, he was attending the postmortem and that Tim's ringing meant he had some news to pass on. He did, though the news took Ray by surprise.

'Hello boss, just wanted to let you know that our new superintendent is arriving this afternoon.'

This was totally out of the blue, as the rumour mill, since it had become general knowledge that Adam was moving on, had been going full pelt; most of the gossip had been that, as part of cost cutting, the force was not looking to replace Adam.

'That is totally against what we had thought, is it not?'

'It seems to have taken everyone by surprise, sir. I just thought I would let you know to allow you to try and plan things so you can be here.'

'Thanks, Tim; I should be there, though I am not going to rush Graham. I think we are going to need as much help as possible on this one.'

Ray ended the call with mixed feelings, even though over the years he had had plenty of disagreements with Adam; he certainly always felt it was a case of better the devil, you know. His own work ethic meant he would carry on working as he always did and would deal with the new superintendent with respect; long gone were his days of trying to impress senior officers.

He entered the nondescript door that led to the mortuary and made his way along the corridor. He was as amazed now, after countless visits, as he was the first time, that even though this department was in the older section of the hospital, the walls and corridor seemed to sparkle under the lights. It also felt very airy. He pushed open the double doors to the main area and, at the same time, took a deep inhalation of breath as the familiar smells assaulted his nostrils. Over the years, he heard many officers giving advice to young officers on how to combat the smell at a postmortem; he had never found any of these working for him, so he took a deep breath upon entering and then attempted to control his breathing. The glare of lights on white tiles and stainless steel was even brighter here. Graham was alongside his assistant Dennis, and they were both kitted out in their usual green scrubs.

'Hello gentlemen, I hope you can give me some good news.'

Dennis looked across the table, 'He is definitely dead if that helps.'

'Thank you, Dennis, helpful as always.'

Ray found he could not help the laugh that followed; they all knew how a sense of humour kept them sane due to the sights they saw.

'That will do, Dennis. I can tell you, Ray, that the victim died before he met with the combine.'

'That is a relief for any family member to know once we locate them.'

The situation regarding identity was not going to be helped by the fact that the body was naked; along with any clothing, any form of ID had also been removed. Ray knew this could make it a long process to get the victim's name. Graham made his way around the body on the table, explaining to Ray as he went about the findings.

'On examining the body, he has been strangled, and looking at the ligature marks and the depth of them, this was undoubtedly the cause of death.'

Graham carried on explaining that, given the lack of blood at the scene, it was obvious the victim had been killed elsewhere and the body dumped after death. Graham added, 'We have taken a set of fingerprints and sent them away for comparison; if you get lucky and he has any sort of criminal record, it will identify the victim.'

When Ray knew he had all the information he was going to get for now, he said his goodbyes and left to make his way back to the station, feeling some apprehension at meeting the new superintendent. As he was on the way out the door, Graham added 1 more piece to the puzzle, 'I did, as a matter of course, send blood samples to toxicology; it will be a slow process, but you will eventually find out if there was alcohol or drugs in his system.'

Ray acknowledged this with a nod to his head, and he could not help but think about how easily his role was made due to everyone else involved in the chain knowing exactly what was needed. He arrived back at the station and was immediately struck by the noise and hubbub in the front office; he took a guess that the new arrival was in the building.

He spoke to Jim, the desk sergeant, who was a constant at the station and had been for several years even before Ray arrived.

'I take it our new arrival is here, Jim?'

Jim looked up from his paperwork and smirked as he passed the news on; everyone in the station knew how Ray and Adam had had their run-ins.

'She certainly is.'

Jim was well aware that he only needed these 3 words to convey his feelings to anyone who listened. Despite being an excellent desk sergeant, always keeping everyone informed, and running a very organised front office, Jim was old-school and had not really moved with the times. The thought of a female superintendent would seem totally out of place. If you asked some of the other officers, they would have said that was why he was still only a desk sergeant. Ray was not inclined to get into a conversation in a public office about these issues, so at the same time as letting Jim know he had heard the comment, he continued walking through the door and made his way upstairs.

He was not surprised to hear the noise levels were just as high in the different offices as he walked past. He knew it would be planned very cleverly for the arrival of the new superintendent to coincide with the changeover of shifts between morning and afternoon. This automatically meant that a maximum number of staff would get to meet the new person. It was not an event that had happened very often during his career, as when working his way up the ranks, he had found himself in stations where the staff levels were very stable. He was aware of the format of how the rest of the day would pan out. The new arrivals would make their way round the rooms, meeting the different officers in charge of each section. Despite wanting to get on with things, he decided the best course of action was to be in his office and available when required. He made his way across the CID room and spoke as he walked.

'Right, come on, everyone; I am sure you have work to do.'

The comment was enough to quieten the room down as he went and sat behind his desk. This was not a position he was totally at ease with. As usual, the first thing he noticed was the pile of paperwork that required his attention. As he started to move some of the papers across his desk and sign some as needed, DS Sheila Carr came to the doorway.

'I presume you have heard the news, sir.'

'Yes, Jim took great delight in telling me. Have you seen anything of her yet?'

Despite the nature of the comment, Ray tried to keep his tone natural, 'Not yet, no. I do know the chief constable is with her, so, take it, he will be making the introductions.'

Ray was always pleased when he could find an excuse to avoid paperwork. He did not have to wait long before he could tell by the murmurs from the office that there was a visitor. He had never been one for standing on ceremony, so rather than wait for the group to make their way to his office, he went out to meet them along with the others. As he appeared at the doorway, the chief constable looked his way.

'Detective Inspector Ray Keane, please meet Superintendent Angela Johnson. She has joined us from Leeds.'

'Very pleased to meet you. This is our CID team; it may be smaller than you are used to.'

'Thank you, D.I. Keane; it is a pleasure to meet you. I am sure I will get to know you and the team better over the next few days. I have heard good things about the team.'

The superintendent had the attention of everyone, as she explained that she would officially be in place in 2 days' time. Her plan was to arrange a meeting with him so he could bring her up to speed with any ongoing cases. With this said, herself and the chief constable swiftly said their goodbyes and left the room the same way they had entered. Ray stood at the front of the room for a few moments and allowed the chatter of them all giving opinions on their visitor to finish, by clearing his throat he soon had the attention of them all.

'Okay, you will all have a chance to chat later. For now, we have work to do. I am sure you would all like it if I could give a positive report in 2 days' time to our superintendent.'

He looked around at the team, and his first action was to welcome a new member. It was one of the last things Adam had agreed to before leaving; this was that W.PC Jill Addy was to be made up of a Detective Constable and join the CID. Ray had pushed for this for a while now, as he had been impressed by her work on a previous case known as Tower of Silence. Tim made sure Jill felt welcome by commenting, 'You don't need to wear those clothes again.'

This brought the usual laughter before Sheila added, 'I am hoping, Tim, that you mean she can wear her own clothes rather than a uniform.'

Jill blushed slightly before answering, 'I will make a note for tomorrow.'

'Okay, that will do. Right, up to date news on our victim, we are currently waiting to see if his fingerprints are in the system. The postmortem confirmed he had been strangled elsewhere and then moved to the field.'

'Did they take fingerprints, or just send the arm along?'

'Tim, you have been spending too much time with Dennis; I think you are developing a mortuary sense of humour.'

'Sorry sir, I have started to contact local farms to see if anyone is missing a worker.'

'Okay, Tim, I know it is obvious, but let's run some checks on missing persons in general. We should not assume at the moment that just because he was found in a farmer's field, that it was his line of work.'

This brought a collective groan, as missing persons was always a bit of a nightmare. It could be a couple of people reported in the area or a couple of hundred.

'All of you know how things are going to go initially, once we get the ID we need a picture of anything our victim had been doing. While we wait to get there, I want you to ask around if anyone is missing someone or are there rumours of trouble that could have led us to the field.'

Jill spoke up, which pleased Ray that she felt confident enough to be heard.

'Can I ask, sir, what are your initial thoughts?'

Ray decided to make the most of the question by replying, 'That is good to hear, Jill, that somebody is interested in my opinion.'

This got the response he had expected of some subtle groans and laughter, as he knew all his team would always respect his point of view.

'I think that our victim got himself mixed up in something bigger than he could handle. The way the body has been stripped before being dumped so we cannot identify them quickly. And the fact that whoever was hoping for the body to be demolished by the combine suggests a particularly nasty piece of work.'

This comment seemed to flick a switch in Tim, who quickly added, 'Was there not a case in Lincoln a couple of years back where some drug dealers dumped the bodies of people who upset them? The 3 victims were all naked.'

Ray was suitably impressed, as he also now remembered the case; it had been brought to their attention when a case of their own had seen a body turn up in the river that ran through the centre of Lincoln. It transpired that there was no connection, but it showed that Tim took notice of things.

'You are quite right, it could be worth a phone call or a check through the computer, to see the outcome, if any, of that case. They can provide us with help as we move forward.'

Ray looked up and saw that several of the team were working on their computers to see what could be found. The incident board that had been set up in the corner of the room was still fairly bare. This would be added to frequently over the coming days, and things would stay a mystery for now until the results from the tests Graham had done were back. He coughed to get the attention before saying, 'Right, give it another hour today, then all be here for a briefing at 8am tomorrow.'

Ray went back to his desk and thought he would spend his time on the mountain of papers, and when he checked, there were several emails that had arrived while he had been talking. He knew the whole team would make the most of finishing at a reasonable time. As the case gathered pace, the working days would get longer. He had always found that the adrenalin kicked in to allow you to work the hours involved, and you also never knew what was going to turn up.

Chapter Four

While the police were hoping for information that would start to build up a picture of their victim. There were several people sitting at a table in the middle of a room; that was their living accommodation. These 4 people, 3 men and 1 woman, were sitting with coffee in their hands, all thinking the same thing, that Sergei Romanov should have sat with them. It had now been 2 days since any of them had seen him. The group of 5 had always thought of themselves as a team. They had been travelling to the UK to work for the last 4 years from their homes in Latvia. The work was to harvest vegetables for the winter.

The 3 men were only slightly concerned. Sergei had been known to go off in the past; usually it would only be for a few hours, and he always came back with a smile on his face and some alcohol for them all. The lone female was more concerned as she realised the length of time he had not been around was totally out of character. Maria Shon was also the only one of them who was aware of the things Sergei got up to. She knew he had used drugs in the past, though he soon worked out that he could make some money from selling them. The 5 of them had been working together for several years in and around their home villages. Then the opportunity came about to travel to a farm just outside Long Sutton and spend 3 months harvesting different vegetable crops.

The money they earned meant a great deal to their families left at home. It suited them to spend a few months of the year working hard, then have time to be at home in Latvia. The farmer was very happy with their work and always asked them back the following year. A lot of the work was always described as backbreaking; despite the use of modern machinery, the days were spent with the majority of the time bent down. They often spent the shift crouched under a machine while cutting crops; the farm they worked on was called Long Bank Farm. They soon realised on their first visit that they would be looked after and not exploited like so many others were.

For a lot of people, the living accommodation would have been classed as very basic; for the team of workers it was a step up from what a lot of immigrant workers, were used to as it was warm and dry. The 5 of them had been friends in Latvia for several years and had all met while working on local farms. Maria and Alekesji lived in neighbouring houses and had been friends since childhood. They met with Sergei and Vetaujis on a farm while harvesting 6 years earlier. The following year, they were joined by Andris, who lived over the border in Estonia.

They found that they formed easy and instant friendships; meeting up each year to work, even though she never expected it, the lads became very protective of Maria. During his first year of working at Long Bank Farm, Andris showed interest in being more than friends with Maria. She made it clear from the beginning that this was not something she wanted; he accepted this, and they all remained friends. It was not long before they all knew Maria was capable of looking after herself, and she proved this on one occasion when a local lad in the pub they frequented tried pushing his luck too far one evening. He realised his mistake as he picked himself up from behind a table while hearing laughter from the rest of the patrons. Because of the way she handled herself when speaking, even the lad himself accepted that he had been in the wrong.

The houses and farms they had worked on in Latvia were all in poor regions of the country; the work was hard, and the pay was very poor. When Sergei heard about the opportunity to work in the UK as well as live there for a while, it was appreciated. The money they would be able to save would also help their families immensely when they returned home. They had to deal with a certain amount of prejudice, especially in their 1st year, but by the time they had been working for a month and with the farmer letting others know how pleased he was with them, they were soon accepted. Other farmers were also asking if they knew of any friends from home that might like the work. Now, each year they return, they are greeted as friends.

As they sat around the table, Maria was the first to voice her concerns, 'So, where do you all think Serg has got to?'

Andris answered, sounding quite blasé, 'You know Serg, he most probably met a local girl and has enjoyed himself a bit too much.'

Vitaujis added, 'He will walk back in soon, especially as he will want his wages.'

As long as Maria knew they were most probably right, she was not convinced.

'Do you think we should tell the boss or even the police?'

Very quickly, Alekesji replied, 'We do not want to get the authorities involved; do not be silly.'

Maria was taken aback by his response, but she also understood what he meant. Despite them all knowing that the UK police were totally different from home, and even with nothing to fear, it was difficult to think of any dealings with the authorities due to some of the atrocities they had come across in their homeland.

'I know how we all feel, but this is so unusual for him. I am just worried.'

Others could see how she was feeling, so Andris decided he needed to settle things down.

'Ok then, how about if he is not here for work in the morning? We voice our concerns to Jack.'

Jack was the owner of the farm, and they got on well with him and his family.

'That sounds like a good idea. He can then decide if he wants to report it. It saves us from being directly involved.'

Vitaujis felt this was the best and felt happier once the others agreed. Having reached an agreement, they all decided it was time to head for their rooms, as it would be the usual early start in the morning. They had been working solidly for nearly 3 months and knew they were now approaching the end of the harvest. As they went their separate ways, Maria could not shake off the feeling that things were not right. As she sat on the bed, she shivered with the thought that there was no good news to come.

48 hours earlier, everyone had been laughing and joking as soon as they knew they would be heading home to their families. Despite the major problems of a global pandemic, which at one stage had threatened to stop them from

travelling, and the restrictions that had led to them having to comply with them, this had been a good harvest time. Jack was relieved to learn he could have his usual workers on site. The weather had been reasonable, and everyone had been happy with the crops that had been grown. The day's work had finished, and even though they were tired, they all agreed that a meal and a drink at the local pub, The Red Eagle, would be a good idea, especially as they were still allowed to, not knowing if this would still be the situation before they left.

The evening had been really enjoyable, until Sergei met up with some of the local lads he had gotten to know over the years. The landlord of the pub had needed to point out to them all that he could not serve them just drinks due to the restrictions; this was met with some arguing as the group all felt they were ok living in a rural situation. The landlord was not prepared to take any risks and asked them all to leave. Once outside the pub, the greetings with the others were all very friendly; along with his work colleagues, everyone called him Serg. The fact that he, in particular, had been accepted into the group of locals gave Serg a certain arrogance. Others soon accepted that this was how he was, especially when he always returned to the hut with drinks. As they left the pub, they knew it would be difficult to get Serg to agree that the evening was finished; already, he had a bottle of drink in his hand that someone had passed to him.

'Are you coming, Serg?'

'No, not yet. Stay and we can carry on the party outside.'

'Come on, you know we have work tomorrow.'

As Maria finished speaking, she saw a flash of anger cross his face, then he stopped himself and just said, 'You lot go; I will see you later.'

'Come on, Maria; he will follow as always.'

None of them were aware that this would be the last time they would see him alive. As they made the short walk back from the pub to the hut, Maria voiced her concern, 'Do you think we should go back for Serg?'

'Come on, Maria, you are not his mother. He is a big boy and can do as he wants.'

Alekesji then added, 'It will be him with the headache in the morning, so stop worrying.'

While this conversation was taking place, Serg was enjoying himself as more bottles of drinks were handed around. It would have been a lot safer if he had only taken the time to check his surroundings; he knew all the people he was drinking with but had taken no notice of the 2 men off to one side who were just watching.

Sergei had enjoyed his time working in England, especially starting 2 years ago, when he made friends with some locals who supplied drugs that he was happy to use. It got even better from his point of view when he was invited to join them in selling the drugs. He made a point of keeping Maria out of the loop, or so he thought. The other guys working alongside him were happy to part with some of their wages and enjoy the high feeling they got; in fact, they all told him that on particularly heavy workdays, it made it seem easier. As seemed to be the case a lot of the time, drugs were involved in anything; they saw no wrong in partaking and no thought of any health problems it could lead to.

Serg was happy with how things were going; he was making a bit of extra money from the price he was selling it for. Unfortunately, as seemed to always happen, arrogance and then greed took control. By talking to the people who were happy to supply him, he was able to get more drugs along with selling to his mates; he started to sell to other workers on other farms as well as some of the locals. It never occurred to him that he was starting to tread on other toes. Despite doing all he could and thinking he had kept Maria out of things, she soon realised something was going on. She tried talking to him about it one day, though he just brushed her concerns away, telling her, 'It is none of your business.'

The situation he was about to find himself in could have been avoided if only he had listened to her. All of these thoughts were far from his mind, as one of the others said, 'So Serg, have you got any stuff for us?'

Even though he thought they were away from anyone, he still lowered his voice as he replied.

'Yes, I have; you know how it works. If you show me that you have the cash, I will then let you have the stuff for your fun to begin.'

'Sorry, Serg, I just could do with some.'

'Yes; I know, but we don't want to ruin things, do we?'

Part of the problems that were about to land on Serg were down to the fact that he had no idea where the drugs came from. He had not given any thought to the fact that he was a small cog in a chain. Also, the person he handed money to, was another small cog. The news that he was not only using but selling the stuff to had filtered down the chain until it reached a thug called Darren Plant. Even though he was just a thug, you would never know it by looking at him. He was always very smartly dressed, and as the old saying went, he never got his hands dirty.

Darren had always managed to stay out of line with any police investigations, despite his name being noted numerous times in interviews. The 2 men, who were currently watching proceedings, were happy to bide their time as Serg and the others were standing at the rear of an old car forecourt when no one noticed that the 2 men had crossed the road and gone separately to the sides of the building. The 2 of them kept very much in the shadows. They watched as Serg handed over several packets, then, in return, took hold of a large amount of cash. It was once this had happened that the men let themselves be known.

The locals, who now had the drugs, ran off in several directions, though they didn't need to worry as no one was interested in them. As Serg made his move to run, he saw the man in front of him; it was only as he turned that he realised there was another person waiting for him. Before he knew what was happening, he had been grabbed, and his arms were pinned to his side in a vice-like grip. His survival instinct kicked in quickly, and he managed a few words.

'Look, I don't know who you are, but there is money...'

This was as far as he got, as a fist hit hard into his stomach as he doubled over in agony and felt himself dragged and thrown into the back of a van. 1 of the men got in with him and roughly pinned him to the floor by putting both his feet on Serg's chest. The other person had obviously gotten in front as the van lurched forward. By now, Serg was scared; nothing had been said by either of his attackers, and that just increased his anxiety. He had no way of knowing where they were going or how long they would drive. Suddenly the van stopped, and the person with his feet on Serg just released the pressure slightly. Instinct kicked back in, and Serg saw a chink of opportunity. He pushed himself to one side and scrabbled towards the doors. The thug in the van with him reacted quickly. Serg felt rather than saw 2 hands grab him around the throat; it didn't take long for him to realise this was his last moment alive. Slowly, the pressure on his neck increased, and he felt dizzy. He didn't feel much more, and slowly, life drained away as he urinated, lying on the floor of the van. As his body went limp, slowly the hands were released from around his throat, just as the driver opened the doors.

'Is he dead?'

'Yes. Now help me get his clothes off, then we can dump the body.'

Both men, who were not adverse to using violence to keep their bosses happy, were surprised at how difficult it was to undress a dead body. One of them had been killed before, but this involved a knife and leaving the body where it fell. The other one had never been near a dead person. Even though it was obvious no one was around to hear anything, conversation was kept to a minimum, and neither used the other's name. Giving the driver a moment to gather himself, the killer added abruptly, 'Come on, get a move on. We need to get this dealt with.'

Showing how violent people's minds worked, it had been the idea of their boss that once they had killed Sergei, he was to be stripped and placed in a field of corn, which would soon be harvested. As they finished getting the clothes off, the younger one went a shade of green as he realised what was going to happen to the body next. He decided it would be a good idea not to say anything yet. As they made their way along a track to a field, as they had been directed to, he found the courage to speak, 'Can't we just dump him in the river? No one needs to know.'

The killer, who was now driving, looked across with a sadistic grin as he replied, 'Good idea. I'll let you explain that one to the boss when someone drags a body out of the water.'

He was quick enough to know he would find himself in a similar position to the body in the back of the van, so he gritted his teeth and said no more. The driver pulled the van into a lane off the road by a small gate. Their next problem, they saw, was how to get the body into the field before anyone saw them. The one benefit was that, despite there being several farms around, neighbours were at a good distance from each other. They moved to the rear doors and felt as it was now dark; they were happy that they would not be seen. As they pulled at the legs of Sergei, they both realised the meaning of the expression, a dead weight.

It was too soon for rigor mortis to have set in, but there was no give in the body. The killer was well-built from a lot of time spent in the gym and taking all sorts of steroids and other drugs, so he took charge, and between them they manoeuvred the lifeless body to the lip of the door. Their instructions of what was to happen that night had been very clear, that as they came to dump the body, they were to get it into the field as far as possible but without disturbing the crops too much.

Fortunately for them both, farmers in the area were used to people walking either by themselves or even with dogs across fields, ignoring the fact that crops were growing. They decided luck was on their side as they carried on and, at one stage, dragged the body into the field. Knowing that harvesting could carry on into the night, it was hoped no one would notice the disturbance. They quickly made their way back to the van and were driving away as they saw the headlights of the combine come onto the field. Chris Small, who was sitting in the cab of the harvester high up, saw the van and cursed, but as it was already pulling away, down the road, he knew he would not find out who it was.

Chapter Five

Ray was not surprised to see that he walked into a full CID room at 7.30 the next morning to find everybody was already looking at computer screens, either to check for responses to emails from the previous day or to see if any news added to the police system overnight was of any use. When Ray started in the force, the idea of health and safety amounted to a sergeant checking that all the officers on his shift were wearing the appropriate clothing. Slowly over the years, things had built up to the point where he now felt there was a fine line between sensible precautions and red tape getting out of hand. As he progressed through the ranks and became more aware of his role in ensuring a duty of care for his team, he made a conscious effort to always check that things were right.

In recent years, this had varied from little things, such as checking that office chairs were fit for purpose, and now, in the modern world, it also involved checking how much time a person spent looking at a computer screen. He did his best by rotating the team so that no one member spent all day at their desk. He knew that it was progress to have everything available on a computer, but he kept in mind that even after a day's work had finished, looking at a screen was not. It could be that someone was relaxing by surfing the internet or, as he now found, just reading a book. A few years ago, he could not imagine not holding a paperback to read and relax, but now he had a whole library of books to read, all stored on his iPad. As with a lot of things that had changed in his life recently. It took some time to accept the way things moved on, but it was so much more convenient to have the books at the touch of a screen.

He had not noticed at first that Sheila was not in the office, though she followed him in after a few moments with tea and coffee for them all. Again, he was impressed by how small actions like this helped keep morale good for them all.

Ray acknowledged some of the team on their way to his office; they all knew and respected his morning routine. There would be a briefing during an ongoing case, but he would always make a point of first checking his in-tray, which is never, ever empty. This was due to a combination of the number of papers that crossed his desk and also his dislike of dealing with paperwork, which he sometimes felt was nothing short of a tick-box exercise by the powers above. Emails would be scanned and the majority answered later. Ray liked the fact that, having spent a lot of time working with the same doctors and forensics, they all knew he preferred reports initially on paper. The top envelope contained a quick summary report from Graham. As Ray glanced through it, he was pleased to read that they had a positive start to the day. He made a cursory glance at the rest of his paper mountain, which seemed to breed overnight, and decided it could wait. He made his way out to brief the team and get the day underway.

'Good morning, all. I hope you all had a good rest last night, as I think this case will start to pick up pace from now on.'

Ray brought them all up to speed on the results from yesterday and then gave them a crumb of positive news.

'Graham has let me know that early signs from a toxicology test show our victim had used drugs. So start putting the word out and listen for any information you get regarding drugs on our patch.'

Even the newer members of the team knew how Ray felt about drugs.

Several years ago, his father was fatally injured by a stray bullet from a passenger in a car that had been cornered by the drug squad. The driver had decided to try to get away by crossing his father's field. The wrong place and the wrong time come to mind.

The audible increase in noise in the room was good in that they now all felt they had a starting point. Ray spent the next few moments outlining each member's work for the day, and after telling them all to be back for an evening briefing at 17.00, he left them to get on. He returned to his desk, inwardly objecting but knowing he had to spend some time on paperwork. Some of these papers involved him completing forms that would wrap things up from the last case. This had been particularly difficult for the entire team, but particularly for Ray, as it had been the senseless murder of a former D.I. and a friend. As he started to look at the papers and take a moment to scan emails, his desk phone rang. As always, he saw this as an escape route from the paper mountain. He answered as he as usual even though it was an internal phone, the person ringing would know who should answer.

'D.I. Ray Keane speaking.'

'Good morning, Detective Inspector.'

Ray recognised the voice of the new superintendent, despite only having met her briefly.

'Superintendent, what can I do for you?'

'I thought this might be a good time, before you get swamped with the case, to catch up and introduce ourselves properly.'

Ray had never had any issues with superior officers, nor did he look to progress any further up the ranks, as he was happy to still be involved in daily cases on the ground. He did admit to himself that he was slightly nervous about meeting and working with the new superintendent, only due to the fact that he felt that, as much as he had had disagreements with Adam over the years, they did get along reasonably well and understood how each felt about the job. Having agreed that he would make his way upstairs, he took a moment to ensure he was presentable. Despite not being the sort of officer who wanted to show rank by wearing a uniform, he was from an era of people who felt better when dressed in a shirt and tie.

He left the CID office and went into the corridor on the next floor, expecting to see someone sitting at the desk outside the superintendent's office. Apart from being surprised to not see anyone, he saw the desk was still empty as it had been left when Adams' old secretary had decided to retire when he left for his new role. The next surprise for him was that the office door was open; in all the time Adam had been in office, the door was only open to enter or exit the room. Superintendent Angela Johnson was sitting behind her desk, and again he was taken aback by her jacket hanging on a hook behind her; he could only remember seeing Adam without his jacket on once in all his years. Ray knocked on the frame of the door and waited, 'No need to stand on ceremony, Ray; please come in.'

'Thank you, ma'am.'

He knew immediately, from the look on her face, that he had said the wrong thing.

'First thing, I am not royalty; so, either superintendent or, as I would prefer, Angela will do.'

'Sorry, Angela, I am just not used to being so relaxed in this office. I noticed you have not got a secretary yet either.'

'You can certainly relax here, unless you are not doing your job properly, and I will not be having a secretary; I am perfectly capable of organising my own diary.'

As she made the comment about doing the job properly, Ray noticed the slight smile pass her lips; he felt the idea of a new superintendent was not to be as bad as he had first thought.

'This is certainly going to be different from before, Ma...' Ray stopped himself mid-word and said, 'Sorry Angela.'

'I realise it will take time for people to get used to the way I work. Though I am hopeful everyone will be able to adjust without any major problems.'

When Angela went on to briefly give Ray a potted history of her time and progress in the force, he found himself feeling relaxed for the first time ever as he sat in the office of the station superintendent.

'I am sure we will have plenty of opportunities to chat, but for now, can you bring me up to date on this latest case?'

'It is still early days, though we have had a couple of pieces of information that should help us start moving forward.'

'I know from what I have already been told that you have a perfectly good team working for you. I just ask that you keep me in the loop. If you can email me when you are holding briefings, I may put in an appearance, if possible. If not, my door will always be open; so, all I really need is a message each day on progress.'

Ray knew his next comments would show a lot about how the new superintendent would be supporting them.

'How do I stand, as far as finances, if I need either some extra uniforms or overtime to assist us?'

'As long as I do not feel anyone is taking advantage, you concentrate on solving the case and leave budgeting to me.'

Ray could not believe the feeling, like a breath of fresh air, so he decided it was a good time to take his leave.

'I will get back to the team, and we will speak later.'

'Good, just keep me informed.'

None of the team sat at their desks in CID had ever seen Ray return from the superintendent's office with a smile on his face. Usually, he was frowning, and there would be a moan about the latest little gem Adam had come out with. Tim saw his moment to keep the obvious good mood going, 'We may have an identity boss.'

'Okay, give us all the details.'

'Downstairs, just put a call through from a young lady. Maria Shon is a Latvian farm worker, and there are five of them altogether. One, Sergei Romanov, has not been seen for just over 24 hours.'

'It is not long for someone to be missing, especially an adult.'

'I realise that. She told me that it is not unusual for him to disappear for a couple of hours, though this has been a longer period of time. He's also usually a very reliable worker.'

The rest of the phone call had given Tim enough background about the five workers and the farm they worked on, so he now passed this on to the rest of the room. The farm he worked on was no more than 20 minutes away from where the body had been found.

'Okay, initially, take Jill with you and go and see what else they can tell us. Do not forget for now; keep it vague about what we know.'

The way Ray worked with his team, no one took it as a slight on character about their work when he just reminded them how to progress. They all knew of officers who had been caught out just by saying the wrong thing, even if it was seemingly an innocent comment. Tim was just glad to be getting out of the office and doing his bit towards moving the investigation forward.

Suddenly, it struck Ray as well that they had started to make some progress. It would be slow at first, and they were all used to the feeling that sometimes an investigation felt like 1 step forward, then 2 back.

'Tim, make it part of the conversation to see what you can find out about any drug use. I have a horrible feeling; it is going to play a major part in everything.'

While others continued to put together the information gathered so far, Tim and Jill made their way to the car. As they started their journey out of town, Jill took the chance to ask Tim about his time working in the force and particularly his recent time in CID.

'You know this area well, don't you?'

'I should do; I have lived here all my life, and local knowledge helps in this job. That is the other reason I like working with the boss, as he is also a local person, though he did spend his early career working in other areas.'

Jill still lived with her parents and had decided to transfer to King's Lynn when they moved from Kent. She liked the area and was now fulfilling her dreams of being a successful police officer. Tim found he was enjoying the conversation, so he continued.

'Are you enjoying being part of CID?'

'I really am; it was what I always wanted to do.'

'Are any of your family in the job?'

'No, I just decided it was for me. We had a policewoman visit our school to give a talk. I spoke to her afterwards and knew that's what I wanted to do.'

The conversation carried on as they drove towards their destination. The good weather seemed to be continuing, which meant it was a pleasant day to be heading out.

'I admit, I find it hard to believe sometimes that a day can be as nice as this while we are investigating what is obviously a horrible crime.'

Tim laughed as he replied, 'You'll get used to it and find you appreciate it being good weather when you are trudging from door to door, maybe not getting anything helpful in the way of information.'

They pulled off the main road and made their way down an unmade road to the farm they needed to be at. Tim thought to himself that farm vehicles might not notice the state of the track, but his car certainly did. Tim parked the car beside some of the farm machinery, and as they got out, they took in the surroundings. As always, there seemed to be an abundance of bits and pieces of machinery laying around, some undercover, while other bits looked as though they had been outside for an age. Across the yard were 2 buildings that looked like the hundreds of holiday accommodation buildings that adorned the countryside and seaside areas. He realised from part of the phone conversation that this was, obviously, the workers living quarters. As they made their way towards the buildings, there was a call from behind them, 'May I help you?'

Tim introduced them both, 'I am Joe Warner; I own the farm. So, what can I do for you?'

Tim explained about the phone call from Maria Shon and that they would like to talk to her. Without realising that he was helping them already, Joe told them that he was surprised and found it hard to explain that it was unusual for Sergei not to report for work. Joe appeared willing to talk, so Tim decided to let him carry on for a while. He told them that he had used the same work force for the last few years, due to them being good workers and not causing him or the locals any problems. This sounded to Tim that if their victim was Sergei Romanov, he may have just been in the wrong place at the wrong time, but he knew he would wait before making any judgement.

'Can we speak to Maria first, then the others?'

Joe pointed in the direction of a large shed and said, 'They are all in the field behind there. My farm manager, Neil, is with them.'

As Tim and Jill moved away, Joe showed a slightly different side to the conversation so far, 'Just try and remember that time is money, and while you are chatting with them, they are not working.'

Tim decided he would be polite for now.

'We will keep it as brief as possible, sir.'

Jill spoke as they made their way carefully across the field.

'All heart, isn't he? Worried we might hold things up. What about the poor sod we picked up from the field?'

Tim fully understood Jill's frustration but replied.

'He is not aware of the body yet. We also know how hard it is for some farmers. Hopefully, if we don't take too long, it will keep him on side.'

They soon reached the group working in the field, and Tim showed his warrant card as he introduced himself again. Neil, the farm manager, took charge of the conversation and introduced Maria to them, he pointed to the others saying, 'That is Alekesji, Vitaujis, and Andris.'

Tim couldn't help but feel the 3 male workers were not overjoyed to see them; on the other hand, Maria just seemed happy to have someone listen to her concerns.

'Have you heard anything yet?'

'Not yet, Miss. We need to get more details from you all.'

It was Andris who spoke next; 'Maria is the one you need to talk to; she is the worried one.'

Tim saw that this response pleased Neil as he followed up with, 'That would be best; the others could continue working.'

'If it is okay with you, is there somewhere quiet we could talk?'

Tim directed this comment at Neil, as he still felt it was best, at the moment, not to upset anyone. He had learned by watching Ray that this could help when needing to question people who didn't particularly want to talk to the police. He also noted how Ray could apply pressure just from the tone of voice and the nature of a question. He was not aware of it, but Ray and Sheila had both commented on the fact that Tim had developed a good style when interviewing people. He found that engaging a witness in a conversation worked very well for getting information rather than asking direct questions. His manner, at present, was working as Neil appeared relaxed enough with the situation to say, 'Maria, take the officers to your kitchen area. Take your time, so hopefully we can get things sorted.'

Maria moved towards Tim and Jill, then pointed across the field.

'This way. Is there any news?'

Tim realised this was the 2nd time she had asked this and knew he would have to broach the subject of the body they had found. He didn't really want to do this in the middle of a field. So, without answering, he walked in the direction she had indicated and left her to follow Jill by her side. Tim thought to himself that Neil, having mentioned a kitchen area, would possibly get the offer of coffee. Maria had caught up with him and led them to 1 of the caravans they had spotted earlier. Maria led them inside, and though it was not fancy, everywhere was clean and tidy.

Tim was pleased that he had been right as Maria put the kettle on immediately, then asked if they wanted coffee; Jill took over at that moment. Having worked as a family liaison officer several times, she was accustomed to the order of things and was aware that Tim would want to question Maria as soon as he could. Tim was just about to start talking when Maria interrupted and took a minute to explain the living arrangements. She had this caravan to herself, and the 4 men shared the bigger one between them. She laughed as she added that they seemed to spend more time in the evenings in her kitchen area, and this was where most meals were eaten. Jill had finished making the drinks and joined them at a dining table. Maria sat on one side and indicated the chairs opposite. Tim started the conversation that he knew was going to be awkward.

'I have to tell you that just over 12 hours ago, we found the body of a male. It was in another farmers' field.'

Maria looked as though all the energy had left her body and fell forward to put her head on the table. Tim knew it was hard but carried on.

'We have no ID for him yet, but after your phone call, we think you can help us.'

Maria looked up from the table slowly, and Jill saw there was no colour in her face and tears were forming. She continued the conversation as Tim paused.

'It would be helpful if 1 of your group could come and identify the body.'

At this thought, Maria just shook her head violently, 'I would not like to, but one of the others may.'

'That would be okay. Do you happen to have any photos of the person you called about?'

Maria was struggling to speak, and they both noticed she appeared to be thinking very hard before saying anything else. Slowly, she uttered a few words, 'Was he murdered?'

Tim responded first.

'Why would you ask that?'

'If you knew anything about our upbringing at home, you would be able to answer that for yourselves.'

'It is very difficult, I realise, but until we know exactly who he is and have more details, I am only prepared to say that it is a suspicious death.'

Despite the sobs that were now racking her body, Maria got up and went to a drawer in a unit beside her. She reached across to pass them some photos, and even though the people photographed were much younger. Tim knew they had found their victim. He left Jill to console and talk to Maria while he went outside to ring Ray with the news. After telling him, well done, Ray told him his next move; while they were speaking, Tim realised that he was going to upset the farmer. They would need statements from all the others quickly, while their memories were fresh. It would be easier to conduct these interviews at the station, but Ray told him that in the circumstances, as long as he and Jill felt they could do things correctly, they could interview the others separately at the farm.

Tim was relieved, as this would mean keeping disruptions to a minimum. He would get Jill to take notes, mainly due to the fact that her shorthand was a lot quicker than his usual strangled writing. He was always happier typing up reports, as his handwriting had never been good. He always remembered a parent's evening at school when a teacher described his writing to his parents as looking like someone had pulled some of the legs off a spider, dipped its body in ink, and let it try to run across the page. As he got older, he preferred to think it was because his brain worked faster than his hands. He preferred to record the conversations on his phone. They would still need to arrange a formal ID, but this could wait until they had talked to each person. He thought that while talking to them, he could make a judgement on who would be best to ask to do this ID.

Chapter Six

After the phone call from Tim, Ray felt positive that the case was now underway. He knew that identification meant that there was now grief being caused to a family and friends. Knowing who the victim was gave him a familiar feeling; they now had a target to work towards. The conclusion he would aim for was justice for anyone who knew the people involved. He went out into the office, making his way to the white board at the far end. He could feel the eyes of the others watching and holding their breath. It soon became clear he had something to add to the information; it was obviously important. Below the picture of the deceased, he wrote the name Sergei Romanov, then turned to face them all.

'We have a name. Hopefully, once Tim and Jill return, we will know a lot more about him.'

The noise level automatically rose in the room at this news. Ray gave it a moment, then cleared his throat, which was all it needed to silence the group. He went on to explain as much as he knew so far from Tim, then told them all to start looking into the background for anything to do with Sergei. Once Tim filled in the gaps, they could also check on the others.

'Let's just remember, though, that it is great to have a name; we still have an investigation to run. I would like to see as much as possible added to this board today.'

Unfortunately, as always seemed to happen, for every positive they came across, a negative moment followed. None of them were aware yet, but within 24 hours, the first negative would cause problems. Ray left them all to get on and returned to his desk. He was surprised to look up as he sat down to see Sheila coming into the office. He was more taken aback by the wide grin on her face. It had taken a while for them to slip into a routine of working together, especially as she had been the replacement for Jenny. This had happened when Jenny had taken a transfer to allow their relationship to develop.

It was not entirely a necessary move, but they both knew how office romances were frowned upon. It had taken Ray time to get Sheila to understand how he works, while at the same time getting her to be part of the team. Several times he had been frustrated and wondered if it would work out, but slowly things had fallen into place. Now she was becoming a valuable member of the team. He could tell immediately that she had some news to pass on, and she obviously felt it was important to address him upon entering; the usual greeting of sir, which he had tried on several occasions to get her to dispense with, was this time replaced.

'Ray, I really think I have something.'

He had full respect for all the officers in the station and accepted the term sir. Though he would try to get his closest colleagues to feel equal, he encouraged the use of first names.

'Do not keep me in suspense then; what has got you so excited?'

'Sergei Romanov is in the system. It's nothing major, but it's enough to draw our attention.'

'So, has this just been flagged up due to his name, or should we have picked it up earlier from fingerprints?'

Ray was fully aware of how the media followed everything nowadays, and even though it was only a matter of hours involved, if it got out, then questions would be asked why they hadn't acted quicker. The reply put him at ease.

'It is his name; he was not fingerprinted as he was only a witness to a drunken brawl in the Red Eagle.'

'When was this?'

'It was 2 years ago, and it just so happened that it took place the night before Sergei went home to Latvia after working the harvest.'

Sheila explained that she had searched the computer for any mention of his name, and it appeared in the police constable's notes regarding the events of the evening. Sergei had literally been leaving the pub when the police arrived, having been called by the landlord. There had been no indication that he had been involved, fortunately for the team; the constable had been very precise in taking notes. He noted that Sergei had been with 4 other people, and Sergei in particular had been very jumpy, just seeming to want to get away as quickly as possible. The constable added afterwards that when following up, all 5 people had left the country; due to none of them being actively involved, that was the end of their connection.

'What are the chances that the names Tim has on his return match the others mentioned?'

'Fairly high I would think.'

Sheila went to move back to her desk when Ray had a thought, 'Sheila, it may not be much help, but just have a quick look and see what else you can find out about Sergei, such as how long he has been travelling here and how he first got work. It could paint us another picture of him to compare with whatever Tim has.'

Ray knew how they all found this part of an investigation tedious, but finding out as much as possible about a victim or a suspect in any crime played a big part in achieving a satisfactory end result. He also noticed that sometimes it was this work that was needed to keep everyone focused on the details required. Despite what others seemed to think, and in the case of the media, even reporting sometimes. There was no getting away from the fact that police officers were only humans. Along with the other emergency services, they saw and dealt with things on an everyday basis that stayed part of them forever. He knew already, with the little information they had, that if it turned out that the case revolved around a falling out over drugs, some officers and lots of members of the public would be of the opinion that they got what they deserved.

Over the years, Ray had heard these thoughts expressed and always felt the need to point out that a crime had still been committed. He was sitting at his desk, and though he was looking at paperwork, he heard the noise levels increase as Sheila told the others what she was following up on. The general opinion was that it had to be a move forward. He wanted to get to the next stage under way, so without appearing to be checking up on Tim, he made a call to get an update. Tim answered almost immediately, 'Tim, how are you progressing?'

'I must admit, sir, that it was a bit slow at first; we also met with some resistance, but we now seem to be getting there and should be finished soon. I can confirm from seeing the picture that the victim is definitely Sergei Romanov. One of the men who worked with him is willing to do a formal ID.'

'Sheila has also found some information about our victim, following on from you getting a name. Please finish up there as soon as possible. Arrange the ID for the morning as it is only a formality; then make your way back and be ready to bring us all up to date.'

'Certainly, sir, I will see you soon.'

After having had a long conversation with Maria, who, despite being very upset, had felt able to talk and had given them a lot of information to work through. Tim felt the need to clarify exactly what their relationship had been. Maria very quickly pointed out that it was purely friendship through working together. She had stated that there was no desire on her part to get involved with any of the others. The 3 men were less forthcoming. At first, Tim thought this possibly had a bearing on the fact that drugs were involved, but were they also involved? Slowly, while talking to them, he knew this was not the case. It appeared they had good reasons of their own for not wanting to be involved with the police in any matter. Alekesji told them he was willing to view the body just for confirmation.

In the end, they all made similar comments, saying they really didn't have any idea what Sergei had been doing. They said initially, on hearing the news, they thought it could be a hate crime, even though they did feel accepted by the locals. Acting on the information so far and the way the body had been left, there was nothing to suggest a hate crime.

Tim moved quickly to dispel this idea, as he knew none of the team would want that message to start being passed around. Tim asked them all the same question and received similar answers back, was it possible that Sergei had been involved with anyone outside of their group? All the answers were cagey at best, and automatically he knew there was more to find out. He felt that Maria would be the most helpful but that she would be more talkative alone than with the men around. After finishing up with the initial statements and having had a quick word with Neil, the farm manager, he rounded things off by talking to the group as a whole.

'Thank you for your time today. Sorry to hear of the loss of your colleague. It's likely we will need to speak to you again, though we will contact you when needed.'

It had taken some persuasion, but they had managed to get mobile numbers from them all. This would be helpful as and when they need to talk again.

'Alekesji, we will arrange a car for the morning to complete the ID. Someone will give you a call to arrange a time.'

Even though he had offered to do this, his reply was just a grunt. Tim could not help but feel the other men didn't want too much involvement.

As they made their way back to King's Lynn, the conversation revolved around the morning's work. Jill was the first to speak.

'I can't help but feel there is a lot more we haven't been told yet.'

'I totally agree, though we can leave it to the boss to decide the next move. I also think Maria can tell us more. Alekesji may also be more helpful tomorrow on his own.'

'Once we get back, I will get the interviews transcribed so everyone can read them. Though you can tell them most of it at the briefing.'

Tim enjoyed becoming more involved within the team; he knew that others were impressed by his work. He still found it slightly uncomfortable to have to stand in front of the room to pass on information, despite the encouragement he got from Ray. He didn't know it yet, but this evening's briefing would include extra pressure. They arrived back at the station, making their way upstairs to the CID office, they had about 30 minutes before the briefing was due to start. This would give Jill time to start typing up the interviews. They would be available for any of the team members to print off to read, though the majority of officers nowadays read them on the screen of their computers. Tim also had the opportunity to speak with Ray.

He was surprised to see the room was already quite full, as others were working on computers or on phone calls. He noticed 3 uniformed officers on phones at the back of the room, so he assumed Ray had been able to get some help from some other departments. He recalled attending a briefing for the first time, having been seconded to the team while still in uniform. At the time, his impression of the office had been formed by stories he had heard from others, and if he was honest, even slightly influenced by television programmes, this meant that CID officers had little time for anyone in uniform. He soon realised how wrong he had been. Years ago, he would have been correct in his thinking. He was soon made aware that Ray liked to integrate everyone to get the job done.

This had made its mark on Tim, who soon knew where he wanted his career to go. He made a point of welcoming and making sensible use of the extra team members. As he made his way to the inner office, acknowledging others were on their way, he recognised the uniforms from around the station. He entered Ray's office when he saw he was on the phone, so waited just outside until Ray indicated for him to go in.

'Afternoon Tim, do you have all the information for us to tie everything up by the end of today?'

Ray smiled as he finished speaking, so Tim knew he was joking. He decided to play along by replying, 'Not quite, sir; may take us until the morning. I do have some information for you to use at the briefing.'

If Tim hoped this would get him out of doing it, he was soon proved wrong.

'No, you don't. This is your information, so you get to run the show and pass it along. So, come on, let us get their attention.'

It had happened so quickly that Tim had no time to be anxious, even though he realised that the news he gave would be new to Ray as well. He felt his nerves move up a notch as they went to the front of the room. As he went to speak, he saw Superintendent Angela Johnson appear in the doorway, and Tim took a moment to pause and look over at Ray in case he wanted to say anything. The superintendent took the edge off things; Tim realised she had been given notice that he would be running the briefing.

'Carry on, sergeant.'

These 3 words made everyone aware of who was standing at the back of the room. It was interesting for Ray to note how, even in the short space of time that Angela had been in the role, the atmosphere of her being in the room was totally different from when Adam had been in place. Tim cleared his throat and was pleasantly surprised by how easily he found the words flowing as he addressed them all.

'DC Addy and I carried out interviews today with the 4 other people who worked alongside our victim on a local farm. It is about 2 miles away from where the body was located.'

He went on to explain that a picture they had been shown confirmed their victim as being Sergei Romanov. Once he had covered all the important points of their discussions, he finished up by adding, 'Jill is currently transcribing the statements for you all to see. I will add photos and names to the incident board.'

'Thank you, Tim, and Jill. So, all of you now have plenty to be working on. If the early report from the postmortem is clear enough, we need to be looking at a possible drug link. From what Tim has told us, it sounds as though Sergei enjoyed mixing with the locals at the pub more than the others. Another point to follow up is that Sheila has found Sergei's name flagged up after being interviewed as a witness to an affray at Red Eagle in the past. I need you to look into this as it could suggest others are not being as open with us as they could be.'

The mood in the room was positive, and Ray was able to lighten it even more with his next comment.

'Tonight, Tim and I will have a drink at the Red Eagle, all in the name of research. We will start to put the word out as to how we are dealing with things to see if anyone comes forward. Once the rest of you finish up, get some rest and be back here bright and early.'

People started to move about the room, and Ray made his way to his office, indicating for Tim to follow. As they went in, Superintendent Johnson walked in as well.

'Very impressive presentation, sergeant.'

'Thank you, superintendent.'

'I do not want to tell you about your job role as Detective Inspector, but is it a good use of resources for you to visit the pub?'

Ray still wasn't sure how to react around the new super, so he just went with instinct.

'The team is all going to be busy over the next few days and possibly weeks. I can visit the pub on my way home and take some of the pressure off them.'

Ray felt good that once he explained his reasoning for his moves, Angela was happy to accept that he was not just acting on a whim; there was a good reason for his actions.

'Right, I will leave you all to get on.'

She left the office, acknowledging Ray personally, 'Just keep me in the loop.'

'No problem, superintendent.'

'Tim, I hope you are happy to join me at the pub?'

'It is a hard job, but someone has to do it.'

They decided to take separate cars, as this would make it easier for their journeys home later. There were several shouts of goodbye from the others, along with a couple of calls to have a drink for us. As they made their way out, Sheila was working at a computer.

'Sheila do not work too late. It is going to be busy enough soon.'

'I know that I just want to finish up some background checks.'

Tim and Ray drove to the Red Eagle. Over the years, Ray had heard lots of people tell him that you can always spot a policeman. It was certainly a feeling he had as they walked into the lounge bar of the pub; all eyes turned towards them, and conversations ceased. After a few moments, chatter started again at various tables. Ray made himself known at the bar, and the lad serving explained, 'My name is Mike; I only work a few evenings. It might be better for you to talk to Jerry; he is the landlord.'

'We will do that if you let him know we are here. First, you can get us some drinks, and we have some pictures you can look at.'

Tim noticed how much confidence Mike had first shown, had now been replaced by signs of nervousness.

'As I said, I don't see how I will be of much help to you.'

'You never know, sir; pour us both a pint and then relax.'

Ray just knew that Mike was hiding something. They just needed to find out what. He served the drinks and initially waved away the money offered. Ray very quickly indicated they were paying for the drinks, so Mike accepted the note, and as he stood at the till, he pushed open a door beside him and called through to Jerry. By the time he turned back to the bar, Tim had placed a couple of the photos they had for him to see. Ray was quite happy to let Tim lead the conversation as he took a mouthful of beer.

'Just take a look at these, please. Do you recognise any of the people in the photo?'

One picture was of Sergei on his own; the other showed all the workers Tim had spoken to and included Sergei. It was taken earlier in the year when they first arrived back in the UK.

'They may have been in here at some stage, but I just serve people their drinks. Apart from that I don't get involved.'

They both had the same thoughts, that it was a village pub, and Maria, along with the others, told Tim they had become regulars there, so it was hard to believe that Mike did not know them. They were also aware that bar staff usually knew as much about regulars as there was to know. Mike walked away to the end of the bar to serve another customer as Jerry walked through the doorway that Mike had shouted through.

'Good evening, officers; allow me to get you another drink.'

'No, thank you, sir.'

Ray accepted in the job. How differently people reacted when faced by police officers. The main responses they saw were either nerves or suspicion, or in the case of the man facing them now, it was a confident bluster, which Ray always felt suggested past experience with the law.

'So how can I help the people who keep us safe?'

It would not have mattered how hard he had tried; Jerry would not have been able to disguise the sarcasm in his voice. Ray moved the pictures in front of him, 'Do you recognise any of these people at all?'

'Yes, they are regulars here during the harvest season. They work on a nearby farm; they never cause any trouble, except for him.'

As he spoke, he pointed to Sergei, 'There have been a few occasions recently where I have had to keep him in check.'

'In what way?'

'Only that, I think he has got himself mixed up with some unsavoury characters. There was one time I thought I saw him trying to sell something; due to the group around him at the table, I wasn't sure, though they were all acting shifty. I just politely pointed out to them that I didn't want anything underhand going on here.'

'So did you think to report this at all?'

'No, I can deal with things myself. I just told them all, in particular him, that they could pack that lark up. He didn't make a fuss and left with some of the local lads. The next time he came in, he was as polite as before.'

'I need you to remember, when did you ask him to leave?'

Jerry took a moment, then replied, 'It would have been about a month ago.'

'When was he last in here?'

'2 or 3 nights ago. I think they were all looking forward to the end of the harvest and getting back home.'

'Well, I am afraid that particular gentleman is going to be making the journey home in a totally different way to his friends. I can tell you we found his body in a field, just after it had been in contact with a combine harvester.'

The colour visibly drained from Jerry's face, 'Was he drunk? I thought they would all know their way around the farmers' fields.'

'He may well have had a drink, but his body being where it was is being treated as deliberate.'

'That is terrible news. I don't see how, but if I can help anymore, just ask.'

Ray decided they had gotten as much as they were going to get from the evening. Jerry went on to tell them that none of the locals, who were friendly with the farm workers, were in this evening. They finished their drinks and were preparing to leave as Ray's mobile rang. His first thought was that it would be Jenny. Looking at the screen, he was surprised to see that Sheila was calling.

'Sheila, are you still at work?'

It was as though by him answering without announcing his rank and name as usual, threw her off her train of thought.

'I was just getting ready 15 minutes ago to finish up when the desk sergeant put a call through. I don't think it's good news that we have another body.'

Just for a brief moment Ray reverted to some humour, 'Can we not give it to someone else?'

He could hear the smile in her voice as she replied, 'Sorry sir; it is too much like the last one for us to pass over. Even with the minimum of facts I have already, I am convinced it is connected to Sergei.'

Chapter Seven

Ray had realised very early in his career that he had not taken on a job with regular hours. It was true that as he had risen through the ranks, he no longer had to work shifts; he was also aware that if he chose to go for further promotions, he would be more likely to follow a 9-5 pattern. He already knew this was not going to happen through choice; he enjoyed being part of the team on the ground too much. Sometimes, though, he did wonder if criminals were conspiring against him having a home life. He knew that with darkness falling, there would not be a lot they could achieve tonight, and then again, he also knew it would be a late finish. Having asked Sheila to text him the details of where they needed to be, he told her that he and Tim would meet her there. During their conversation, his mind switched into overdrive, thinking of all that would need arranging.

'Sheila, get a patrol car to the area as fast as possible to cordon things off. We will not necessarily need a full team. Call Lisa and Graham; they can arrange who they need once on scene.'

He ended the call, looking at Tim, who had picked up pieces of the conversation.

'You did not really want to go home yet, did you?'

'Of course, not, sir; I would much rather spend the time with you and a dead body.'

Before he could continue, his phone bleeped to indicate a message. The text was from Sheila, with the details he had asked for, the body had been found by a dog walker on the edge of the river at Sutton Bridge. Ray made the same connection as Sheila had; this was no more than 5 minutes away from where the 1st victim had been discovered. He turned his phone around for Tim to see the screen.

'Tim, this is where we need to be.'

'I know that part of the area, sir; it is slightly further along the river. If I remember correctly, it is past the dock area, where the river starts to head out to sea near the lighthouse.'

'Okay, we will meet the others there. I will call Jenny, then the superintendent from the car.'

He never mentioned Tim ringing anyone, as he knew he lived alone; there had been no mention of a girlfriend while they worked together. Tim confirmed this by adding, 'At least I don't have to check in with anyone.'

Ray was not the greatest lover of modern technology, but at times like this, he embraced it for its help. Bluetooth connections meant he could make his calls while driving to the scene. As expected, Jenny totally understood the situation.

'I will get a hotel room tonight rather than arriving home, who knows when, then having to leave early tomorrow.'

Ray had always carried an overnight case in the boot of his car. This meant. that he was always able to stay out for a night when necessary. He finished the call by telling Jenny he loved her and would speak tomorrow. Then he called Angela.

'Good evening, Angela. Sorry to disturb your evening.'

As he spoke, he realised he knew nothing about her personal situation, though the way she answered the phone suggested she was always in work mode.

'I presume you are not ringing to tell me you had a good time in the pub.'

'Not quite. I think the landlord may be of some help in the future. Unfortunately, I am ringing to let you know, we have another body.'

'Are these bodies connected, do you think?'

Ray went on to explain the location and said he found it hard to think of anything else due to having 2 bodies in such close proximity.

'I just wanted to let you know the situation; I think it will be a long evening. You can have an update in the morning.'

In the short space of time of knowing her, he was not surprised by the response.

'You can fully update me in the morning, though I would appreciate a call as soon as you know if they are connected. It doesn't matter what time.'

Ray and Tim followed the satnav instructions to the area; Ray led the way as his car was equipped with blue lights in the grill and a siren if needed; the journey didn't take as long as previously due to the starting location. Soon they came across the bridge and turned to start driving along the river. There had not been a lot of traffic, and on this road, there was even less. The next thing Ray saw was the flashing light bar from the top of the patrol car, reflected across the water. Being a still evening, the reflection spread out across and down the river. They were now past the busy port area, which had been eerily quiet, and heading out towards the lighthouse. If they followed this road, they would arrive at the estuary and then the North Sea. Ray pulled his car into a passing place alongside the patrol car. Tim went further along and parked at the roadside. As Ray got out, he could see Sheila's vehicle making its way towards them.

The 2 officers on patrol were from Long Sutton, and Ray didn't recognise either of them. They were both young officers, and as he showed his warrant card, they introduced themselves, 'PC Newby, sir.'

'PC Wilson.'

'Good evening to you both. Who is that sitting in your patrol car?'

'That is John Deal, sir. He was walking his dog.'

Ray noticed the Labrador that was busy sniffing the ground at the side of the car.

'Apparently his dog was running along the edge of the river and discovered the body.'

'Have either of you been to look?'

PC Newby quietly replied, 'I went down, sir. Then I decided I'd better wait for you to arrive.'

'Is this your 1st body?'

'Yes, sir it is. PC Wilson is yet to have that pleasure.'

'Well, in that case, you take contact details and a brief statement from Mr Deal. While PC Wilson, you can join us.'

Sheila had now joined them, so along with the light from the police lightbar, they all switched on torches and made their way towards the body, following PC Wilson, who had been watching when his colleague 1st went down. Ray could not help but notice the PC slowed his pace as he approached. The body was naked, as in the 1st case, apart from the temperature dropping, which suggested no one would consider the idea of lying around nude.

It looked as though the person had been walking along the edge of the river and decided to lay down. PC Wilson stood to one side, and it was obvious that this was as close as he was comfortable being. Ray always encouraged his officers to deal with the harsh reality of the job, and dead bodies were just about the worst. The only thing he could think of as being worse was if the body was a child. He would not push anyone if he saw that it would have a detrimental effect. This was something he remembered from when he was first in the job. Some senior officers found it amusing to see a young officer struggling to cope with their 1st body. He looked at PC Wilson and spoke.

'Thanks for showing us this, you can get back to the car. Forensics and the doctor should be here soon and direct them to us.'

'Yes sir.'

The 3 of them approached the body, carefully watching where they stepped. The body was close to the edge of the water; immediately, Ray's thought was that whoever dumped it there had been disturbed. He would have thought the plan had been to dump the body in the river, then let the tidal flow deal with it. If the body had been dragged out to sea, it would have been highly unlikely any remains would have been found. As Ray moved to look closer, Tim pointed as he spoke, 'What is that at his waist?'

Ray could see something tied to one side of the body; as he went to examine it, he heard a disgruntled voice, 'I hope you are not thinking of contaminating my crime scene, D.I. Keane.'

Ray stood up sharply.

'I would never dream of doing that. Though if you can have a quick look at the body, I would be interested as to what is around his waist.'

Lisa looked across at him.

'Always someone wants a favour, and working quickly is not in my nature. I work thoroughly.'

This had all been said to no one in particular, and Ray could tell by the tone in her voice that there was no malice meant by the comment. Lisa would not be rushed in any aspect of her work; she always did her best to accommodate the jobs that seemed to queue up for her. She checked that the area where they were standing had not been disturbed, causing them to lose any valuable evidence. Satisfied that all was good, Lisa crouched down by the body.

'Whatever it is, there is no way it was being used to weigh down the victim.'

Slowly and deliberately, she used a pair of scissors to cut through the plastic tie that held a small bag in place.

'I will give you this to examine but do it away from my crime scene.'

'Thank you, quick question; do you think he was left here on purpose or was the intention to drop him in the water?'

'Firstly, I don't classify that as a quick question, though I think you could be right. His body is too close to the edge for it not to seem like the idea was to get him in the river.'

Along with Tim and Sheila, he was about to start walking back towards the cars; even at this time of night, the 2 PC's, from Long Sutton, were having to move cars along as word seemed to be spreading and people were coming to see what was happening. Suddenly Lisa called after them, 'Ray, I will need to wait for Graham before I do anything else. Take a look at his feet.'

They had all been distracted by the package, which, apart from seeing the body, was naked, hich was another strong connection with the other body. Now, as Lisa pointed out, they could see a plastic bag that was held in place with a tie identical to the one around his waist, though this bag covered his feet.

'I can tell you without removing this; his feet are tied together.'

The voice from behind them was very familiar, as Graham said, 'That will be for me to look at then.'

They all turned to look as Graham had joined them, and he carried on walking to where Lisa was standing over the body. They exchanged a few words, then Graham looked up at Ray.

'I think, given the lateness of the hour and the fading light; the best thing is to get the body moved to the mortuary. Scanning the area, I don't think any of us are going to find anything that will be much help.'

Ray agreed with all this.

'The best we could hope for from forensics is if they found any footprints. Though looking around it is a well-walked area, there will literally be hundreds of prints.'

'I would like to just mark this area so I can come back in daylight; you never know what could be waiting here to be found.'

Ray knew Lisa well enough that she wanted to cover all eventualities.

'To save you from disturbing anyone else on your team. You can make use of the P.C.'s, who were first on the scene, if that helps.'

Lisa agreed that was fine. Graham had already made arrangements on his journey over for a team to meet him at the site with a mortuary van to remove the body.

'Shall I meet you at the mortuary, Graham?'

'I really don't think it is necessary, Ray. There will not be a lot we can do tonight. So let us all start fresh in the morning.'

Ray was not sure how he felt about leaving things overnight, though he realised it was getting late, and Graham was correct that there would not be a lot more they could do.

'I can give you 1 nugget of information to mull over and start with tomorrow. Looking at the body briefly; he has been killed in the same manner as your other victim.'

There were now too many coincidences for the 2 bodies not to be linked. Ray looked over at Tim.

'I know it has been a long day, but we need to know what substance is in that bag. I know we are all thinking along the same lines about what it could be. Can you get hold of someone at the laboratory and just get an initial finding on it?'

Tim took this request in stride.

'That is no problem, though you may need to arrange for some strong coffee to be available first thing tomorrow.'

They all looked at their watches, and Sheila added.

'You mean later this morning.'

Tim was already on the phone as he went towards his car. Fortunately, the people who worked in the lab kept similar hours to themselves. This meant that they could always get access in a hurry. The other reason he had no issues with doing this was that it was on his route home. If he could get details now, it would allow him to have some news for them at the morning briefing.

As Tim made his way back to town, Ray got things arranged as best he could. He was able to leave the PC's on site as they were on a night shift. He told Sheila to get herself home, even though it would only be for a few hours. Having spoken to both Lisa and Graham, he made his way to his car. As he drove towards the town, even though he felt it was unnecessary, he rang Angela. The voice that answered was as alert and bright as if she had been sitting at her desk during the day and not being disturbed in the early hours.

'Just an update for you. The cases are definitely linked, and there is a high possibility that drugs are the reason.'

'Any idea on who this latest victim is?'

'Not yet, though Graham has told us, he was also strangled. We will know more as the day progresses.'

'Are you heading home?'

'No. I shall use the hotel I have used before. There will not be a lot of sleep; the briefing will be at 8 AM.'

'Thank you, Ray; I will see you later.'

Chapter Eight

Ray found he was having to deal with feelings of frustration, and this was something he had never really gotten used to over the years of leading investigations. He just had to do his best to control his emotions while not allowing the team to be aware of them. Invariably, this would happen whenever a 2nd victim turned up. Just 24 hours ago, there was a feeling of optimism around everyone, and due to some good detective work, they had a name for the 1st victim. There was a link with drugs to follow up on after the toxicology results so far; they had not been the most helpful people, but the landlord of the Red Eagle and his barman had given them some more information to be working on.

Suddenly, the investigation was thrown into disarray by this discovery. Even allowing for the minimum amount of facts, it was blatantly obvious there was a connection between the bodies. The work now would primarily be to find the link. There was also an issue now with the extra workload to spread across the team. Despite all the assurances that staff would be available, Ray was wise enough to know that finances would be scrutinised. There was always a feeling of 2 steps forward and 1 back when investigations developed, like this one looked like it was going to. His 1st job of the morning had been to make himself presentable.

The hotel he had stayed at knew him well, and even if only for a few brief hours, he had managed to grab some sleep. Breakfast had been some toast and coffee in his room, courtesy of the night porter. He had rung Jenny early, and just talking to her lifted his spirits. His next job, and crucially the one he felt was important this morning, would be to keep the team motivated. Knowing that Tim and Sheila would both be feeling tired, he knew he wanted to let them know he appreciated their work. He was pleased that he need not have worried about this. They both came into the office just after Ray and before anyone else. He was happy to see that they both looked fresh; he knew that without going over the top, Sheila could cover a multitude of sins with a small amount of make-up. Tim was almost bouncing as he walked in. Ray wondered how much caffeine had been needed to achieve this effect.

'You are both looking bright and breezy this morning considering events last night.'

Tim was the first to reply with laughter in his voice.

'It is all for your benefit, sir. You can deprive us of sleep, but you won't grind us down.'

'Glad to hear it, especially as I think we will all need our wits about us today.'

As he finished speaking, the rest of the team filtered into the room. Ray was happy to see that, due to being early himself, D.I. Dave Hulme, who ran the night shift, was still in the office. Ray did not get round to ringing him last night, though he wasn't surprised that Dave knew what had happened. He was surprised, though, by his source of information. Apparently, Dave had a phone call from Angela after Ray spoke to her. This did mean that some vague details had already been added to both the incident board and the computer system. The noise of conversation amongst the others immediately increased as they noted the addition of information.

Ray wanted to get things moving as quickly as possible this morning. He knew there was going to be a lot of work needed, and they also had to keep in mind the original investigation. He moved to the front of the room and was about to speak when 2 arrivals stepped through the doorway. 1st in was Angela, who, like the others, did not appear to be suffering from her interrupted sleep from the previous night. Just behind her with an enormous grin on her face was Lisa.

'D.I. Keane, before you get underway. I just had the pleasure of meeting Lisa from forensics, and she tells me she has some important news for you.'

The majority of the team knew Lisa; the ones who were unsure just added words of acknowledgement to the others greeting her. Ray would normally pass on information from people such as Lisa or Graham after he had spoken to them, so it was extremely rare for of them to put in an appearance at the station.

'This is a rare honour. Since you are gracing us with your presence, am I correct to assume you have good news?'

'Well, I certainly hope it will help you. When I finished up last night, 1 of the PC's you assigned to help, who I will just add, were both very helpful, noticed this as we were walking away from the scene.'

She held up an evidence bag in which they could all see a small card.

'This is a gym membership card. Now I know the cynical members of your team will think it could have just been discarded by anyone.'

'I must let you know, Lisa; I do not allow cynicism in my office. It will be taken at face value and certainly treated as a positive.'

'Of course, I understand all that, Ray. The reason I don't think it has just been thrown away is because it was on the ground under where the body was lying.'

'So, is this the time our criminals have been careless? I take it that we have a name to work with, possibly also a picture?'

'Sorry, no picture, though you do have the name Nick Crowe as a starter. I can also tell you there is a date of birth, which, looking at the face of your victim, would match up.'

'A name is a good start. Tim, see if our system gives us anything.'

There was a voice from the back of the room. Ray looked it up and acknowledged PC Dan Carol, who assisted them at the conclusion of the last case.

'Go ahead, Dan. What have you got?'

'I know that name, sir. His family, if you can call it that, live in Long Sutton.

Well, sir, the expression from a broken home is nowhere close enough. It is not just broken but almost demolished.'

Ray could see that Dan was not sure about carrying on talking as he was new to the room.

'Carry on; you give us your knowledge. While Tim sees what he can find out.'

'Dad has been in and out of prison most of his adult life. His mum has been known to entertain male friends whenever dad is away. He also has an older brother who, the last I heard, was also doing time after a botched robbery.'

Tim called over from his desk, 'Bingo. We will only need Graham to get us a set of fingerprints, as Nick Crowe is in the system, along with the rest of the clan.'

'Thank you, Lisa. I have to ask; did you find anything else that may help?'

'That is known as pushing your luck. Though you are unlucky, I can't help anymore at present, as there was nothing else at the scene.'

Lisa took her leave. Unusually, Ray had to raise his voice to get the attention of the room back.

'Right, we have a lot to go on; just remember, we also have a lot still to learn. Are these victims definitely connected, and if so, how? As soon as possible, I want the incident board to have as much detail as we can about Nick Crowe, along with anything else about Sergei.'

There was not a lot Ray could say or do to keep the murmuring around the room down. He knew that, as well as chatting about the latest developments, the team was experienced enough to already be scanning details on computers regarding Nick Crowe.

'Okay everyone; I want you all on computers or out on the streets, getting as much information as you can. I can leave it to you to decide the best course of action for you. Tim, along with a couple of PC's I know, C.C.T.V. will be limited, but there are traffic cameras on the A17 plus at the bridge crossing. Time is still vague, but start looking for anything suspicious. It certainly appears that our perpetrators were disturbed; you may just spot something.'

The thought of sitting and staring at endless traffic on a computer was always dreaded by the police, but some officers, and Tim was showing he was one of them, had the ability to sit and stare at the screen, then seemingly from nowhere spot a vehicle or person that was of interest. PC Dan Carol made a move towards the computer when Ray stopped him.

'Dan, as you know a little about the family, you can join me. First, we will go and see if Chris Small knows who owns the land by the river. It would surprise me if he does not, as the farmers seem like a close-knit community. Sheila, can you attend the postmortem? After we see Chris, we will visit the Crowe family.'

Everyone who needed to move did so, to their respective positions to carry out their instructions, Ray spoke to Dan.

'Give me a minute to just glance at my emails. Then we will move.'

After a quick look and deciding there was nothing that couldn't wait. Ray and Dan made their way to the car. While he was waiting, Dan made use of the time by calling Long Sutton police station and getting the most recent address for the family. During the journey to the farm, Ray got Dan to tell him as much as he could about the family. It turned out Dan came across the family while on patrol one night in King's Lynn town centre. Following a call about a disturbance, he and another officer had to arrest the Crowe brothers for fighting in the street. Due to the fact that they were only brawling with each other, there were no charges brought.

Dan had taken it upon himself to spend some time looking at the background of the brothers; this was now allowing him to update Ray about them. It appeared that, despite the family situation, Nick had shown some promise in his early years at school that there was the possibility he could break the mould he had been cast in. Unfortunately, due to the life of his family, when he got the opportunity at 15 years old to have some money and what he felt was the respect of others, he saw it as too good a chance to miss. As seemed to happen so often, by the time he knew what was happening, he was further in than he wanted to be.

Even so, the fact that he had money and was being talked to instead of yelled at outweighed any reservations he had. It was turning out to be quite an unpleasant story, as Ray had heard many times. Any more Dan could add would need to wait as they pulled into the yard at the farm. They were lucky that pulling in just behind them was Chris at the wheel of a tractor. They got out and waited while Chris parked at the side of a shed and made his way over.

'Good morning, Inspector. Do you have any more news on your victim?'

'We do, sir, we now have a name, and he worked on one of your neighbours' farms. That is not the reason for our visit now, I am afraid.'

As Ray went on to continue; Chris said, 'I was just about to go in for a tea break. If you would like to join me, you can then tell me the reason for the visit.'

Ray had always found that, as long as he had a supply of coffee throughout the day, it was always a good day. As usual, there was also a supply of cakes to go with the drinks. They sat at the table, and Ray brought the conversation around to the events of the previous evening. The 1st piece of luck for them was that Chris owned the land where the body had been found. Currently, he rented the land out to another farmer, who used it as grazing ground for his cattle.

'I heard that something was going on last night; I just didn't know what.'

Once Ray had explained the discovery, Chris phoned the other farmer to arrange for Ray to go and see him. There is an outside chance he may have some information to help. After finishing their coffee and getting directions to the other farm, Ray and Dan left. Chris, who was happier as the discovery of where Sergei worked meant that his field could now be completely harvested as the police no longer needed access. The other farm was only a few minutes away. Unfortunately, there was not a lot the farmer could tell them. Basically, there was a system of fences in place so his cattle could roam freely during the day, and in the evening, he would bring them back into sheds on his property.

'I brought them in at their usual time last night, 6 o'clock; there was nothing I noticed untoward. Certainly not anyone dumping a body; I have had problems in the past with fly tipping, but then again, we all have at some stage.'

Ray could not help but feel this line of inquiry was a dead end. His thoughts were that they needed to speak to Nick Crowe's family, hopefully as a way of moving forward. Having said thanks to the farmer, they started on the short journey to Long Sutton. As they drove past the site where Nick's body had been found. Ray noticed Lisa's car parked on the side of the road. He pulled in beside it and went to see exactly what she was looking for.

'I did not think you would be back here; from our earlier conversation, I thought you had found everything you were going to.'

'I just decided it was worth another look in daylight, just in case. It does seem to have been a wasted journey, though.'

Ray turned to go back to the car when she said, 'Or then again, maybe not.'

He looked up to see her holding 2 small packets in her hand, which she had retrieved from very close to the edge of the riverbank.

'I will get these checked for fingerprints and may have some news for you later.'

'Thanks, Lisa; I look forward to that. I think these next few hours of the investigation are not going to be the best.'

Chapter Nine

As Ray and Dan were making the journey to Long Sutton, along with themselves, there was 1 other person having similar thoughts to them. This went along the lines of what has happened to Nick Crowe. For them, one question was already answered, and they knew where he was. The other person involved in this triangle was his mum. Shirley was quite open when asked if she was fully aware she had not been a great mum; this didn't stop her from wondering why Nick had not been home for 2 days.

Family had never played a big part in the home of the Crowe's; mum and dad had met as youngsters in the town. There was never a lot of opportunity to move away, so it was quite normal for people who had known each other since school to end up married to each other. Shirley had always thought that Stan Crowe was a good catch; there was a lot of jealousy from friends when they first got together. He was good-looking, very athletic, and played rugby and football for the school teams. Unfortunately, she didn't find out anything about his family background until they were engaged and she was pregnant with their first child. It turned out that Stan took after his father in that if he could get something for nothing, he was interested in it. It transpired that even playing sports at school had an ulterior motive, which he knew attracted the girls.

It seemed that family life followed a pattern developed through the years, then handed down from in particular fathers to sons like heirlooms. The rules were seemingly that work was a subject to avoid, as there were plenty of other ways to get money. Living on the edge and staying 1 step ahead of the law were the important things to learn. For Shirley growing up, her family was no different, though her dad did work as a general labourer, usually around the local area on building sites. Once she and Stan were engaged, he was happy for her to meet his parents properly. If alarm bells should have been ringing, they would have needed to be clanging louder for Shirley to have taken much notice.

The pattern of a young girl fascinated by a good-looking boy, who showed her affection and also kept promising a good time, was set down. At first, she was convinced that Stan would be different, especially when he came in 1 day and announced he had gotten a job. They had moved into a flat, which Shirley thought was really lovely. She spent her time making it look nice, and the main reason behind it being allocated to them was due to her being pregnant. Her life had been rather sheltered, so to her, the fact that the small block of flats was now home was all that mattered. Unfortunately, even though the flats had only recently been built as part of a push by the local council for social and affordable accommodation, they were already showing signs of wear and tear. It was soon apparent to most people that the flats were living quarters for people on benefits, usually youngsters with no prospects.

For Shirley, who was fast approaching her due date, it was home, and that was all that mattered. Within weeks of moving in, she gave birth to Jed, a strapping baby boy, and once back at home, she was disappointed by Stan's reaction, which was basically, we can now have another baby to get more money. This was how, at the age of 19 Shirley had a boy approaching a year old and was expecting another. If she had thought things were different after Jed was born, it really changed when Nick arrived.

She had only been home with them both for a matter of days when there was a knock at the door, and police officers arrested Stan in connection with some stolen property. His denial was pointless, as 1 of the items on their list was a stereo system currently sitting in the living room of the flat. Stan's attitude towards it all being okay lasted right up until the point he appeared in court. Any idea that it was only a 1st offence vanished with an overzealous judge who sentenced him to 6 months in prison. This started a cycle that would last for years. The idea of proud parents having their sons follow them is okay, though not so in practice when the sons become career criminals.

Shirley knew very quickly that she had to do her best for her and the children by looking on the positive side of things if they all were to have any kind of life. This attitude stood her in good stead; this was the idea that she was still young, she had 2 lovely boys who she doted on, and still she believed life with Stan would be okay. Stan kept his nose clean, and his sentence was reduced to 4 months when he was given parole. Soon after getting home, though, he was off out at all hours, and despite what she told herself, Shirley knew he was up to no good. On an odd occasion, she was brave enough to mention anything was always met with the response along the lines of, you look after the kids, and don't worry about me. Soon he was in trouble with the police again and was very quickly back in prison.

Her life took another course when, at a mother and toddler group, she met a girl whose life was just like looking in a mirror. Once Shirley got over the shock of the girl introducing herself, 'Hi, my name is Candy.'

Shirley thought about who the hell calls a child Candy.

'Hi, I'm Shirley.'

They both had 2 children; though Candy had a boy and a girl, the children enjoyed playing together. This meant the girls could talk while the children were occupied. Over the days, they got on well together. Candy explained she was on her own with the children, and their dad had soon cleared off once she was pregnant for the 2nd time. After meeting for a few weeks, mainly at the group, then arranging to go for a coffee, Shirley found she enjoyed the company. Shirley had always kept her private life just that private; slowly, she started telling Candy more. One morning she asked a question that had been niggling away at her, 'So, how come you can afford all the nice clothes for you and the kids.'

Candy smiled sweetly as she replied, 'I don't pay for them.'

Shirley physically felt herself move back at this comment. The one thing she had always promised herself was that she would never get involved in anything criminal.

'Don't look so shocked, girl. My male friends pay for it all.'

Shirley was now intrigued, 'When you say male friends, what do you mean?'

'You have led a sheltered life, I think.'

Candy went on to tell her that she had always attracted the opposite sex and decided she might as well make use of this ability.

'I had men making comments, then advances towards me, once they knew I was on my own. A few nights a week, once the kids are asleep, I entertain them.'

Shirley started to take notice; she had had a fair number of comments from men. Even some of her female friends had told her when Stan was first inside that she needed to think more of herself and that she had to remember that she was still young and attractive.

'How do you arrange all this?'

'It is easy after a few times of listening to their lewd comments. I invite them back to the flat; either they run a mile or they want more details. I think you would be surprised at the number of married men I see.'

Seeing her reaction, Candy continued, 'You should give it a try.'

'I don't think so. Isn't it dangerous? What would Stan think?'

'Oh yeah, because Stan is always thinking of you, isn't he? It is no more dangerous than when we used to meet boys in a club, then go outside in the quiet for a quick grope.'

It did not take long for Candy to work out what sort of man Stan was. She already knew that Shirley would just have a life of trouble if things carried on as they were. She wasn't necessarily thinking that she should leave Stan; just kept herself occupied and rewarded while he was in prison, which it was obvious would be a big part of the future. She could tell that Shirley was interested as she continued to ask questions, 'Do you use your real name?'

'I do, and if you like, I use it as advertising. You should see their eyes light up when I slowly look at them and introduce myself. Hi, I am Candy, and I guarantee I'm as sweet as.'

Shirley roared with laughter at this, 'And does it work?'

'Oh yes, every time.'

'I don't think I could use my name.'

'You don't have to; most of them aren't interested in your name. I tell you what I have a guy that would suit you for the 1st time. How about I arrange a meeting? I'll make it easier for you, and I'll look after the boys.'

'I'm really not sure.'

'Just think of the extra money.'

This was enough to convince Shirley to agree; while thinking to herself as thousands of women had in the past, if I don't like it, I will stop. Quicker than she expected, it was all arranged for 2 nights time. Shirley answered the knock at the door nervously, wondering what she was doing. Without even thinking, she looked at the good-looking man on her doorstep, and licked her lips seductively, without a thought she said, 'Hi, I'm Shirl. Come in.'

Time passed in a flash, and her only thought was that it was not too bad. Within 40 minutes, the man was dressed and walking out of the bedroom, saying, 'I hope we can do this again.'

If there was any part of her mind that wanted to say no, it disappeared as he put a £50 note on the table. This set the pattern for her future. Over the years, as Stan spent more time in prison than at home, it allowed her to make sure the kids were always fed and dressed. When Stan was at home, he showed very little interest in her or the kids. She even wondered sometimes, when he was out, if he was one of the types of married men Candy had talked about. Time passed, the boys grew up, and her nightmare life continued as Jed followed in his father's footsteps, even to the point once when, due to an error by the courts for 2 days, they shared a cell. Shirley still had high hopes for Nick at the time, as he showed a lot of promise in his early years at secondary school, something Jed had never done. Unfortunately, all these hopes were seemingly dashed in a matter of days when Nick totally changed.

He was 16, and Jed was 18. Jed was again in trouble with the police, and Stan was back in prison. So it was down to Shirley when she opened the letter from the school. The letter told her that there had been occasions recently where Nick had been spoken to about his behaviour; there had now been an incident, and he had struck another pupil. When reprimanded by his teacher, he lashed out at him as well. Therefore, the school had no option but to suspend him for 2 weeks. Sitting at the table, Shirley couldn't believe the words in front of her. Nick had always been her ray of sunshine; her hopes for him just seemed to be disappearing as she read the words on the page. She had just finished the letter as Nick slammed his way into the flat; any hopes she may have had that he would show some remorse dissolved as he glared at her and saw the letter.

'Nick, what have you done?'

'Don't worry about it, mum. The kid deserved it.'

'I hope you are going to drop that attitude before you go back.'

Shirley actually felt as though she had been slapped as he replied, 'I ain't going back; there are better things to do with my time.'

'I hope you are not serious.'

'Deadly serious. I want some of the money that dad and Jed get.'

'Great, look what good that does them.'

'Yeah, well, they aren't careful enough.'

'Oh, so suddenly, as far as the criminal world is concerned, you are a mastermind then.'

There was no reply to this as Nick stormed into his room and, within minutes, was back out. As he walked out the door, he levelled another comment at his mum that hit her hard.

'At least you can keep yourself busy now without wondering if we can hear at all.'

Shirley had no idea what to think; life had thrown plenty at her. She always seemed to manage, but now, with the letter from the school and the barbed comments from Nick, the wind had literally been knocked out of her. Within weeks, Nick seemed to completely change; he was staying out all hours, sometimes bringing people back to the flat who she didn't know. Suddenly money was appearing with no explanation, and despite all her fears, Nick seemed to be enjoying himself.

She soon knew there was no going back, and Nick had made it clear he had no intention of going back to school. A phone call she had with the headmaster came across as though he was relieved by the news. Her decision about it all was that there was only one person she needed to concern herself with, and that was her. Her friendship with Candy had lasted throughout the years, so it was a help that she had someone to talk to. Despite all the complaints about her life, every time Candy suggested she get a divorce and move on, her answer was always the same, 'They still need me, so I will always be here for them.'

Candy's reply was standard, 'They just want you as a housekeeper.'

They both knew nothing would ever change. Shirley settled into a routine of basically living for herself. Despite comments from Nick, she still carried on entertaining men, so she was never short of money. She still had the idea that she was discreet about things. Occasionally, there would be rumours around the estate that she did her best to ignore. Sometimes, if someone caught her at a bad moment, she would react and defend herself, usually by telling whoever it was to mind their own business.

Nick, meanwhile, had got mixed up with a gang of youths, who were all of the opinion they knew how to avoid the police and also had a good time. The group all did some run-around work for a local thug. At first, all Nick saw was the money he got for not doing very much. He was fully aware, due to his family's past, of what went on in the real world; he just never gave it much thought as to what was in the parcels he dropped off around the area. Being young, it didn't seem odd to be turning up at someone's house in the early hours of the morning, he would even be invited in for a drink; sometimes there was a party in full flow.

The attitude of them all was that we are enjoying ourselves, getting lots of money, and no one was being harmed. Unlike his dad and brother, whom he knew knocked people about as part of a robbery, to him, the harm caused by people using the drugs was invisible. He was feeling pleased with himself; time passed quickly; and his family settled into a routine. This basically meant even though they all officially lived at the same address, they led totally separate lives. Nick thought that by buying his mum the odd present, that should be enough to keep her happy. He really didn't understand that presents and money were not something his mum was short of. Her attitude towards him had gotten slightly better since he left school, though he knew she felt let down.

It was as if she just had to accept how things would be. He continued to hear rumours about her lifestyle; he chose to ignore them, as he was happy as he was, and she seemed content. He also knew she could not rely on his dad.

Nick thought everything was on the up when, one evening, he got a message that Darren Plant wanted to see him at his house. All Nick ever knew was that Darren was the man in charge as far as the drug trade in the local area was concerned. His 1st thought was had he done anything that could have upset Darren? He soon pushed that idea away, as he knew Darren would not get his hands dirty dealing with problems himself. When he first started to deliver the parcels, the guy who transported them to him went to great lengths to let him know what would happen if he got any ideas of not doing as he was told. Nick made his way to the address that had been given; even though it was not far away from his flat, it may as well have been on a different planet. Darren lived in a mansion; as Nick looked at it from the driveway, he wondered how many times the flat would fit inside. The door was opened before he went up the steps, and he was surprised to see it was the guy who always delivered the packages to him.

'Good evening, Nick; Mr Plant is waiting for you in his study.'

Standing and looking at the surroundings, Nick couldn't think of anything to say. Then as he went to speak, the guy cut him off, 'This way, you don't want to keep him waiting, do you?'

Nick followed, then walked into the study to see Darren sitting in an upright leather chair. Nick's thought was that if that were in my bedroom, there wouldn't be room for anything else.

'Nick, come in. Sit down; do you want a drink?'

Slowly, he found his voice, 'No thank you, Mr Plant.'

'No need to be so formal, Nick; I have heard good things about you. I think we can make better use of you than just a delivery boy; also, I am sure you would like to earn more money.'

If anyone who didn't know the situation were to have been listening in, they would have thought it was a business meeting and that some lucky person was being offered promotion.

'I would like you to start accompanying Jack on his runs for us. There is a bit more to it than just delivering the stuff. You would be surprised at how closely we have to watch people to make sure they aren't trying to put one over on us.'

It was as if Nick was being offered something with one hand and being warned on the other. He had now found his voice, 'So, what does Jack do?'

'Let's just say he enforces the strict rules I like people to work by. He also doesn't talk to anyone about his role.'

Nick could tell by looking at Jack that his way of ensuring rules were followed easily involved inflicting pain, if necessary, while at the same time enjoying it. Nick had always thought of himself as well-built, he had taken after his dad, though he would be described as medium-built when alongside this giant of a man he was now to work with. He was sensible enough to know he didn't have much choice in the matter; having been invited to this inner sanctum, if he said the wrong things, he would be sorry, so just thought about the extra money.

'I think I can handle that sort of thing.'

'Good. Jack will show you the ropes. You may need to do some driving for him as well.'

Darren went on to explain that from now on, Jack would let him know what was required. Nick soon realised the meeting was over as Darren reached for his drink while Jack opened the door to the study. Nick went to leave when Jack stopped him, saying, 'We may as well start your training tonight.'

That first night was an easy start for Nick; it involved driving around in a nice car and Nick watching while Jack made sure the people they met understood the situations they were in. Over the following months, Nick found his feet and enjoyed a feeling of power, as well as spending the extra money he now had. The 1st time he witnessed anything more, it was a shock. Himself and Jack were talking to a lad who was a similar age to what Nick had been when he started delivering. The difference was that this lad thought he could have an opinion. Nick was shaken at the speed at which Jack moved to slap the lad around the face, then picked him up and threw him across the room of the flat they were in.

'Do you now understand what you need to do?'

Through a split lip and with one eye already closing up, the lad mumbled a reply, 'Yes, I'm sorry.'

On the way out, Jack said, 'Sometimes they just need a reminder of how to show respect.'

After getting over the shock, things settled down until the incident with Sergei, which ultimately led to Nick being found at the water's edge. This was also the reason D.I. Keane, along with PC Dan Carol, was now parking outside the block of flats where Nick was known to live with his parents.

Ray had never understood the thinking behind building blocks of flats like these ones and then housing people who were always going to be in trouble all together in close proximity. The flats at Nelson Court, opposite the police station, had recently undergone a major refurbishment and certainly looked better for them. Though the crime rate amongst its residents was higher than anyone liked. Ray was fully aware that it was overall a bigger problem to solve than any solution so far suggested or implemented had managed. He just felt sympathy for everyone who was indirectly affected by the criminals. They parked the car at the side of the road.

Ray looked around as they got out. The block of flats was not as large as Nelson Court, though there were plenty of similarities, such as the odd boarded-up window or door. The small communal garden at the front, which he was sure was in the eye of the designers, would have been a pleasant space for people to sit or children to play. It looked like a subsidiary of the local council tip, including several old bikes, fridges, and a washing machine. They made their way to number 9, with Ray thinking that despite all he could see around him, it was not a visit he was looking forward to.

Chapter Ten

They knocked at the door, standing back to wait for an answer. If the woman who answered was the same person who Dan had described as Shirley Crowe, then Ray was taken back. Standing in front of them was an attractive middle-aged lady with a small amount of make-up applied, also smartly dressed. He introduced himself, 'Good morning, Mrs Crowe, I am Detective Inspector Ray Keane.'

As he was speaking, he showed her his warrant card. Dan took his card out and turned it towards her as well.

'We are from the CID team at King's Lynn police station. Can we come in?'

Most people on the estate would recognise a policeman at 10 paces and would certainly not like to have them standing on their doorstep. Shirley was definitely not used to policemen knocking at the door and then being so polite. For just a moment she was unable to answer, and very quickly she realised they had to be there about Nick, partly because their demeanour told her this. She found her voice, 'Hello, I'm Shirley. Most people call me Shirl. Come in.'

She turned away, so they had to follow her into a hallway, then through a door to the living room. Shirley sat on a chair and pointed to a sofa for them to use.

'So, what is the point of your visit? I thought you kept track of my family.'

Ray had always realised it was better to be straight with people, especially when delivering bad news. Also, in an instance where he was speaking to people who had no trust in authority, he wanted them to take in the news without being defensive.

'I am really sorry to have to tell you that late last night, a body was discovered by the river in Sutton Bridge. We have reason to believe it is your son, Nick.'

There was a look of disbelief on her face, quickly followed by a wail, and tears followed. Shirley slumped back further into the chair, then rocked forward. Ray gave her a moment to digest the news.

'Would you like the PC to make you a cup of tea?'

There was no answer, just a nod and a finger pointed towards what was the kitchen. Dan went through, and Ray heard the kettle being filled. Slowly, the tears subsided, and a trembling voice asked, 'How can you be sure it's Nick?'

Before he could answer, she carried on. Ray was happy to just let her speak.

'I know you all know Stan and Jed, but as far as I know, none of you have had a lot to do with Nick.'

The words kept tumbling out, 'You said you had reason to believe it was Nick, so you could be wrong.'

'We will need a formal ID to take place, though at the scene we found a gym membership card with a name and date of birth, which is why we are here now.'

As he finished speaking, Dan came back in with the tea for Shirley and also a photo in his hand. He handed the drink over, then turned the picture towards Ray. It was obviously a

111

couple of years old, but there was no mistake; it was the person they had found last night.

'I am really sorry, Mrs Crowe. It is definitely your son we have found.'

The tears started to flow freely again. Ray had to admit to himself that he was surprised by the reaction going on what Dan had told him about the family. He then thought there was no getting away from things. Shirley was a mum; despite everything her husband and sons had put her through, she still had feelings for them all. Slowly, she gained control of herself, and he could see she was digesting the news he had just given her, her face taking on a different look. They both knew, having seen it many times before, that there was a hard side to the woman sitting in front of them.

'I just hope your lot will put aside any differences against my family to catch whoever has done this.'

Ray always found it amazing how different groups of people reacted to the sort of news he had just delivered. The majority of people who heard the news that a body had been found drew the question of what had happened, as a lot of the time death would have been accidental. The criminal family had the automatic reaction that someone else had to be involved, and despite their feelings towards the police, they expected everything to be done to get answers.

'There are several questions we need to ask. First though, is there anyone we can contact to come and be with you?'

The reaction was as he expected, with a harshness to her voice, 'I'm quite used to dealing with things on my own. So, just get on with your questions. Then you can get back to doing your job.'

'I can assure you, Mrs Crowe, that all of my team is working hard to discover what happened to Nick.'

The more they talked, the more Ray knew they would not get a lot of help. As they continued, it was as if Shirley was growing in confidence and, at the same time, showing her feelings towards the police.

'As you have pointed out, we have not had any major dealings with Nick. Also, most of the dealings with your family have been with the local police. We need to know as much as possible about Nick and who he has been mixing with.'

'Nick was the shining light in my family until recently, when he changed. But before you all jump to conclusions, he was still a good lad.'

Over the years, Ray had lost count of the number of times he had heard this scenario, along with another favourite expression of how someone's child had been led astray. The one thing anyone who worked alongside Ray knew was that he could be compassionate, though he had certain lines he would not allow to be crossed. The conversation appeared to be heading in that direction, so very swiftly he laid out some facts that he hoped would get them the right answers. He knew his next statement would cause more grief but felt it was important, 'Mrs Crowe, before you continue, I think it is only fair that I tell you some facts we are already aware of.'

He could tell immediately by her look what sort of reaction he was about to get, so he continued before she could interrupt.

'Nick was found strangled and his body dumped. We think whoever did it was disturbed; his feet had been tied together, and also tied to his waist was a bag containing a small amount of drugs.'

Ray could tell by her look that she was not totally surprised. He also noticed the look on Dan's face of shock that he felt Ray was being very harsh. Her answer was to prove Ray was correct in his actions; her first words showed the attitude of the family, 'They were certainly disturbed.'

Before either of them could correct her view of things, she continued, 'I did wonder if something was going on with drugs.'

Dan had been taking notes of the conversation, though he stopped writing to look up at this moment. Ray had to decide how to move forward. Shirley seemed happy to talk now, as he didn't want to slow the process down by returning with her to the station. While Shirley was not a suspect in any of the inquiries, he felt they would get more information by allowing her to sit comfortably in her living room.

'I need you to think back over the last few months and tell us who Nick has been mixing with.'

'This is really hard for me; I need to know what happened to Nick. You are the last people I thought I would ever help.'

'I understand your feelings; if it helps you, I think his death is connected to another we are investigating.'

'You are not thinking Nick had anything to do with that, are you?'

Ray had to admit it was not something anyone had mentioned so far, though if drugs were behind the deaths, then it was a possibility. At the moment, he just wanted to keep Shirley on his side.

'There is nothing to suggest that. Like I said, what would really help us is knowing as much about Nick as we can.'

'I don't think I can be of much help; for the last few months, he has hardly spoken to me. It would appear he thinks the same as the others; I'm just here to clean and cook. Even though that has stopped, he seldom eats here. Or should I now say ate here?'

This comment choked her up again, so Ray took a minute before asking, 'Has he brought anyone back to the flat?'

'There have been people here, but we haven't been introduced. Usually they come in with Nick, go to his room, and just as suddenly leave again.'

He could not help but feel they were not getting anywhere, 'I really need to know some names if you hear anything. Or places they may have gone.'

Shirley looked directly at him; he could see she was struggling with her conscience. He knew exactly how her husband would react if he knew she was talking to the police. There was one other option he had that might just persuade her to talk, 'If you can tell me what you know, I can arrange a special visitor pass, so you can be alone with Stan to give him the news.'

Ray knew how precious visiting times were; the chance to visit alone instead of in the communal rooms they were used to was inviting. Shirley looked relieved at the idea already in her mind, as she thought it could in some way help her relationship with Stan. Anyone outside looking in would know how foolish these thoughts were; she even hoped they could help Stan to reform his life. This last thought would eventually turn out to be as far away from real life, even more than she could imagine. Suddenly, it was as if the thoughts of Stan outweighed any idea of betraying someone by talking to the police.

'There was a name, though the way it was said, Nick was talking about someone rather than talking to the person.'

'Okay, that could help. What was the name?'

'He mentioned Jack; I only heard it once.'

'It is a starting point. My next question is, can we look at Nick's room? I hope you are not going to want me to get a warrant.'

It was as if Ray had preempted her thoughts, as she took a deep breath before replying, 'I suppose as you are here, you might as well get everything out of the way.' She pointed across the hallway, then added, with some venom in her voice, 'Don't make a mess.'

This really was an understatement; when they pushed open the door, it looked as though the room had been ransacked. Ray had never had children to think about; basically, going on what friends had said, the room looked like what he would expect the majority of young adults who still lived at home to look like. Both of them put on latex gloves before entering, and Dan said, 'Not sure if these are going to be protection enough.'

Ray did wonder if they had to get forensics to go over to the room, and there was no telling what they might find. The first thing they both noticed were several pizza boxes on the floor, some with lids open, and they could clearly see pieces of congealed food. The boxes were joined by a collection of beer cans in various states of being started.

'Dan, whatever you do, be careful what you touch.'

'Honestly, sir, I can't say I want to touch anything.'

'I know; I think we can just do a cursory check for now. We can arrange a more detailed search later if needed. Just look for the obvious, possibly a mobile phone or laptop. Also, anything that suggests drugs are around.'

Slowly, Dan made a start on uncovering what, was the bed; it was covered in clothing, and he could see a couple of pizza slices. His only thought was that surely no one would want to sleep in this bed. As he pulled a jacket across from the far side, he heard something metallic scratch against the wall. The jacket had no pockets, so placing it to one side, and in his mind deserving a medal, he knelt on the bed and reached between the mattress and the wall. His bravery, as he saw it, was rewarded as he withdrew a mobile phone. The reward he got as he turned back towards Ray was not what he had in mind. As he held out his arm to pass the phone across, he saw the sticky mess of a piece of pizza hanging from the sleeve of his jacket.

'If I didn't already dislike pizza, I would now.'

Ray could not do anything but smile as he replied, 'Well done, pizza guy. I think we are going to have to move the bed.'

As they started to pull the bed away from the wall, having heard the noise Shirley said from the doorway, 'Just exactly what are you hoping to find?'

'Anything that may help us discover what happened to your son. As we have found a phone semi hidden behind the bed, I am going to need to get a team out to go through this room.'

Shirley went to protest, though she already knew it would be pointless.

'Just do what you have to; I need to get to see Stan to tell him about Nick.'

She wasn't too worried that they would find anything to incriminate Stan or Jed, who had both learned early in their criminal careers to not keep stuff in the flat.

'If you make the phone call you promised, I'm going to see Stan. You 2 can wait here; I trust you will only take what you have to. Shut the door on your way out.'

Her attitude seemed to keep changing, which Ray put down to her way of dealing with the grief.

'We will treat everything with respect, Mrs Crowe. I will get a uniformed officer to stay by the door until we are all finished and until you return.'

'Great, that is all I need is a PC Plod advertising that the police are here.'

Ray was amused when she was worried about appearances to neighbours when he was willing to bet that they all knew her family's business and that police officers were regular visitors to see Stan or Jed.

'We will be as quick and tidy as possible. If you feel you need it at all, we have a family liaison officer who could come to visit you.'

'I don't think that will be necessary. You just find out how Nick died.'

Her emotions seemed to have changed again, and all he could see in front of him was a grieving mother. He was about to say more when Dan spoke, 'Here we go, sir; this could help.'

In his hands, he had an iPad and several small packets of white powder. Shirley could do nothing about the shocked look on her face; it was quite obvious. For all the criminal connections via the family, she did not know what Nick had been up to.

'I can tell you; I have never seen any of that stuff before today.'

Her reactions over the last few moments helped convince Ray that she was telling the truth.

'We will get this stuff looked at by our specialists and hope it helps us. I can assure you that despite our differences, I will do everything I can to find the people responsible.'

As Shirley was gathering herself and getting ready to leave, she looked at Ray. The look in her eyes was one of despair; this really was the side of the job he did not enjoy.

'I can tell you that I did hear Nick on the phone 1 evening arranging to meet someone.'

'Do you know who or where this was?'

'No, all I heard was a mention of something red.'

Suddenly, Ray had something to work with; it would be too much of a coincidence if it was anything else. It had to be that Nick was talking about the Red Eagle. This felt as though not only could it be a breakthrough, but it also suggested a very strong connection between the 2 victims. Ray decided that, as they now had a picture of Nick to show once the forensic team arrived, he and Dan would pay another visit to the pub and this time apply more pressure to the landlord. He felt, despite the seemingly helpful attitude on his last visit, he was holding something back. He rang Sheila to get an update on how the others were doing, and she told him that they felt things were coming together slowly and that she was getting ready to leave for the postmortem. He explained about his morning and the proposed visit to the pub.

Finally, he arranged for them to have a brief meeting before the evening briefing. As he hung up and put his phone away, Lisa and her team arrived. Dan passed over the pieces they had already found and leaving them to get on, they made their way to the Red Eagle.

Chapter Eleven

As Ray and Dan were making the journey to the Red Eagle, hoping to get more answers to move things forward. Sheila was getting into her car for a trip that, in her opinion, was always a worse visit than telling relatives about a deceased member. This was her appointment at the mortuary. She found out very soon in her career that offering sympathy to a distressed relative was something that came easily. Others have always noted how she seems to have the talent to offer the right words at the right moment without going over the top. This had led to one of her first roles being as a family liaison officer, though she had no desire to stay in this role she did see it as a vital part of her training.

Standing in a mortuary and watching while a body was dissected was never a choice she made. She just always understood the need for it, and she was amazed after attending her first one at how much they could learn from the details the pathologist could determine from the examination. Sheila never had a problem as a young officer attending these things. Her thoughts had always been to leave it to the doctors and then read their reports.

Often over the years, she listened as doctors got annoyed by questions being asked while they worked. She had soon become aware of it. In her words, "dinosaur senior officers" who found it funny to watch the reactions of a probationer officer dealing with the cutting up of a body. Her superior officers soon realised they were wasting their time trying to cause her upset. It helped that she was never afraid to stand up for herself. Being a police officer and a successful one was something that was very important to her.

After the call from Ray, it was obvious there was a connection between the 2 victims and that drugs were playing a big part in the case. Due to the traffic system that seemed to have a mind of its own in King's Lynn, the short journey from the police station to the hospital was a start stop affair.

It always amazed her that none of the traffic lights in the town appeared to be synchronised. Since her transfer to King's Lynn was recent, she knew no different about the traffic in town. On her first experience of a car journey alongside Ray, who was driving, he pointed out that a few years back, several people were of the opinion that the local council had been offered a special deal on a job lot of traffic lights, then just felt they needed to put them all up in town.

It never took much, especially during the summer months when people were heading to the many coastal resorts, for the town to become gridlocked. She soon learned to leave plenty of time for any journey she had to make, particularly to the mortuary, as she had developed a good working relationship with Graham and didn't want to keep him waiting. Sheila parked her car in one of the few designated parking spaces, then walked the short distance to push her way through the old wooden doors that were marked with a sign with peeling paint that read now as the ortury.

The hospital appeared modern, but everyone knew it needed a revamp. She thought this part would be the last to get that. There was still a feeling of entering a very old building, though these ideas soon disappeared upon entering. Everywhere was either bright white tiles or gleaming metal tables and fixtures.

Dennis, who had been the doctor's assistant for as long as anyone could remember, was waiting for her in his usual attire of surgical scrubs. As always, when not in the room for the examinations, he had a packet of sweets in his hand. These, along with a grin, were offered to the person attending. He had always seemed disappointed but respectful that Sheila was one of the few that would take the proffered sweets.

'Good afternoon, Sheila. How are you today?'

'I'm fine, thanks, Dennis. Hopefully, I will be even better if Graham is able to tell us more.'

As always seemed to happen in the mortuary, she never heard the footsteps behind her, then jumped slightly when someone spoke, 'I will only be able to tell you what the body tells me.'

'Thanks for the shock, Graham. I think we are just hopeful we get something to be a starting point. Why are these places always so quiet?'

Both of the others laughed; even that felt out of place here.

'I think even we would be worried if our clients started making too much noise. Shall we get started?'

The body was already laid out on the table and looked very pale under the harsh fluorescent lights. As Graham and Dennis got to work, Sheila was always asking questions that helped move conversations along. Though she knew they liked to concentrate when working, she also knew they didn't mind her talking, 'How did you come to choose this line of medical work?'

It was Graham who answered, though Dennis was nodding his head in agreement, 'After studying at medical school, I was always fascinated by the things a body can tell you, and they don't talk back.'

Sheila smiled as she thought it was a very good point. The postmortem process continued slowly at first as Graham made his way around the body, with Dennis taking pictures as Graham pointed things out. The process was also being recorded as Graham spoke details into a microphone hanging above the table.

'I can tell you that he is a well-nourished young male; there are no signs he has been living rough. There are signs of past drug use; his nostrils are showing early signs of damage.'

'Could that have contributed to his death?'

'Now, DS Carr, you should know better than to jump to conclusions.'

Dennis smiled at the reproach, even though there was no malice in the comment, 'Even though I can see damage, it is not recent. Any issues with drugs can take a long time to heal. I would say it has been a while since he was using it.'

Sheila was busy taking this information in, and while thinking it was not of a lot of use, she realised Graham was still talking, 'This is going to be of more interest to you, I think.'

Graham was pointing to an area at Nick's neck when Dennis moved into her line of sight to take his pictures, and Sheila moved to one side to see, 'What have you found?'

'There are equal-sized marks on each side of his neck; they are from where pressure has been applied by hands.'

'Are you saying he has been strangled?'

'I am saying that on the initial examination, it is highly probable.'

'That has to be our link with Sergei; they were both strangled.'

'I am afraid that it is a job for you to find a link. I'm just giving my informed opinion as to what happened.'

'I accept that, just so I can keep Ray happy. Are you saying his death was similar to Sergei?'

'Yes, they were both killed using the same method. I will also tell you this suggests you are looking for a very self-minded individual.'

If it was possible, the look on Sheila's face was asking the question before she uttered a word.

'What does that mean, self-minded?'

'It is really my way of describing the type of person you are going to meet when your detective work locates them. As I have told people before, strangling someone can be interpreted as very personal.'

Graham stopped his examination to explain more, and he told Sheila his own theory on things.

'If I were to shoot you, I do not necessarily need to be close to you, stabbing you; it is still possible to have some distance between us. To strangle the life out of you, I would need to be very close and for a considerable time.'

He could see her taking this all in, so to allow her to fully understand, he was happy to continue.

'The 2 victims have been strangled from the front; this means your killer was looking them right in the eyes. He would also be very powerful. It is not easy to strangle someone to death; it takes time. This means that all the time you are doing this, you are no more than a few inches away from your victim. I personally would think it is very upsetting for a normal person to hear the life being taken out of someone else.'

Sheila stood, shaking her head as she took in all the details. Meanwhile, Graham carried on with the postmortem. Eventually he got to the feet and slowly removed the plastic bags that covered them. This revealed that as Lisa had said, they were tied together. This had been done with some cable ties.

'So, what happened first? Was he strangled or were his feet tied together?'

'It is impossible to tell. Taking into account where the body was found, it suggests the feet were tied together with the intention of dumping the body in the river, meaning the person would not be able to kick with his feet properly. As to why, you would need to ask that question of your killer.'

Graham moved on with the task at hand, which now involved cutting up the body and examining the organs. Again, as with the outward appearance, the organs showed someone who had used drugs in the past, along with a drinking habit associated with most young adults. The postmortem ended with Graham saying, 'I will get my report sent to Ray as soon as I can. Though you have all the basics to be going on with.'

Sheila thanked him, and left the room, removing her green overalls as she stepped into the corridor. Dennis was just behind her and acted as expected.

'Would you like another sweet?'

He expressed his disappointment at her reaction as she took a handful, saying, 'These will remind me of our time together today.'

Both of them were grinning as she pushed the door to move outside. As always, she took a moment to allow her eyes to adjust from the harsh brightness inside to normal daylight. There was going to be plenty for them all to discuss at the briefing later. There was also going to be a press conference, which would be the first one the new superintendent had led. The fact they had a connection between the victims would help Angela at the conference; it would allow them to squash any rumours that there was a serial killer on the prowl. This was a term that police officers never liked being used, as it made already difficult investigations even harder.

While Sheila put together in her mind all she had learned from the postmortem, Ray and Dan were on their way to the Red Eagle. Ray was hopeful that with a photo of Nick to show the landlord and the overheard conversation by Shirley, they would find a strong link between Nick and Sergei. Over his years in the job, his attitude towards any criminal activity involving drugs had changed, and as a young PC he felt that his superiors had accepted that you never caught the main players as they were too careful. It always seemed that any arrest was celebrated, even though it may have only been a minor character. The stock answer whenever he questioned things was that at least they had taken some drugs off the street.

It was never really satisfying for Ray to hear this answer, as he knew that within 24 hours, someone else would be supplying the area they celebrated, supposedly shutting down. On his way through the ranks and with better techniques, he felt it was better to be patient and get the bigger fish. Recently, there had been some high-profile cases in bordering forces where they had achieved some convictions of important characters. No one was naïve enough to think the problem would go away, but these court appearances had gotten a point across. As soon as they knew there was a drug connection between the victims, along with the fact that Nick was only young, and until recently, according to his mum he had been doing okay at school, with her having high hopes for his future.

Ray was determined that even if it took a bit longer, he would like to use their resources and aim higher up the chain. At the same time, he was fully aware that pressure would start to build via the media to make an arrest, especially once they went with the storyline that the cases were connected. The pub car park was a lot quieter in the afternoon than when Ray and Tim had last visited. Inside were a few hardy drinkers, who Ray decided were in positions at the bar that they were most probably in most days. No one appeared to take any notice of them as they approached the bar. Jerry, the landlord, stood ready behind the bar. Ray would not be surprised if he was the only one working, as it certainly did not look busy enough to warrant paying another person's wages. As Jerry looked up, the ready smile for a customer disappeared as he saw who was waiting at the bar, and he took a deep breath and turned his eyes upward, 'Back so soon, we must have made a good impression.'

'We are not here to socialise or give you a review.'

This caused a different look to appear on his face, 'How can I help you, officer? Not that there is a lot I can add since your last visit.'

Ray placed the picture of Nick on the bar, avoiding a few patches of spilt beer. He looked very carefully to see if there was any reaction. Observing body language played a role in police work, usually as a way of forming a question based on a person's reaction. Ray was the first to admit he was still sceptical about this, though since having been with Jenny, who had done several courses on the subject, he was more open with his thinking. It helped now that from the way Jerry looked at the picture, then quickly glanced around the room as though looking for something to distract him, he had recognised Nick.

'I think he may have been in here.'

'I really do think you need to try harder, sir. We know he has been here.'

Ray could see the confident attitude was being replaced by a concerned look, 'Now that you mention it, I do remember seeing him. I think he used to hang around with the farm workers you were asking about.'

This was the link Ray had hoped for, though there was still the niggling feeling that Jerry was holding something back.

'I am going to make it an easy decision for you; either you tell me everything you know about this lad and any others that use your premises, or I will get the drug squad to pay several visits, which is a sure way to help your trade.'

'There is no need to be like that. Yes, I do recognise him; he is a regular, and I would say he knew the group you were interested in. If he comes in again, do you want to know?'

'I can assure you he will not be in again, as we found his body nearby, to where we found the other victim.'

129

Any bravado there may have been left in him, along with the colour in his face, all disappeared at the same time.

'I am sure you can understand our concern. We have 2 bodies that appear to be linked, and a major connection is that they both visited your pub.'

'Hang on a minute. I hope you are not suggesting I had anything to do with it.'

It was not a line of inquiry they had even considered, though Ray could see it was a good way to get some more background information, so played along.

'Well, no, sir. We had not thought of that, but now you mention it. Can you tell us where you were on the dates I am about to mention?'

Seeing Jerry get flustered as he was, gave Ray some light relief on a very difficult day.

'I can assure you, Inspector, that apart from a weekly visit to cash and carry, I am here 24 hours a day, 7 days a week.'

'I think, sir, you will be in the clear, though you need to realise we would appreciate any help you can give us.'

As Ray finished speaking, Jerry looked towards the door. As it opened, there was a lot of noise as several young lads came in.

'Alright, Jerry, set them up. We feel like a session is in order.'

Ray had always impressed upon his team that solving any case was down to good detective work plus a little slice of luck. He was about to get some of that luck. Speaking afterwards, PC Dan Carol could not explain why he had done what he did, but he was happy to accept others' praise that it was intuition. As the group moved towards the bar, he walked away and placed himself by the door. Jerry's next words led to the next part, 'Inspector, these lads may be of help; they went around with Nick.'

At the mention of the word Inspector all the group turned to go to the door.

'Going so soon, lads.'

Just the tone of Dan's voice made them all stop. 1 of them decided to be brave by trying to move to one side of Dan and out of the door. Ray could see that Dan was dealing with the situation; he gave it a moment to settle down and then took control.

'Do not be silly. We would just like a word with you all.'

The authority in his voice was enough to silence them all, and they stopped moving. He looked at Jerry, 'Landlord, how about you serve your customers? Then we can all sit down and have a chat.'

Once the noise level had settled down and they were all sitting around a table, the young lads all took a mouthful of their pints. Ray explained how he thought they could help; he already knew from their reaction that they knew Nick. He still made a point of showing them the photo and decided there was no point in sugar coating things, so he told them about the discovery of the body. Again, while talking, he took notice of their body movements. All the group except 1 appeared shocked by the news. There was some chat amongst themselves about Nick, then Ray focused on the 1 who was acting as though he didn't care.

'What is your name?'

'I'm Ian, not that it has anything to do with you.'

'You are right there, though I would hope you would want to help us find out what happened to your friend.'

'I don't know where you got the idea that we were friends. I've known him from seeing him around.'

Ray could see that this was liable to become hard work, so rather than let things drag, he took it to another level.

'I will tell you what is going to happen; you can all give your contact details to PC Carol. Just a warning; he can always tell if someone is not being truthful. Ian, you can join us in the car and take some time to think while we're on our way back to the police station.'

The bravado was still in place, though it slowly vanished as Ian realised the seriousness of the situation.

'I might be able to help you, but there is no need for me to go to the police station.'

Ray took Ian to one side after telling Dan to join them once he had finished.

Ray saw the chance to get this wrapped up, 'Just for everyone's benefit, I will record our conversation on my phone.'

The thought of not visiting the station meant the cockiness returned, 'Whatever. Just ask your questions.'

'All I need you to tell us, Ian, is how you know Nick and what you all got up to.'

'As I said, we just saw each other around.'

Ray took out a copy of the photo of Sergei, 'Did you also just see this guy around?'

Ian had obviously heard about Sergei; the colour drained from his face as he realised that what had happened to Nick as well was connected.

'I only hung around with them for something to do; I never was involved in any business dealings they had.'

'You were aware they were doing something then?'

'Well, when we first met, Nick was always in here scrounging drinks, and then all of a sudden, he was buying for everyone. I, along with the others, were only guessing where the money came from.'

'So, were Nick and Sergei working together?'

'Not that I knew. Sergei started last year when he was here. We all knew he used drugs, so he started offering to sell a lot cheaper than we usually paid.'

As Ian finished, he seemed to realise what he had just said, 'Not that I used a lot.'

'To be honest, Ian, I am not particularly interested in your drug habits. I would like to catch the people further up the tree who supply. I really want to find out who is killing people and dumping their bodies on my patch.'

Ray could see the relief on Ian's face, 'Have you any names you can give us?'

'Not really; all I know is that Nick started to drop packages off, and he also kept telling Sergei to be careful. I really liked Sergei.'

Suddenly, it was as if he remembered something, 'The only name I recall Nick mentioning was 1 night in here recently. Nick had had a skinful, and as usual, started telling us how well he was doing. A couple of times he said he was meeting Jack.'

'Any other names?'

The fact they had now heard the name Jack twice felt important.

'He did also mouth off that night by saying Jack was the muscle, though he intended to be like Darren.'

'This is really vital, Ian; did he mention a surname?'

'Not that I remember.'

Ray accepted that, for now, he had all he was going to get from Ian. He had the feeling that the name Darren was another step up the chain of command.

'Okay, Ian, we may need to speak to you again. If you hear anything else, then contact me. I will not lecture you about drug use; just think about what has happened recently to people you know that were involved in some form of drug trading.'

As Ian re-joined his pals, Ray noticed the bravado had returned, as he started to tell them how he had given the police some vital information, though it didn't mean he was a grass as he had done it of his own choice.

As they left the pub to make their way back to King's Lynn and the press conference, which would be followed by a very busy briefing, Ray could not help but have a little bit of fun at Jerry's expense.

'We may need to talk again, Jerry. Also, just think about what you allow customers to get up to; otherwise, I know some colleagues who would like a chat.'

As they went out of the door, Dan couldn't help but say, 'His face is a picture, sir.'

Chapter Twelve

Arriving back at the police station, there was a real hubbub of noise greeting them through the car windows. The area outside the station and towards the car park at the rear was crammed. Neither of them needed to ask what was happening; the press had arrived ready for the news conference. It was still 45 minutes until the start time, though everybody wanted to be sure of a prime position. The news about the discovery of Sergei had been released officially, but the discovery of a 2nd body was still only a rumour. Ray thought that in this day and age of technology, why would people still follow television or printed news? If anything happened, it seemed to appear on social media immediately.

The only thing keeping it quiet about Nick was the time he was discovered and the area where he was left. The locals, who had been around the previous evening as the police went about their work, were interested in what had happened but did not necessarily want it broadcast. The press conference had originally been planned to launch an appeal for information regarding Sergei; this had now changed, though the crowds of reporters were unaware of any of this at present.

Ray and Dan managed to get into the station without being accosted by any reporters. Ray would usually leave the media work to the police press officer, and TV appeals had always seemed to suit Adam, who had liked nothing better than shining his uniform buttons and ensuring his tie was straight. Ray left Dan to go and join the rest of the team at CID while he made his way to see Angela. The decision he was about to make would take everyone in the station by surprise; they all knew his feelings about the press, he always felt they were quick enough to report any negative articles, though there was never the same focus on any good news stories.

Even at the last press conference he had attended, when Adam announced his departure as they wrapped up the last case, rather than make it a story about the result of the case and point out the good work Adam had done at the station. The headline the following day had been about the fact that the criminal had been killed in an accident but that the police had not been aware he was back in the area. He felt this made his point about his opinion. He made his way upstairs, still stopping, as he could not get used to there being no secretary at a desk, and the door to the superintendent's office was standing open. It had always felt that going to see Adam was a closed affair, requiring an appointment.

Also, while in the office, it felt as though the person being talked to was being constantly assessed. The feeling so far since Angela was in place was more relaxed, and Ray felt he was just reporting back as he did to the team. Angela was busy writing at her desk, so he knocked on the frame of the door as he walked in, 'Good afternoon, Ray. How are things going?'

'Without putting any pressure on anyone, I would say it is moving in a positive direction.'

Before he explained what he had found out, he gave his reason for first coming to the office.

'This is not meant in any way disrespectful, Angela; I do not know how many times you have faced the press. I wanted to offer to join you this afternoon.'

'I take it that I should be honoured, as I know how you feel about the press. It would be appreciated. I am sure I will recognise some faces, though you can point me in the direction of the local reporters. I find it helps to have a good relationship locally.'

'I will go and get ready. Once the press have been dealt with, there will be our evening briefing, which you may like to attend. Going on my own day with the calls I have received from others will be busy and hopefully fruitful.'

Ray left Angela to prepare, having told her he would meet her downstairs in 15 minutes. One of the benefits of the police station being housed in such an old building was that there was plenty of room. The conference room they would use was bigger than some of the CID offices Ray had visited over the years. He went into the CID room and was greeted by a similar level of noise he would expect to get from the press. If Angela had been surprised by Ray's offer to attend the press conference, the team around him were absolutely gobsmacked. They all knew Ray avoided the press like the plague; he had even upset several reporters over the years by telling them in no polite way to clear off. The only thing that appeared to redeem him was that none of them could do anything but admit he was a good policeman who got results. Once the varying words of shock had subsided, he spoke, 'Right, the briefing will follow my chat with the press; it will be busy. Before I get back, the ones that need to be able to update the incident board. Dan, you can put in there the basics of what we found out today.'

Ray had expected banter regarding him and the press, though he did not want any of them getting distracted. Before the noise level could rise again, he took control, 'Okay, on you all get. I will not be long.'

He quickly detoured to his office, scanning his eyes over his emails, none of which were of any major importance. He also grabbed a coffee. He felt the purchase of a coffee machine for his office had been a good idea. Coffee was a mainstay of his day, so having a machine to allow it to always be readily available felt right. Some of the others had remarked that he was too impatient to wait for the kettle to boil in the kitchen area, though these same people were happy to use the machine as well. He had pointed out that he had no problem with them using it, as long as everyone made sure it was always filled up. Ray left them all doing as needed; with so-called words of encouragement ringing in his ears, he went to meet Angela. They both walked into the room to be greeted by a wall of light as cameras flashed, taking pictures that would be on news broadcasts and in papers.

Before they had even reached their seats, questions were being shouted across the room. Fortunately, the lady who was in charge of the media office was very good at her job; even though Ray recognised her previously, he couldn't recall her name. She was part of a new programme that forces across the country were encouraged to use; this was to employ people who had previously worked in the media to deal with anything press-related. As usual, this had been greeted with scepticism by the old-school as to why have someone with no police experience talk about what was happening in an investigation.

Very quickly, though, it became obvious, especially to officers like Ray who didn't enjoy working with the press, that it relieved a lot of the pressure that built from the outside when dealing with the day-to-day running of an investigation. The other help was a good media officer who knew exactly what the press wanted. Slowly, the flashing lights eased off, 'Good afternoon, ladies, and gentlemen. I think most of you know me. I am Susan, and I am the press officer for King's Lynn and the surrounding area. The majority of you know Detective Inspector Ray Keane; also here today is our new superintendent, Angela Johnson. Angela and Ray will take you through the details so far; there will then be an opportunity for questions. To make things easier, please keep things civilised and avoid shouting over each other.'

Ray was impressed as the reporters sitting facing him were all taking notice of what Susan was saying. He had heard that previously at another station, she had a reporter removed for constantly shouting out questions designed to try and catch out a detective; that same reporter had found himself not invited to any recent press conferences.

Angela got proceedings under way by introducing herself, and he was impressed by how easily her words flowed, but in comparison to Adam, they did not appear to be just about her, 'Ladies and gentlemen, I'm Angela, and I moved here 2 weeks ago. I really hope we are going to have a productive working relationship. As I always tell my officers, if you do your job to the best of your ability and I do mine to the same standard, everyone will get along fine. You were all given press releases when you arrived; these detail our progress into the investigation into the discovery of Sergei Romanov recently.'

A reporter sat beside a cameraman with the name of a television company emblazoned across its side and went to speak. They all soon found out that Angela was in charge. Literally, the guy got as far as opening his mouth when she cut him off, 'There will be time for questions at the end. I'm sure if you want a full story, you can wait with the others.'

This brought laughter from around the room, 'Now, there have been some developments for us to pass on; I will just reiterate that it is still early days in the investigation. D.I. Keane will now bring you up to date.'

'Good afternoon, everyone. First, we would like to appeal for any information people may have regarding Sergei Romanov, in particular his movements over the last few weeks. We have found out he was fairly well known in the area, and along with 4 friends, he has been returning to the UK for several years to work on a local farm.'

Ray's next comment did something that rarely happened, this was that he took members of the press by surprise.

'We have also, in the last 36 hours, discovered another body; this was a young lad by the name of Nick Crowe. Initially, we thought it was a separate incident. I can tell you that information that has come to light today has confirmed they are connected.'

This time, there was little Angela or anyone else could do to keep the reporters in check, as more flashbulbs erupted and questions were screamed from all corners of the room. Eventually calm was restored, and as it became quiet again, one person from the back of the room took his chance to speak.

'So, is there a serial killer roaming the area?'

'Categorially, no, there is not. I can tell you that both victims were killed in the same manner. You will understand our inquiries are still piecing information together.'

The response from Ray seemed to indicate to the room that they could all start asking questions. The 3 people sat facing the cameras decided without words to each other that for now they would answer questions. Angela, who had hoped to get to know which reporters were local before the questions started, skillfully went with the flow and, without realising it, pointed at a young lady to ask her question. Ray recognised her from the local town paper.

'So, if there is not a serial killer, do you not expect any more bodies?'

Ray took a moment to think before he answered and decided that he was possibly mellowing, as previously his answer would have been a few snapped words, 'I am sorry to have to say, the only people who use the expression serial killer are yourselves. Someone can either take the life of 1 person or 101 they are still killers. Both of our victims appear to have been killed by the same person, though our early investigations show there is a likely drug connection behind the reason for their deaths.'

A few of the regular reporters were just as surprised as Ray himself by this new response to questions, so they saw it as a chance to get a bigger story splash for their editors. The press conference carried on, with the majority of the press getting to ask questions that, between all the answers, built up a picture for them to give their audience. Ray saw an opportunity to wind up the press conference and get back to the team for the briefing.

'Just before we finish up, ladies and gentlemen, I will add that it is looking increasingly likely that there is a strong link to a local drug dealer being involved. I hope you all feel the same as the force does about the damage caused to lives by drugs. I can promise you that our main priority is to find the killer, though I will have a team searching deeper. I want to find the person responsible for circulating and living off the misery caused by drugs. You all know the importance of information, so please let your audience know we are here to listen.'

Angela took control to finish things up, 'I am sure I will speak to you all again. Thank you for your cooperation.'

As always, some of the reporters tried their best to get another question answered, but to no avail as the three of them made their way out of the room. Outside, they all stopped, and Angela addressed them both, 'Ray, I am impressed. Going on what I had heard, I did not expect you to be so polite.'

Ray smiled, 'I can be very polite until any of them overstep the mark. Which they have done with regularity previously. We just hope their reports bring us some more details.'

'Susan, you did very well. If you want to come and see me tomorrow, we can discuss anything they put out tonight. So, if needed, we can prepare another press release.'

They all went their separate ways, with Angela adding, 'Ray I will be along to the briefing shortly, though you can get started if you need to.'

'I will just check everyone is ready to go, then we can all be updated on what we know so far.'

As Ray made his way through CID, to his office with the intention of quickly checking emails and casting his eyes at his in-tray for any post, in particular an envelope he would recognise as being the postmortem results. He was greeted with several comments, all of which followed a similar pattern; the majority were about his newfound friends in the press, and any banter between them always helped to relieve the pressure felt during a case. One of his favourite descriptions of the situation had come from DI Steve Edwards, the man who Ray had first worked under, and recently Ray had had to solve his murder. Steve had always said a murder investigation was like a pressure cooker; it bubbled away until it was ready, though if you didn't release the pressure at the right moment, the lid would blow and it could take a long while to clear up the mess.

His in tray was its usual mountain of paper, and despite his time spent trying to clear paperwork, this tray always seemed to have a way of multiplying itself. He did wonder if he could dare to ask Angela; if she did not want a secretary, then maybe he could use one. He felt it was too early for the full report from Graham, though he knew they would get a detailed explanation in a few moments from Sheila.

There was an email from Graham with some basic information regarding the fact that both men had been strangled. The words that interested him were that Graham had concluded that the imprints of finger marks on the necks were very similar, even though he was not 100% certain. He pointed out that when they arrested someone, he would be able to carry out tests to confirm his thoughts. Ray could hear conversations starting to develop outside, so he knew the team would be starting to talk about what they had each found out throughout the day. This was a sign for him to get the briefing underway to enable the main details to be reported accurately. Ray went out, and without having to say anything, his action of just going to stand by the incident board was enough to get the attention of the room.

'Okay, I know you all have had a busy day; so, let's make a start and get these boards updated. Sheila, you can start by giving us the details of the postmortem.'

'Graham is convinced we are looking at 1 person committing the killings. Both were strangled, and pressure marks from the killers' hands are similar on both victims.'

She went on to explain how he felt that Nick had been a user in the past, though currently no one could see the bearing of this. Though Ray knew the pieces they had put together about Nick today would show this was important.

'He also felt that the feet may have been tied together, initially with the intention of the body being dumped in the river, making it extremely difficult for the victim to escape. He would not commit to the question of whether the victim was strangled at first or as an afterthought. Telling me that was a question we would need to find the answer to.'

'Anything else to add for now?'

'Only really something for us to bear in mind. The killer is very dangerous.'

This brought a quick response from several voices in the room, 'Aren't they all?'

'That was possibly not the right word to use; from his findings, Graham could tell both men were strangled from the front. This means that while he was committing the act, our killer was face-to-face with his victims. Summing up, Graham said it takes a particularly nasty type of person to do that.'

Ray felt it was worth taking a moment to reiterate that point, 'So, just remember, when we get near to a conclusion, I do not want anyone playing the hero and thinking of tackling this man alone. I know it sounds like health and safety advice;

I do not want to lose any of the team; we all know the dangers, so take it all in.'

He was about to continue when he saw Angela in the doorway, 'Carry on, Inspector. I am only here to catch up.'

Ray looked over at Tim, who, as well as listening to Sheila, was also watching his computer screen.

'Any news from the traffic cameras yet?'

'Nothing yet, sir, unless you want me to start reporting to the traffic section the amount of dodgy driving that is going on.'

'Right, well, keep looking. We will leave reporting people's driving habits for a quieter moment.'

This brought the expected response of muted laughter, and Ray noticed that the laughter also included Angela. He could never have imagined Adam laughing as part of the team. He was convinced that there was going to be a good working relationship develop.

'Tim, you keep searching. I can tell you that Dan and I had a fruitful day, in as much as his mum felt that Nick was the blue-eyed boy in the family. She is wise enough to know he has recently gone off the rails.'

Ray knew he wanted to get as much information as he could across to the team. He was also aware that a lot of them found it easier to take in information once it was on the boards; they could then cast their eyes over it several times and then follow up on anything when needed.

'You can all get the details later if you need to ask Dan, who will give you the details. Just to finish up, we also visited the Red Eagle again.'

Sheila broke in quickly, 'You are becoming a regular there, sir.'

'Thank you, Sheila; I just wish I had the time to sit and enjoy a pint. We visited as Shirley Crowe overheard Nick arrange to meet someone there. The landlord, who last time appeared to be helpful to a point, was more forthcoming this time, especially once I suggested I could get the drug squad to start visiting.'

Ray was about to tell them about the mystery character called Jack when Tim called out from behind his computer.

'We got it.'

'I hope it is not catching. What have you got, Tim?'

'You remember Chris Small said he had seen a white van driving away from his field the night he discovered the body? The night, Nick was found there was a white transit coming over Sutton Bridge and then turning left along the road to the lighthouse.'

'Can you see a number plate at all? There may well be lots of white vans using that route, though you know I do not believe in coincidences.'

'I can see a partial plate; it begins WA5 and ends AP. We may get lucky with DVLA, but unfortunately, as soon as it turns left, we lose sight of it.'

'Good work, Tim, you, and others. Keep on checking; you have a target now; as surely, they would have to drive back out to the main road.'

Tim didn't want to dampen any good feelings by saying they could use one of the back roads out, though this would depend on them being local and knowing the area, so instead he kept things upbeat, 'We will keep checking the cameras; the best bet is if they turn out onto the bridge and we get a good look at them; if they go left towards King's Lynn, we will have to search harder.'

Ray acknowledged all this with a nod, then got back to his own information, 'We possibly have a name to work with; Nick's mum had overheard mention of the pub, and she also heard Nick talking to someone in the flat, saying he was to be working with Jack from now on.'

He carried on telling them that the landlord at the Red Eagle had also heard mention of Jack. It had not been any of Sergei's group who had used the name, but several groups of younger drinkers. When pushed, he admitted knowing that there was drug usage in the area, though never in his pub. This was something Ray did not believe for a minute. Jerry said he thought it was likely Jack was a dealer.

'I want us all to proceed with caution; as I have just told the press, our main objective is to find and arrest the killers of both Sergei and Nick. If, while doing this, we can get information to break a drug ring, then even better. I do not for a minute think Jack is the brain behind this, but he could be the muscle. If we find him and storm into arresting him, we all know he will go for no comment in the interview room.'

Ray looked over to give Angela a chance to speak, which she took, 'Just to say, you are all doing a good job; keep it up and let's get the result we want. But safely.'

'Okay, finish up for this evening, unless you are working on anything in particular that is urgent. Get home and be back here at 7AM.'

There was some chatter as the room slowly emptied, with people making their way home. Even though it had only been just over 24 hours, Ray was looking forward to getting home and seeing Jenny. Angela came over as he was getting ready to leave, 'Try and get some rest this evening; we can do more tomorrow. It does feel as if you are moving things in the right direction.'

Ray smiled and had to admit he liked this new situation, where the work of the team was encouraged as being good police work and not just trying to make figures look good. He did not feel totally comfortable yet to tell Angela that there was a good chance himself and Jenny would be going dancing in the evening; he just knew it would be a chance to relax for a few hours.

Chapter Thirteen

As the team made their way out of the crowded CID room, having discussed the deaths of Sergei and Nick. 2 other people were in much more comfortable surroundings, discussing the same thing. Darren Plant sat in his study, in his usual leather armchair, with a glass of fine whisky sitting on the elegant table beside him. He had the appearance of a very relaxed businessman at the end of his day. This was the total opposite of the emotions that Jack was displaying; he was currently pacing up and down by the French doors, which looked out across a very neat garden.

Jack had arrived 20 minutes earlier, and apart from a few words of greeting, nothing else had been said. Jack just continued with his pacing; it was Darren who took the lead, 'Jack sit down; you will wear a hole in my nice flooring.'

Killing someone was not new to Jack; so far, each time he had taken someone's life, he made it right with himself that he had done it to protect himself and a very lucrative business. Jack had met Darren 6 years previously, and they had gotten along well from the start. Jack was well aware of the situation between them. Darren was the boss, and Jack was the hired help. He knew very well that while Darren was happy to give out orders and reap the benefits, he would never get his hands dirty. Jack had spent a short while in the army; at the time, his thoughts were that it was a good use of energy, while several other people observed it was a way of controlling his anger issues. He had been the type of child then teenager who appeared to be constantly angry with something or someone, as Jack was to discover, though in as much as the army was able to channel these emotions into good work.

A mix of constant anger and energy didn't sit well within the regulations of army life. It was a fixture of a life in which officers hoped to channel both emotions to develop a career soldier. Everything started off promising enough; initial reports from instructors were good, with several comments along the lines that, if we can smooth out the rough edges, there is the making of a good soldier. After completing his basic training, he received details of his first posting, a tour of Afghanistan. It should have all passed relatively quietly, but as the conflict had changed from previous tours, it was now more of a peacekeeping mission.

The reports that followed the incident were not fully helpful, as there was conflicting analysis. One report said that Jack just appeared to lose his temper, then lashed out at another soldier. A more detailed doctor's report after Jack returned home concluded that a combination of early-onset post-traumatic stress disorder and a minor case of sunstroke had led to the altercation, which left Jack bruised and battered, while the other soldier had suffered a mild concussion. However, as anyone interpreted the response, there was only ever one conclusion, Jack was to be medically discharged.

After leaving the army, Jack spent a lot of time alone; this was thought of as the worst thing he could do. If ever there was a positive side to his anger, this allowed Jack to see it. He decided he was not going to let things get the better of him; somehow, he managed to keep on a steady track. He had never been a heavy drinker, so he avoided the pitfalls of alcohol, which had taken over the lives of so many others in his position. He dabbled in what he saw as social drug use, and this was the event that led to him meeting Darren. He had been wandering the street near his flat one evening, having arranged a meeting for someone to supply him with some cocaine. He was surprised that his image of a drug dealer, someone dressed rough and looking as though they needed a good wash, had been destroyed by the guy in the smart suit, who handed him a packet and took the money in return. Jack had no idea why, but he felt he wanted to talk to this person, 'Can you introduce me to the right people so I can do what you do?'

The reply was exactly what he needed to hear, 'You fancy earning some money, do you?'

The idea of earning some cash was very appealing; even though his payoff from the army had been substantial considering the short time he had served; he knew it would not last forever. It was to take a few weeks of meeting others first, as though there was an interview process to go through before it was arranged for him to meet Darren. His first 2 meetings with Darren took place in a pub in town that was always busy, and no one took any notice of anyone else. Except for Jack, who was constantly scanning the room, Darren noticed this, and eventually it was the first time Jack impressed him.

'You seem nervous, Jack. All you spend time doing is looking at people; you are not heavily using are you?'

'No. It is a throwback to my army days. I like to know who is around and how many. It has saved me from a couple of beatings in the past by keeping me one step ahead.'

'I think you would do well in my organisation. I need someone who I can trust to keep an eye open to protect me.'

The 2 of them got on well immediately. Jack because he could see the potential to earn some good money, and Darren who saw hired muscle who would be happy to hand out the warnings needed without asking too many questions. The first time he visited Darren at his house, Jack was as impressed as most visitors were. If this was the result of money earned through dealing, then Jack was more than interested. Slowly, they fell into a routine of work, and Jack was suitably rewarded for his work. One of the first things Darren made sure Jack understood was that he would not get anywhere if he sampled too much merchandise.

'If you play it right, you can enjoy the finer things in life. The thrill of a nice meal with a good bottle of wine served to you in a lovely setting is much better than the quick few minutes high you get from snorting powder up your nose, and you are the one in control.'

Jack found it easy to slip into his role; he found following instructions was just like being back in the army. A lot of ex-servicemen found it difficult to not have orders to follow. Working, they all had a very strong ethic; this meant they could get work, though if struggling with issues, it needed understanding, and invariably, this was where problems developed. The other bonus for Jack was that he was getting more money in his hand at the end of the week. He also enjoyed wearing smart clothes, and with the respect this earned, Darren made sure he was kitted out with shirts and ties as the first thing he did; again, this had echoes of army life.

Darren was very happy as well, in that he now had someone at his side who, apart from his size, didn't stand out as though he didn't belong. There was this feeling that, if needed, Jack could take care of himself and also Darren. News soon spread that it was not a good idea to get on the wrong side of Darren, as this led to a late-night visit with a painful ending, courtesy of Jack. Soon Darren was making offers to other dealers in the region; they felt they could not refuse; more money started to appear, and Jack was enjoying his life. Jack had always had a feeling inside that, with the right encouragement, he could be good at organising things.

It seemed totally wrong that this skill should become prominent while he was working for someone who was happy to break the law. As it was, Jack never saw it as law-breaking; he was just supplying a need. Darren had told him that the people they sold to knew exactly what they were doing. Of course, if anyone, including Jack, was to look closely, it was obvious this wasn't true. They may have known they were taking illegal substances, but for whatever reason they took them, a lot of the time they were not aware of their actions.

Jack had skirted on the edge of the law several times, and as with lots of others, if he had not joined up, he would have ended up in big trouble. Even though it was only for a short time, his time in the army had shown him what he could achieve. This was a big problem for a lot of people who joined up for the services. The main problems arose on leaving the services. You had career servicemen who, after a very successful career, found adapting to civilian life extremely difficult; also, there were an increasing number who were forced to leave early, either through ill health or, as in Jack's case, bad behaviour.

For some of them, the fact that they had always wanted to join up and then it was taken away from them was too much to deal with. Jack had heard of several friends he had made who just could not deal with it and ended up joining a growing number of suicides, along with a lot of these people. On leaving the forces, Jack turned to passing his time with recreational drugs. This had to be a major misleading statement as to how anything that could leave you not knowing what was happening could be classed as recreational. Jack was fully aware that meeting Darren when he did saved his life from becoming a hazy mess.

Some of the problems were also caused unwittingly by the forces themselves, as it would be drilled into young recruits that they didn't need to think for themselves but just do as ordered. This was the main reason why several of them ended up working in a security situation, as they were still following orders; on the other side of the coin, unfortunately, a lot of them ended up living rough. These people came to rely on the selfless work of one of the many charities set up to help them. An amazing amount, of veterans turned their lives around because of these charity workers. After these 2 types of people, there were the few like Jack, who were classed as borderline cases; they lived life on the edge and given the right, or depending on opinion, the wrong, support could go either way.

Jack liked the lifestyle that Darren had; he liked the big house and the fancy cars, though he didn't feel these were as important to him. He did, however, like the nice clothes that he could now afford. He was happy in a t-shirt and jeans but felt more at home in a smart outfit with a nice tie. When he first started working for Darren, jeans and a t-shirt meant he blended in with his surroundings. Over time, Darren started to use Jack more for personal protection and the places they visited—a nice suit that earned respect.

The working relationship was easily maintained, and in the beginning, Jack was the same as many others, who spent their time around the area supplying as required. One evening, Darren called Jack and told him that he had started to hear rumours that someone they supplied was trying to sell the drugs; this was not part of Darren's business plan. He told Jack that he had arranged a meeting to supposedly talk things over. He told Jack where the person would be and arranged for a friendly warning, though with enough force to get the message across. If this notice was ignored, there would be worse to come.

That night, when a bloody and bruised youth turned up at the local hospital, no one took a great deal of notice, as it was explained that he had been in a fight. Police were notified by staff when they arrived and recognised him as a local drug user, but it was logged in the report as a falling out among thieves. Darren was impressed by how Jack reacted to his instructions and was even more satisfied when, a few days later, he got a message from the lad involved an apology for overstepping the mark. This was proof to Darren that Jack was going to fit in nicely; it also meant Darren could distance himself from any problems that may arise from the deal.

If Jack's career path was mixed, then Darren's was totally the opposite. He had a good family upbringing; his father ran several successful businesses; and as an only child, his mother doted on him. The family had always been in a position where she could stay at home, look after Darren, and run the household. His childhood and teenage years were privileged times. Unfortunately, any hope his father harboured for him to follow in the family business disappeared once Darren went to college. At a party, he had his first encounter with drugs. He enjoyed the feeling at the time it gave him, though he was quick enough to see how at one house party of possibly 40 students, there was an immense amount of money changing hands.

Suddenly, he saw a business venture he wanted to be part of. His father's disappointment at not having his son join him led to several family arguments. It was only his mother's feelings towards her boy and the relationship between his parents that stopped him from being cast adrift by his father. No one could honestly say they would willingly set up a member of their family to run a drug business; unknowingly, this was exactly what his father did after pressure from his wife. He installed Darren in a nice flat and still gave him a generous amount of money. It didn't take long for Darren to make inroads on the local scene. He had always been popular at school and in the neighbourhood, partly due to the fact that he always had spare money.

He was the posh boy at school and was happy to be surrounded by large groups of people. It was because of these groups that he found it easy to get contacts to start selling drugs. The money from his father meant he could buy his way into the scene that had always been viewed as a low order of life. For his own life, the money aspect meant he was soon at the top table of organising things to make even more money. This also meant that he learned very quickly that to avoid visits from the police, it was best to put as many other people as possible between himself and any transactions.

This had worked well for him, and he saw no reason that anything should change. It didn't take long for him to establish himself as the top dog in the area. He managed to keep away from the police, and slowly he bought into legitimate businesses and proved to be a successful man. He soon moved out of the flat his father had arranged for him and, with contacts he had made, was soon living in a very desirable property on the edge of the town. He was sensible enough to keep knowledge of his dealings to a select few; none of his neighbours would have been able to tell anyone what he did. They only knew him as a pillar of society who supported local charities; at one stage, there was a picture of him in the local paper at a fundraising event, and alongside him in the photo was the chief constable for the area.

Things continued to move well for Darren, and he enjoyed himself. He had a few people in his inner circle that he trusted, and he saw no problems moving his business forward. When he was introduced to Jack, he saw it as another piece fitting into a puzzle. Over the last couple of years, he had had to be careful as well as clever to stay one step ahead of the law. It had happened recently that every now and then, police forces in an area would get together to tackle a particular problem. It would work through the system; seemingly, businesses that were linked would be targeted, possibly by the people involved. Darren had always found it better to concentrate fully on one side of things.

This helped him retain certain control over it all. The police collaboration maybe that they would target drug dealers, then look to tackle prostitution, followed by house break-ins; these were all things that could make their figures look good, as well as dealing with issues people complained about. This time Darren had to move quickly. He was alerted by someone he had once done a favour for. He got a phone call to tell him that a dealer further into Lincolnshire had dropped his name into a conversation in a pub; this had been overheard by an undercover drugs officer. Darren always had plans in place for just such an occasion and very swiftly took himself out of the area. While he was in hiding, he heard of several raids, fortunately with no link back to him.

The arrangement between himself and Jack worked well; every now and then Jack would have to revert to type and, in his words, give someone a slap just to remind them who was the boss. The previous year, there had been a few problems keeping Sergei under control, and again, Darren felt that Jack had dealt with it all neatly. So far, the last few months had all seemed good. Nick was introduced to Jack and then Darren. Money was coming in at a regular rate; Darren had even started to look for a bigger house. Suddenly everything changed; rumours started spreading that Darren was past it and no longer the big shot.

This was enough at first for Darren to get annoyed. He got Jack to start visiting the usual places and put the word out that nothing had changed. It was while Jack and Nick had been talking to a regular customer outside of the Red Eagle that they heard Sergei's name for being interested in supplying. Jack reported this back to Darren, who was suitably angry that someone he had supplied for a few years and at a good price should suddenly think they had the right to try and take over.

It transpired that upon asking around, Darren learned that Sergei had been offering to sell drugs for another dealer outside of the area, for which he got a cut of the profits. Then, on returning to the UK this year, he had been selling drugs that were being brought into the country from Latvia. Darren knew that once he had this information, he had 3 options for what to do next; the first choice was always the least likely. This was to allow information to be passed to the police and let them deal with it; he was loathing to do this as it could attract unwanted attention. His 2nd option was to cut and run; he knew he could move out of the area and live comfortably, and if he wanted to, he could even start up again somewhere new.

The final option, and anyone who knew him knew this was a choice he would make, was to stay put and use people like Jack and Nick to send out a warning. The idea of a warning was how things led to Sergei being left in the field for the combine harvester to find; possibly Darren should have taken more notice of things when the plan to destroy all the evidence failed. If he thought it was unlucky that the farmer spotted something was wrong before the combine harvester ran over Sergei, leaving the police with nearly a complete body from which to start their investigation. His next problem was people not knowing when to keep quiet. It had always been a problem for Nick to know when to not say anything; he particularly liked to brag about things when they were going well.

It had started at school, when if he got praise from a teacher, his friends would soon be fed up hearing about it all. This continued throughout his life and even led to a couple run-ins with his dad, who felt his problems were compounded by Nick mouthing off in the neighbourhood. He knew it was best to keep quiet sometimes, but he found he couldn't help himself. It reached a point where he wasn't even cautious enough to worry about who might be listening; a prime example of this was the things his mum had overheard and has since told the police about. Unfortunately, for Nick; this information being brought back to Darren happened while he was trying to deal with other things. In the normal course of events, and because he liked Nick, he would have arranged for Jack to have a word and set him straight. Darren was just not prepared to take any risks, so he told Jack to use his own judgement and that Nick needed silencing.

For reasons he couldn't explain, possibly down to his own feelings of anxiety being higher than normal, silencing Nick and disposing of his body was just a bit too much for Jack. The actual act of killing him was not the problem, especially when Jack first tried talking to Nick about Darren's concerns. When Nick responded by starting to mouth off to Jack, including comments about how one day he was looking to take control away from Darren, it became easier for Jack to deal with things as he could only see the trouble Nick could cause. Jack's problems increased afterwards when he had to report to Darren.

All of these events from the past few days were the reason behind the situation that Jack was now in, seemingly wearing a hole in the floor of the study at Darren's. He also knew that Darren was good at sorting things out, but his attitude at present was not helping, 'I'm not sure what you expect me to do, Jack?'

'Well, sorting out what happens next would be a good start.'

'You have not made things easy, have you? I asked you to get rid of 2 bodies, even giving you a clue on how to do it.

Both times, you have left the police with plenty of clues to help them.'

'Hold on a minute; you are not suggesting I planned it deliberately, are you? I don't see it as entirely my fault; you reckoned a combine harvester would run over almost anything without anyone noticing. Then getting disturbed by a late-night dog walker as I was about to dump Nick in the river was just unlucky.'

'Be that as it may, we still have the initial problem—that others are seeing a chance to muscle in on my turf, and now we could get the police sniffing around. I think it could be for the best if you were to disappear for a while. The way you are getting stressed, a holiday could help you relax.'

'What are you going to do if I go on holiday?'

'I think in the current situation, the less you know about my intentions, the better. I do not want to know your plans either. Disappear for a few weeks; don't contact anyone. Then you know which phone to call me on, and we can then see how things are.'

As Darren finished speaking, he pulled a large amount of cash out of his pocket, placing it deliberately on the table before pushing it towards Jack. As far as Darren was concerned, this should have been the end of the matter. For him, having money available and the ability to put distance between everyone involved should allow things to calm down. He was fully aware from conversations at dinners with superior police officers of how pointless they sometimes felt using resources to investigate drug offences; his hope was that once details were gathered that both Sergei and Nick were involved in a local drug scene, their deaths would be treated as nothing more than a falling out.

Darren was about to make 2 mistakes: first, he had no idea how strongly D.I. Keane felt about drugs; and second, he was not an authority on people's behaviour to recognise the signs of how everything was affecting Jack. In actual fact, to show how little notice he had taken of Jack's demeanour over the last hour while he had been pacing, his last comment inevitably, even though meant with good intention, lit the fuse.

'Time for you to go, Jack. Take the money and find somewhere to relax. I don't expect to hear from you for at least 2 weeks.'

As Jack walked out, his brain was buzzing, and the only clear thought was that I am on my own.

Chapter Fourteen

Ray found the journey home exciting, in that he would get to spend the evening with Jenny. They both understood the pressures of the job, and Jenny was fully aware of how consumed Ray got when in the middle of a case. She hoped that the details she had heard so far about the new superintendent would mean that Ray could get on with things without the added worry of outside influences. With Adam in charge, Ray had gotten more irritated each time he was working on a major investigation. He kept being called to see Adam, who was continually worrying about the cost of everything as well as wanting cases solved to make the numbers look good.

Ray walked in, having rung her on his way home, just as she was getting ready to cook some pasta for their dinner; Jenny had waited until he got home to mention that if they had a quick dinner. They could possibly go dancing. This was something she had introduced him to when they first got together; initially, he was unsure, it was something he had ever considered. Even when attending official dinners, he was happy to sit on the sidelines. He was pleasantly surprised by how much he enjoyed being taught and was pleased to find that it allowed him to switch off from work for a few hours;

during a case, this was something he had always found difficult. Jenny would never push the point, but she was happy when he agreed it was a good idea.

'I will say though, I am not sure how focused I might be. There is a lot going on at the moment, but I will try and concentrate.'

'That is fine. It is not a class, so you do not have to concentrate too hard, and we can always leave early if you want to.'

Ray knew this was always okay with Jenny, though he had to admit in the past that once he got to a dance, he wanted to make the most of the time spent with her.

He also felt it was important that they had a social circle outside of work. Too often, emergency services workers formed relationships that involved as much time socially as at work. The feeling had always been well; we understand what we are going through, and though he felt it did not do good, eventually, on any given night out, the conversation would always turn to work.

Since they had moved into their new house together, going to the classes as they had done in King's Lynn was not as easy. Jenny had soon found out where dances took place in the area, and they had managed to attend a few. On the first one they attended; they met several dancers they had seen before; it appeared they didn't mind travelling for the chance to dance. Ray agreed it was a good idea and hoped to relax slightly. It helped that the last thing Angela had told him was to go home and switch off for a few hours. They ate dinner, and Ray found he had a spring in his step at the thought of going dancing. They parked at the hall, and Ray was pleased to see lots of people they had not met for a while.

They found a free table and sat down, but not for long, as the music started up and Ray whisked Jenny around the floor for a quickstep. One of the reasons he found dancing relaxing was he never got a lot of time to sit around, which would lead to him thinking about work things, attending a dance nowadays meant there was increasingly a number of single people, so there was always a lady to ask to dance. Being how he was when Jenny mentioned dance classes and the possibility of attending a social dance, he took time to read about the history of ballroom dancing. While reading, he learned until very recently, people only ever attended a dance as a couple, spending the evening dancing with their own partner.

It was accepted and expected nowadays that people would change partners easily, which helped encourage the social aspect. It also helped in getting younger people interested in ballroom dancing, which was important for its continued success.

As usual, the evening passed in a flash, and soon they were saying goodbye, with others telling them that they hoped to see them again soon. Most of their group knew what they both did for a living and that getting to a dance was always dictated by whatever case was ongoing. It always seemed to take time to leave the hall, as saying goodbye to everyone took longer than expected. They made their way home, with Jenny feeling good and Ray feeling pleased that they had gone. There was always a ritual to follow when getting home from a dance, which involved Jenny getting into her dressing gown as quickly as was humanly possible while Ray made coffee and toast.

This time, had become a moment where they would discuss the current cases. For Jenny, her transfer to a different CID group meant to be the newest member of the team, so far, she had no involvement in a major case. Ray knew she found this frustrating, though she had settled in well and was finding her feet, so knew it would not be long before she was in the thick of things. Once they were both in comfort mode, Jenny started the conversation.

'So, where are things at in your investigation?'

'Going slowly if I am honest. We did find out more about Nick today, though all it did was confirm what we knew already. There is a definite link to drugs between our victims. Unfortunately, that becomes a sticking point; as usual, no one is forthcoming as to who may be involved further up the chain.'

'Any names to work with yet?'

'Yes, but even that is causing problems because we only have first names.'

'That is not unusual in anything to do with drugs is it? What names have you got? I could ask around the office; someone may just make a connection.'

'It could be helpful; I think with all the action nowadays involving county lines investigations, we may have to spread our wings a bit further on this one. The names we have so far are Jack and Darren. The latest victim, Nick Crowe, was involved; possibly he worked for them and has upset somebody.'

'That will give me something to start on tomorrow.'

As always, Ray found it helped to talk things through with Jenny, and despite the fact they were no further forward, it did feel as if they were moving in the right direction. He finished his coffee, then changed the subject, 'Right, as I spent last night on my own in a hotel room, I think it is time I took you to bed.'

Jenny knew she had a few minutes start, as there was no way Ray would go to bed without clearing the cups away, so she smiled at him as she said, 'Ready when you are.'

Leaving him at the living room door, she ran up the stairs, laughing. Hearing Jenny laugh was the best sound in the world to him. After a restless night previously, as he turned to put out the bedside light, he could feel himself drifting off to sleep. It was a favourite saying from Jenny—that she didn't know how—but he appeared to be asleep before the lightbulb was fully out. He always found that after a good night's dancing, no matter which case was ongoing, he was able to get a good night's sleep. The loud squawking of the alarm clock signalled the start of another busy day.

They had always made a point of allowing time to have breakfast together, feeling that it was important in setting them up for whatever the day might bring. Once they had finished and cleared away, they both left for work with Jenny, promising to ring him if anyone could help with the names and the drug connection. Not knowing it at the time, Ray was to get a pleasant surprise later in the day, which was to involve him working alongside Jenny again. It had taken a while, but he was now used to the feeling of being relaxed without feeling guilty after spending time with Jenny.

This had taken some adjusting to in his thought patterns, even though his wife Mary had always been understanding; he was the first to admit he had, in the early years, been consumed by the job. It had first been a case of wanting to improve via promotion, but as he progressed through the ranks, it became important that he was seen as a good leader. In his mind, the main objective had been to provide a comfortable life for them both. Though they had not had children, it was not something they missed; Mary had always told friends that she knew exactly the life she was marrying into.

He felt that they had had a good life, even allowing for the upset caused by the dementia that he always looked upon as taking her away from him twice; first by the need to go into a nursing home, then when, with some relief, she passed away. If it were at all possible in those last few years, he had thrown himself even more into his work. He now told people that he could not believe how lucky he was to have found Jenny when they first met; it had involved developing a very good working relationship, and he was most surprised when it moved along further. Jenny had given him another purpose, to enjoy life.

The one thing about making the commute to work was that it gave him time to think things over; he switched into work mode as he got in the car. Fortunately, wanting to get an early start to things meant there was not a lot of traffic to contend with. As he drove, he got things ordered in his mind as to how he would like things dealt with during the coming day. His first job of the day would be to go through the full postmortem report, which he knew Graham would have sent over by now. The next thing would be more in hope that possibly Tim or one of the others looking at traffic cameras may have had some luck in spotting the white van they were all interested in.

He pulled into the car park, which at this hour was relatively quiet, and made his way inside. The station was busy with the current changeover of shifts. It was a time as a young PC that he had always enjoyed; there would be time for a brief chat between the officers as they started or finished shifts. It was no different in any of the uniformed services that there was camaraderie, built around concern for your fellow officers. All of them were fully aware of the fact that each day at work, you had no idea what you might face.

Despite his own concerns, whenever the subject of arming officers arose, Ray was happy that they now had extra defences, such as tasers, to call on if needed. Making his way upstairs, he was surprised but not shocked to see Tim already sitting at his desk. He had to admit that he admired Tim's stamina and that even after a previously long day, he was able to look fresh the next morning.

'Good morning, Tim. Any good news for me this bright and early morning?'

'Not much, Ray; good morning to you. We spotted the white van again, though I am having to contact the Lincolnshire traffic team, as once they went back across the bridge. I need the footage from their side of the A17.'

'Okay, well, at least it is a start in that we have an idea of the locality they are working in. Everything seems to revolve around Sutton Bridge and Lincolnshire. Someone obviously knows the area well, with both bodies being left in a similar area.'

'I will keep checking the cameras to see if there is any other sign of that particular van. I can get one of the others to look back around the time we think Sergei was dumped as well. It is more than likely they used the same van, and it would tie in nicely if we could confirm it.'

Ray was expecting the others to start arriving ready for the day, so he took the opportunity to check his desk for post and scan emails. As expected, Graham sent over the full report. He had just opened the envelope and spread the pictures on his desk when the phone rang. It was the duty sergeant who, moments earlier, had seen him come in.

'Ray, I have a call from a prison officer at H.M.P. Sutton Wells. He is asking to speak to you.'

'Okay, thanks; put him through. Good morning, D.I. Ray Keane's speaking; how may I help you?'

'Good morning, Jackson here. I am a senior officer at the prison.'

As the man spoke, Ray formed a picture in his mind. From the tone of his voice, his first thought was that you have got to be ex-military.

'Hello, is that your first name?'

'No, sorry, force of habit, it is Ian.'

'Okay thanks, Ian. How can I help?'

'We have had a request from a prisoner who would like to meet with you.'

Ian Jackson went on to explain that following a special visit yesterday from his wife, which they understood Ray had arranged. Stan Crowe was now asking to see Ray.

'We normally wouldn't respond to a request such as this, but after the news he received yesterday, along with the fact that he is the type of prisoner who never gives us any trouble, we show compassion if we can.'

Listening to the man talk, Ray found it difficult to believe Ian Jackson would ever be described by inmates as compassionate. He decided it could be worth a visit just in case Stan had some information that might be helpful. He hoped this might be the case, as Stan was requesting to see him.

'I will come over later this morning and see him.'

'That would be fine. I will be here until early afternoon.'

Ray avoided mentioning that he could not wait and politely ended the call. He then called out to Tim, 'How long will it take me to get to H.M.P. Sutton Wells?'

'About 40 minutes, sir; you'll like that; it is one of those new prisons; that is all about rehabilitation.'

Ray knew from Tim's tone that he was sceptical about the success of these places.

'Now, now, Tim. You know they all deserve a chance.'

'If only I knew you believed that yourself.'

For now, Ray pushed any thoughts as to why Stan Crowe should want to see him to the back of his mind. After finishing the phone call and scanning emails, he could tell without looking, due to the noise levels, that most of the others had arrived. A couple of the team members had come in carrying take out coffee boxes and a selection of bags containing cakes. Ray smiled as he thought, nothing like starting the day with a sugar rush. He left and stood by the incident board, clearing his throat, and bringing silence to the room. Looking around, he could see copies of newspapers on different desks. It was something that would be discussed as part of the briefing; he had not had a chance to look at any headlines yet.

'Good morning, everyone. I hope you all got as much rest as possible last night.'

The response was almost in unison, but Tim was slightly ahead of the others, 'We did, sir. How about yourself, or were you out tripping the light fantastic?'

This brought laughter around the room, as it was no secret that he enjoyed ballroom dancing and that it was Jenny who had first encouraged him.

'As it happened, DS Jarvis, I did enjoy an evening dancing and it is probably the best way for me to relax.'

They all noted the use of his title directed at Tim, but they could also see the grin on Ray's face.

'Right, time to move on, jobs for today. I need to know anything that can be found involving the names we have so far.'

Sheila added.

'We have not got a lot to go on, have we?'

'It may seem like that, but we all know these people from the drug world do not give a lot away. In the past, we might have only had a Christian name or even a nickname, and then it led to another contact, which helps unlock the puzzle. I am sure we will find out more.'

Ray knew how important it was to keep encouraging them and tell them that they were making progress. He told them that Jenny was going to talk to a couple of officers that did a lot of work on the drug trade, in particular concentrating on the county lines initiative. So far, this had brought some success in closing down lines of communication between dealers. Tim then took over and gave them a progress report on tracking the transit van, he added, 'Before anyone gets too excited, we need to realise that, if we do apprehend anyone driving the van. the chances are that it is going to be falsely registered, but it could be a start.'

Ray could see they were all eager to get on. He quickly outlined the report from Graham, but they had heard all the important stuff from Sheila yesterday.

'I have a visit to the prison at Sutton Wells to see Stan Crowe, Nick's dad. I can only think of it as a follow-on from him getting the news from Shirley yesterday, but you never know if it could be useful. Before we finish, all back here at 17.00 hours, and quickly, what does the press have to say?'

Several copies of the papers were held up for others to see. The headlines in the local papers were all good reports focusing on the drug angle; none of them mentioned the word serial killer, which, as far as Ray was concerned, was a good result. PC Dan Carol was the next to speak, 'One of the nationals has got the story inside sir. They are currently running several articles about the damage caused by drug dealers; you never know how the publicity could help us.'

'That could well be worth keeping an eye on; just also be aware that we may well get our share of calls from the usual group of people who like to be involved in things, though they have nothing useful for us.'

Ray would always remember the first time he had come across a person like this. He found it hard to believe that, due to a number of reasons, someone would contact the police and use their imagination to give an unsuspecting officer details they thought would be useful. Ray hoped he would be there to help his team, as a detective sergeant had been on hand and knew the person who had called and saved Ray a lot of hours that he could have spent following up on things. As they finished up, Angela appeared at the doorway, 'I can see you have seen the newspapers; all should help us in some way. A couple of them also seem to have taken you as a good source, Ray.'

Before Ray could answer, Angela walked further into the room, heading for the coffee and cake.

'Are these going to be spare, just what I need to set myself up for the morning?'

The atmosphere in the room had stayed as it was, which was relaxed but professional, whereas previously, when Adam entered the room, it affected everyone.

'Right, all of you get to it. Angela, can we talk in my office?'

As everyone moved away, Ray spoke, 'Sheila, you as well.'

Angela walked across the room and, without a thought of appearance or where crumbs would fall, took a mouthful of pastry. Once they were settled in the office, she said.

'I take it you are happy with the press coverage, Ray?'

'What I have been shown so far looks okay; fingers crossed it continues on a positive note.'

'Was there something you wanted to speak about?'

'Just to keep you updated. I had a phone call from the prison where Stan Crowe is serving his sentence. He wants to see me. I thought I would take Sheila with me.'

'Well, as long as you think it will help, you know how sometimes it can be uncomfortable for female officers going into prisons.'

Ray acknowledged this comment with a nod, then, with a smile said, 'I think Sheila can give as good as she gets.'

'Don't worry, sir; I will look out for you.'

'I think that clears that issue up, anything else?'

Ray went on to tell Angela about Jenny talking to her new colleagues, and Angela accepted it but added.

'I will ring her superintendent, so he is in the picture. We don't want people to think we are treading on anyone's toes.'

'Thank you for that.'

'Good, it all sounds positive. It will be interesting to see if Nick's dad can help; I look forward to hearing about it later.'

Chapter Fifteen

All police cases involved a lot of links between characters who you would not, in normal circumstances, place together; then, by the meticulous work of all the detectives working together, these people would be analysed to discover the link they had. After a process of elimination, a case would be resolved with hopefully the right result for everyone; the arrest and conviction of only one person who was at the top of the links to all others. Currently, as Ray and Sheila were in the car for the journey to the prison, there were 5 main characters linked into this puzzle that Ray wanted to solve. These people were Ray and Sheila as the main detectives; then there was Stan Crowe along with Darren Plant and Jack, the last 2 being their main suspects.

Even though their thoughts were slightly different, there was a theme running through it all. Darren and Jack were fully aware of what had happened to Nick, Ray, and Sheila were piecing together what had occurred. Stan had the most basic thought, which was what had happened to Nick. From Ray's point of view, this case then had another level, which on their timeline charts very much looked like a family tree would; as further down after Nick, there was Sergei; then there were the people who wanted to discover what had happened to him.

This is connected to the links in that Darren, Jack, and Nick all knew about this. For much of his own team, when Ray started adding to the incident boards to allow timelines to be developed; it could look confusing, but Ray had always found that the more pieces he put in place, the more it helped him think things through to ultimately arrive at a conclusion.

Sheila had already learned that when Ray was in thinking mode, it was best to wait until he showed signs of wanting to talk. It was well known by everyone at the station that often during a case, Ray would take himself off for a walk either through the park or along the river, usually leading to him coming back ready to put bits of the puzzle together.

As they joined the traffic on the main road outside of King's Lynn, Sheila was able to drive a bit more freely. After a few minutes Ray started a conversation, 'So, Sheila, what are your thoughts on the new superintendent?'

'So far, so good. Is that not the saying? She seems to have settled in well, and all the others appear to have taken to her. I never had a lot of direct contact with Adam, though he always appeared a bit starchy.'

Ray smiled as he thought starchy was an understatement to describe Adam.

'It certainly feels more relaxed around the station, though I still feel that for all her friendly appearance, there is a side to her we are yet to see. No matter what she says, she is controlled from above.'

Sheila glanced across at him, 'What do you think today is in aid of?'

'Who knows, I have given it some thought. Though I felt it's better not to pre-empt anything, so best to keep an open mind.'

'Can I ask, is there a particular reason you wanted me along?'

'I always find it is a good idea to have a second pair of eyes around. You may not need to say anything, but just watch out for any reactions from him to anything I say. Also, having heard a little bit about Stan, he may well drop his guard with a female present.'

Sheila couldn't help but laugh, 'So, you want the little woman to stand quietly in the background.'

Ray could not help his reaction to this comment by also laughing, as it showed Sheila relaxing in the environment of working with him.

'I could never imagine you as the little woman in the background. You may feel I missed asking something, so do not be afraid to step in. That could also throw Stan off balance.'

Ray realised as he spoke that, due to Sheila having joined them and been thrown straight into a murder case when replacing Jenny, none of them had had much of a chance to get to know her or her personal situation. He knew now was not the right time, but he made a mental note to put this right as soon as they could after this investigation. The traffic on the main road had been relatively light; they had even been able to overtake the 2 tractors they had been behind. Soon they were pulling into the official parking area at the prison. It certainly presented itself as a new build; the image from years previously of a prison was of old stone buildings with very few windows, surrounded by high walls; the only way you drove in was after being identified and waiting seemingly for ages while large gates opened slowly.

The building they parked in front of could easily have been block of flats or a fancy office building. The main area that could be seen was all shiny metal and glass, with, from the outside, little sign of its purpose to keep people locked up. Neither of them had been to the prison before, though like most police officers in the area, they had heard plenty about it, including many objectionable opinions when it was first built and opened 2 years ago. These opinions ranged from the people who were known as "do gooders" saying it was just the sort of place to help prisoners turn their lives around to the majority of the general public saying how could it be a deterrent to committing a crime as the place spent for punishment looked a lot better than some people's homes.

Ray had always tried to keep an open mind in these types of conversations, despite his own feelings towards some of the people he dealt with daily. He realised that the prisoners located within these walls were supposedly the type deemed not to be a threat to society; a lot of them had been convicted of fraud, which increasingly revolved around everyone's obsession with the internet. Then here were people like Stan, who were compulsive criminals without using violence towards their victims. This would usually be a case of a burglary that happened due to doors or windows being left open. The fact that these sorts of crimes still happened amazed both police officers and criminals, with all the warnings as soon as there was nice weather.

People stopped thinking of security. The home office information about H.M.P. Sutton Wells was along the lines of, we are here to help these people and make them aware of a better life. The only proof that could be offered in support of this was that in the 2 years it had been opened, no one had tried to escape, and there had been no riots. In the world of prisons, this was an achievement. The other side of any argument about lax treatment was dispelled as soon as you entered the doors. The thing was the only people who saw this were the staff and inmates. The staff would always defend their work, but this never washed with the doubters; if the inmates said anything, it was always taken with a pinch of salt, followed by the comment, well you are a criminal.

With them both being on their first visit to the establishment, they were slightly surprised by having seen the outside and thinking being incarcerated here is not a bad outcome of crime. They slowly changed their minds on entering; they had to wait outside the doors, which from the car had looked like all glass. Up close, the strengthening wires and alarm cables could be seen running through the glass. After having had their identities checked, they heard several electronic bolts unlocked, and it was made more chilling by hearing the same bolts locking in place behind them. Immediately, they had to pass across mobile phones and were instructed that if they needed to make notes of any conversations, they should use pen and paper, but they were not to leave pens on the table. When Sheila looked questioningly at this, it was explained, 'You would be surprised at how easily a pen casing can be sharpened into a weapon.'

Sheila's response was similar to remarks they had heard before, 'Surely the idea here is to rehabilitate; that shouldn't be a problem with the category of prisoner you have here.'

'It is not a problem, but we have the attitude; do not put temptation in the way.'

Ray noticed a bristling tone of voice answering, so he stepped into calm things down.

'That sounds like a sensible idea. Is it possible to speak to prison officer Jackson, as he is the one that called me?'

Just as the officer who had been checking them in went to speak, another voice came across the room as a man with exactly the image Ray had imagined said, 'Detective Inspector Keane, follow me through this way.'

The officer who had been dealing with them, looked put out by what was happening, though he never said anything about it and finished by commenting, 'When you are ready to leave, I will meet you here, and you can get your stuff back.'

Ray thought I would like a few minutes with you to discuss your feelings about the other officer; unfortunately, he knew this was unlikely. As they continued waiting to pass through the doors, locking and unlocking as they went, Ray asked a question he already thought he knew the answer to, though he felt it would help him understand things, 'Ian, are you ex-military?'

The response was as though Ian was back on the parade ground, 'Yes, sir, I was a sergeant in the army.'

It was now Sheila's turn to think things through, though they were having similar thoughts, which were that he had liked to throw his weight around in front of subordinates; now you get your kicks from keeping the prisoners in their place. When Ian Jackson took them into a small office on one side of the corridor, they found themselves in it after passing another 2 locked doorways.

'I hope you don't mind; I wanted a quick word with you before you met Stan. Obviously, you are both clever enough to spot if someone, especially a criminal is lying to you.'

Ray was now struggling to keep the sarcasm out of his voice, 'What makes you think Stan might lie to us?'

It was soon obvious that Ian did not like it when somebody appeared to challenge his authority. He showed signs of being flustered.

'I don't mean anything by it; I was talking in general terms.'

'I do not wish to be rude to Mr Jackson; I currently have 2 murders to investigate. So, unless you can tell us anything that might help, perhaps we can see Mr Crowe now.'

Sheila couldn't stop the grin from forming as Ian was put out by the fact that Ray was not going to bow down to him, as he was obviously used to people doing.

'I'm sorry, I'm sure you are as busy as we are, so follow me. I will leave you in the capable hands of another officer while you talk, as I have things to do.'

If this wasn't an obvious sign that Ian felt it was beneath him to stand quietly at the rear of the room, then Sheila didn't know what was. They left the office, and after the repeated process of waiting for doors to be unlocked and locked, they found themselves outside a room. Ian spoke brusquely to another guard.

'Officer, just keep an eye on the prisoner while these 2 police officers have a chat with him.'

As a way of showing his feelings of contempt for them.

'Once they are finished, can you escort them out?'

Ray and Sheila exchanged looks as Ian Jackson moved away without another word. The officer to whom they had been passed to was a totally different character.

'Don't take too much notice of Jackson; every prison has at least 1 officer like that. They have the attitude that if they make life awkward for someone, it gets respect because of the authority. They never seem to realise most people are just taking the mickey out of them behind their backs.'

'Nice to know it is not just us then. What is your name?'

'Officer Coppell, sir.'

Ray found it weird that they never gave a first name but decided to let it pass.

'Just before we go in, officer, what can you tell us about Stan Crowe?'

'Not too much, sir. Even though he is part of the system, this is the first time I have come across him. I will say that if there is such a thing, he is a model prisoner. The type of criminal who accepts getting caught is a hazard of the job. From his records, he keeps his nose clean while doing his time and reading more into it; it is as if he knows when he leaves, he will be back in prison again soon.'

'Okay, thanks. Shall we get on? Then we can all get back to doing what we need to do.'

Officer Coppell pushed the door open, and after Ray and Sheila went in, he closed the door and took up a position to the side where the handle was. Ray looked at the man sitting across from them and saw an image of many faces he had seen over the years in lots of interview rooms. The only way he could ever describe the look was one that was relaxed but with a hard edge waiting to appear at a moment's notice. Ray made the introductions, then said, 'I understand you asked to see me. May I ask why?'

Stan lifted his gaze up from the tabletop.

'I don't think I have had the pleasure of meeting you before.'

'No, our paths have not crossed.'

The one thing Ray wanted to avoid was appearing impatient.

'I am still not sure why you wanted to see me.'

The edge of anger Ray knew was just below the surface started to appear in Stan's voice, 'First, I want to know what happened to my son. Also, what are you doing about it? I know how your lots minds work; it's just another criminal from a family of them, so why work too hard on it?'

'I can assure you, Mr Crowe my team will work just as hard on this part of the case as any other. Is there anything you would like us to know that may help?'

'Gawd, there is a horrible thought, me helping old bill.'

'Well, I would hope you would like to find out who murdered your son.'

'Don't bother trying the pull at my heart strings routine; it won't work.'

Suddenly, it was as if the fight had left his body, and Stan slumped forward in his seat.

'I have never been the best of dads. If I had bothered to take a bit more notice, Nick would've a reason to be proud. Then his mum told me he seemed to go off the rails, which I suppose was no surprise.'

For a few minutes, Stan chatted away about how he thought Nick was going to be different from his brother. He explained how he knew it was odd that he expected his kids to follow his career path and that Jed had seemed happy with this choice. He knew that he had not set a good example, though when Shirl told him how well Nick was doing at school, he had been impressed.

'I just knew as soon as she told me he had got himself involved in drugs it was a slippery slope.'

'I am sorry for your, loss Mr Crowe. You requesting this meeting to me that you wanted to help.'

'Let's stop being so formal, call me Stan. After Shirl came to see me to tell me the news. I asked the governor here if he could arrange a call for me to speak to Jed.'

'Was that not an unusual request?'

'Possibly, when you have been in and out of these places as much as me, you have 2 options. First, you expect things to be as they are; keep your head down, and it has some benefits. Or come through the door with big ideas until you meet someone like Jackson who welcomes a challenge.'

Ray understood this entirely, having heard a similar story many times.

'The reason I called Jed after telling him the news was that I felt if Nick was involved in drugs, he might know. I might be treated like a low life inspector, but I would never get involved in drugs.'

If Ray could get some information from the inside, then hopefully it could give them a breakthrough.

'So, was Jed able or willing to tell you anything that you can pass on?'

'Firstly, Nick dabbling in drugs has been going on longer than we knew about. Apparently, the last time Jed was home, he tried talking to Nick about it. Unfortunately, brotherly love was not a strong bond. Nick basically told Jed, who was he to preach to him about anything? It ended with Nick telling Jed to mind his own business.'

'Any idea how this can help us?'

'Fortunately for you, Jed feels the same way about drugs as I do. To him you can have a good time with a few cans, some cigarettes, and some mates. He told me he doesn't know much about who Nick was mixing with; he heard the name Jack from Nick. Though Jed doesn't think he is the main man, fortunately for you, my Jed keeps his ears open; the last time he heard things, the main supplier in our area was Darren Plant.'

Ray had learned to control his emotions as part of the job, so despite wanting to make calls to the station to get people working on the name, he remained calm. He was surprised that Sheila was not so calm, almost letting out a yelp of excitement at this name.

'So, where would we find this, Darren?'

'Oh, you want me and Jed to do your job now then.'

'That will not be necessary, Stan; though if you are right, the quicker we find him, the better.'

It appeared that if Stan did have a conscience, then anything to do with his sons was where it laid.

'I honestly don't know; as I said, I have always kept as far away from drugs as possible. If Jed is right, then I'm pretty sure this Darren will live in the area, so he can keep an eye on things.'

As if to prove how much notice he was taking, he then added, 'I take it from the ladies' reaction; you have heard these names already. Going on what Jed told me, this Jack is just the hired muscle.'

'Okay Stan, maybe not what you want to hear, but thank you for your help.'

It was as if someone had just slapped Stan across the face as he drew back in his chair, 'Yeah, well, no one else needs to know we have spoken, do they?'

Ray was just pleased that they had a bit more to work with; it had never been his intention to cause Stan any problems, 'No one else will hear it from my team. I will keep Shirley informed, and she can tell you.'

As he was speaking, Ray looked pointedly at the prison officer at the door to indicate he wanted nothing to be said, a nod that showed it had been noted. The next thing Stan said could open up a whole new can of worms. Ray was not sure at this time if he wanted to follow up or not.

'Just do me a favour; don't tell Jackson.'

Ray got up, and Sheila followed his lead, and they both knew there was work to do when they got back. Officer Coppell asked them to wait a moment while he radioed through for another officer to accompany Stan back to his cell. Then he showed them out. After they had gone through the process in reverse, he left them at the gate, saying, 'I hope your journey has been fruitful. Will we see you again?'

Ray could not shake the feeling that there was something going on below the surface, so he replied without committing himself.

'Our paths may cross again. Thank you for your time.'

As Ray and Sheila made their way back from the prison, Jack was making plans to disappear for a while. When Darren first suggested it, his reaction had been that he had no need to get away. Yes, he agreed that disposing of the 2 bodies had not gone according to plan, but at the same time, he was convinced no one had seen anything. There was also another issue, which was that without Darren being aware, Jack had gotten himself a nice little sideline going. It had been successful because he wasn't greedy and got more than enough money from Darren; it was more of a backup plan in case anything happened to Darren.

This involved a lucrative number of people supplying drugs to a couple of prison officers, one of that was Ian Jackson. It came about after a chance meeting in a pub and the link between them both having been in the military. Jack had always managed to make his military career sound better than it was when needed. It now appeared that there were more links in the chain that Ray and his team were putting together. Jack was sensible enough that when Darren threw the pile of money on the table, he took it and agreed to not have any contact for a few weeks. Jack was fortunate enough to have learned in his short time in the army to live on his wits; he was happy enough with his own company, and though he enjoyed the finer things, especially since working for Darren, he was also quite at home roughing it if needed.

Over the next few weeks, he decided it would be a combination of both. The plan he had formed was to use a car that Darren was happy to arrange. He was travelling further up the Lincolnshire coastline, finding a private campsite that, despite some glossy advertising that it had holiday homes to rent, was basically some fields with caravans in place. It would be quiet as there was no entertainment on site, not even a bar; he had used the site once before, a long time ago. He rang ahead and had no problem getting sorted due to the time of year. When booking the caravan for 4 weeks and telling the site manager he would pay cash on arrival, he could tell that he was pleased with the guaranteed income.

He would be able to lock himself away, though he knew of some very good restaurants in the area, so eating was not going to be a problem. The size of the campsite meant that even if there were any other visitors, they would only be on site for a few days, and unlike the bigger complexes that seemed to operate all year round, there wouldn't be any families around. He looked at it, thinking that he would be hiding in plain sight, doing nothing to draw attention to himself. Once he had sorted things out and finally agreed with Darren that they would have no contact for a month, he left and while driving made another call that would eventually point to Darren being right about disappearing; using a very old pay as you go mobile that was never used for anything else, he called another pay as you go mobile; the voice answering was as brusque as ever; the important thing to Jack was that during any chat no names were ever used.

'Yes, what do you want?'

'Just so you are aware, no contact for a month.'

If he was expecting any argument, he was surprised, 'Good idea; you must have good intuition. We had a visit from the police today.'

This was enough to put Jack on alert.

'Right, I don't need details, except was it to see you?'

'No, visiting a prisoner.'

'Okay, get rid of the phone. Just before you replace it text me the new number. I will then change phones as well. You wait to hear from me.'

Without waiting for any sort of reply, Jack ended the call and turned off the phone. He would switch it on again to check in a few weeks. Even though he knew there could be problems ahead, he was looking forward to some time with no contact with anyone else. For himself now, life was good, so he had no intention of doing anything to ruin it.

Ray and Sheila were now on their way to the police station to hopefully put more pieces in place. Jack was heading north away from the area, his thoughts occupied with being ok and safe. Meanwhile, sitting in another caravan, 4 other people were trying to make sense of things. Maria, along with the 3 guys, had been at a loose end since the discovery of Sergei. The farmer had been very good to them, in that normally they would have returned home by now. He had agreed after talking to the police that they could stay in the accommodation, which would normally have been closed up for the winter.

He had even found them some work to do around the farm, though they were all eager to return home. After the discovery of Sergei's body, they had still hoped to be able to leave; the police had made it clear none of them were suspects. Unfortunately, the plans to release his body and all fly home had been curtailed by the discovery of Nick's body. Once the connection had been made, everything was put on hold. Maria looked across the table at the others.

'Just what was Sergei mixed up in?'

'I don't know about being mixed up with; I think he knew exactly what he was doing.'

This reply from Alekesji started quite a heated debate as the others joined in.

'I just think he was only thinking of himself; he made sure we were never around at important times; he just thought he was keeping us sweet by bringing alcohol back with him.'

Andris continued; he had always been the most vocal about where Sergei went in the evenings.

'It is bloody annoying that we can't go home to our families because of him.'

Maria, as always, leapt to his defence, 'I'm sure he had no intention of being murdered.'

'Maybe not; he still must have known he was taking risks.'

After sitting quietly and listening to them all, Vitaujis joined in.

'Quiet all of you. Surely what matters is that our friend is dead, and another family at home will be mourning the waste of a life. Also, have any of us given any thought to the fact that Sergei did mention to anyone about us and where he lived?'

This made them all stop for a minute before Maria said quietly, 'You don't think we are in any danger, do you?'

Alekesji sat upright at the table and, out of a pocket on the side of his work trousers, removed a large and very dangerous-looking knife.

'I will certainly protect myself, if needed.'

The other 2 men didn't seem at all surprised by the knife; on the other hand. Maria was totally shocked.

'Alekesji, what are you doing? Put that away. It won't be an answer to any problem. Have you not seen enough killing?'

'Yes, I have. But having this to hand means I'm still alive, and it stops anyone from taking a chance.'

'How the hell do you get it into the country?'

'I always declare it as part of my working equipment.'

This made the others smile, as none of them had seen him use the knife at work. At some stage in their lives, they had all seen needless killing, and Maria certainly didn't want to see it anymore. It was Vitaujis who got their attention next.

'I think, as the police have not gotten anywhere yet, maybe we should do some investigating of our own. We are friendly enough with some of the locals at the pub, including those Sergei mixed with. Perhaps we can get some answers.'

The idea appealed especially to Andris, who back home, had spent a brief time in a branch of the local secret service. He had appeared to be looking at a promising career but had opted out himself when he decided that some of his colleagues, investigative methods spilt over into violence. It seemed to him that a lot of the time they wanted to get an answer, no matter what. He was sensible enough to know complaining was not an option, so instead he resigned, citing mental health issues. He even moved to another area to distance himself from the others involved. Maria was still not convinced.

'I suppose I could see it helping. We would need to be careful. Anything we find out, we have to report it.'

The others were not entirely in agreement with her thoughts, but when she spoke next, they saw the sense of it.

'If we can find something out to help the police. We could then maybe get home quicker.'

The thought of getting home seemed to be the key to everything. They spent the next couple of hours discussing how to go about things.

The only person involved in all the pieces of the puzzle who did not appear to be worried was Darren Plant. Mainly, this was down to the fact that, to the outside world, he was a successful local businessman. The darker side of how he made extra money was well hidden until Nick started mouthing it off to anyone who would listen. Darren had always been surrounded by people who liked the money he gave them and never spoke about where they got it from. He was happy, if slightly inconvenienced, by having to put the drug trade away for a few weeks and would carry on as normal with his lunches and attending evening events.

The main concern was not having Jack around. Over the time they had known each other, it had made Darren feel safer having him on call. His thought as he walked into his study with a glass of whisky in hand was, I don't intend to let this cause me any major problems.

Chapter Sixteen

The beginning of the journey back to the station was carried out in silence, as both Ray and Sheila seemed preoccupied with their own thoughts. It was Ray who broke the silence.

'What did you make of him then?'

'Partly, your typical career criminal; very bitter towards the law, almost as if it is our fault for capturing him, as opposed to him having broken the law. Having said all that, I think he is also very upset, more so than he was willing to show about the death of his son.'

'Now you can see why I wanted you along to observe. I totally agree with you; the thing that convinced me as to his feelings was the information he was willing to pass over to us.'

They fell back into silence again. Ray was concentrating as the traffic was getting busier and, as most people in the area were used to, on the single-lane roads they were in a queue stuck behind a tractor, with very few opportunities to overtake. After what seemed like a long few miles, the tractor pulled over to allow the traffic to flow more freely.

'So, Ray, what is our next plan?'

'We will get back for the briefing, and I want all of the team working to see what we can find out about Darren Plant.

I also have a job in mind for you; it is delicate, and I am not sure how you will feel about it.'

'I want to say I'm intrigued, though maybe I should wait till you tell me more.'

Ray sat quietly for a moment, as though he were arranging his next words carefully. Sheila was not sure how to react, so she waited.

'It may seem odd at first, but I am mainly going on instinct, which I do not do very often as I like to work with the facts. I had already thought about it, then Stan said something that convinced me to follow the path. I would like to know more about Ian Jackson, the prison officer.'

Ray was pleased with the reply, as it confirmed his thoughts.

'You mean apart from him being sexist and thinking he is better than anyone else.'

'Sorry, I had not noticed the sexist side, but I certainly did notice his attitude.'

'I was basing my thoughts on how he looked at me, and also that all conversation was directed at you. I may be wrong about it, but don't think so.'

The conversation carried on along the same lines as they made their way back into King's Lynn. Sheila was a good passenger in that she could write notes while travelling without any side effects. Ray had always found that even glancing at a map could make him feel queasy. He allowed her a few minutes, then asked her what notes she was making. Sheila explained that she liked to make bullet points ready to pass on to others, plus she was making some of her own observations about Ian Jackson.

'I am still not 100% convinced about Jackson, so it is a case of time management to not allow it to take over our thoughts. Basically, it was because the other officer did not seem keen on him, then Stan asked if we had anything to tell him, not to pass it via Jackson.'

'You might not be sure, sir; though it was very clear he has an attitude. Some prison staff always have the feeling they are so much better than the inmates; he came across with the same feelings towards his colleagues.'

They pulled into the car park at the rear of the station; it showed the strength of feeling that, since the press conference, some reporters were still hanging around on the fringes of the area. The national press and television media were no longer in attendance, though local papers had assigned reporters to keep an eye on things. There were a couple of freelance reporters that most of the officers knew; they would soon alert the major media companies, for a fee, if the story developed quickly. It was some of these freelance people that Ray had taken a dislike to in the past, as he felt they were not averse to doing anything to get a story. As soon as they left the car to walk in, they could hear camera clicks as photos were taken. A young female reporter, whom Ray recognised from the local radio station, shouted out a hastily asked question, as though she felt she wanted to make a point to the others waiting.

'Any news yet, inspector?'

Normally Ray's reaction would be to ignore this type of question, but due to the positive response to his behaviour in the press conference, he decided to act differently.

'At the moment, we have nothing to add. There will be a press release later for you all.'

This seemed to satisfy the girl as well as the others waiting with her. Ray was surprised to hear this as he went in the door, 'Thank you.'

Most of the team were in place in the office, ready for the briefing; all of them were eager to hear how the prison visit had gone. Ray decided that there was going to be a large amount of work to do after he gave them the information he had gotten from Stan. Rather than the usual few minutes of checking his desk, he would get straight on with things. He grabbed a coffee from the machine, then cleared his throat, which always silenced the room.

'Good afternoon, all. Sheila, can you update the boards as we go along, please?'

The incident boards, which just a few days ago consisted of 1 board with a couple of pictures on it had now been added to; in that, there were now 2 boards with several crime scene photos, as well as lots of names that needed checking. Ray did feel they were now at a crucial stage of the investigation, the situation being. They had lots of pieces of the puzzle to work with, and they now needed to get the pieces in place to fit together to form a complete picture. This would allow them to fully understand what and who they were dealing with.

'We now have a full name to work with. Stan Crowe was adamant; he did not like the idea of helping the police. Though the thought of finding out who murdered his son, as well as the drug involvement, won him over. He said his other son, Jed, had spoken to Nick recently regarding the drugs. It is obvious that Nick took no notice, but I got the name of who they think is the main supplier in the area. I need all of you looking into Darren Plant.'

Again, the knowledge that Dan Carol had of not just the local area but also the adjoining counties came to the fore.

'Good luck for us all with that, then.'

'Would you care to elaborate on that, Dan?'

'His name has been mentioned previously in memos from other forces. The main problem everybody has had is that he is a very successful businessman who keeps the right contacts on hand. As an example, I guarantee we will see pictures of him at charity events, standing alongside many top superior officers.'

This brought several groans from around the room, as they were all aware of incidents in the past where a particularly nasty criminal covered their tracks, hiding behind a completely legal business as well as being seen with the right people.

Ray called for quiet.

'Okay, so we could hit some obstacles along the way, but if this guy is the one behind everything we are currently dealing with, then I am happy to do whatever we need to. I will speak to the superintendent about it as well, in case we need some backing.'

Ray continued the briefing by getting information that the others had gathered during the day, which was added to the boards. He was determined to keep everybody focused, as he knew that if they came across too many stumbling blocks, they would soon all start to feel that Darren could evade them. This meant he had to get things moving to prove it was worth pursuing him.

'Tim, how have you got on with tracing the van?'

'Some news, it is registered with a building company. Though I doubt we will find it used much in that trade, as neither postmortem showed residue on the bodies you would expect from it being in a builder's van. Going back to your information and what Dan has told us, I have a feeling that as I search further, I may well find a certain Mr Plant listed within the company.'

'Good, it sounds promising, so keep on it. Something else for you all to know, though for now, this information does not leave the room. Sheila is going to spend some time looking into the prison officer who first contacted me, and we both feel there is something not sitting right with him. Stan Crowe does not want any messages sent through this guy; another prison officer we spoke to did not have much good to say about him either. I will point out that, at present, it is only an instinct. His name is Ian Jackson, so if any of you hear anything, let Sheila know. Does anyone have anything to add?'

Sheila turned from the board to face the room, 'The name Jack was mentioned by Stan. It is reasonable to think it is the same person whose name we have heard already. We still have no surname to work with; ask around; we need to find him.'

None of the people ready to start working to locate Jack were aware that he was currently close to 70 miles away and sat inside a caravan, which, despite the look of the exterior, was actually very clean and comfortable. Jack was thinking this would suit him quite nicely, though only for a few weeks. He would be looking to resume normal service as soon as possible.

Ray finished off the meeting by pointing out that, even though he knew they were all aware of their roles for the first thing in the morning.

'I will talk to Angela as long as she agrees. I think it would be a good starting point for me to have a chat on a relaxed basis, Mr Plant. If he is involved with a legitimate business, I do not want to move mob-handed to only miss out on getting evidence.'

Some of the team went back to working at computers, gathering information to check, and a few said their goodbyes for the day. Ray never made it a point that the team stuck to fixed hours; the main reason being that it was not easy to do, especially once embroiled in a murder case, where the investigation controlled everything. He knew the ones going home would carry on searching the internet or meeting people to see what could be found. They would also be the ones who would be in early the next day. Ray left the room to go and speak to Angela; his feelings were running high as he tried to get things in order on how best to approach things.

It was always a balancing act when a supposedly local success story had a background people knew nothing about. He already knew that the first thing to happen would be Darren calling for a solicitor to be present. This put everyone on edge immediately, though from his point of view, it offered protection. He found Angela sitting behind her desk, talking to Susan, the press officer. He gathered from what he heard on entering that they were discussing the next press release. Even with his feelings towards the media, he knew the importance of keeping a major case in the headlines; otherwise, it could easily slip into a few lines of a report inside a paper and get forgotten.

He knew of at least 2 cases that had been solved by other forces; the conclusion of each had happened due to people who had been out of the area and not seen press coverage. On returning home to see the headlines, they had then given the police information that had been just what was needed. Angela looked up as he walked in.

'Good evening, Ray. How are things progressing?'

'That is the reason for my visit, Ma...' Ray stopped himself; the relaxed attitude still took some getting used to, 'Sorry, Angela.'

'That could be good timing; do you have anything we could add to the press release?'

'I think at the moment, our information needs to stay with us; that is the main reason for me coming to see you.'

Susan took this as her cue, 'I will leave you to talk, as long as you are happy, Angela; I will circulate this release in time for tomorrow's print.'

'Thanks, Susan; we can speak again in a couple of days and possibly be able to send out details of what Ray is about to reveal.'

Ray took his place in the seat as Susan got up. He felt this next conversation would be another test as to finding out how Angela worked. He knew if he had been talking to Adam, any response would be based around the force looking good as a result of any outcome, due in part to how Adam would view Darren as a businessman. Adam always felt it was important to keep people like that on side with the police. He would be thinking immediately about avoiding any embarrassment to the force and himself if they had been at any event that revealed unsavoury characters having also been in attendance. Regarding Darren, he already had Dan looking into his background and ready for any meetings he may have with him. Currently, no one on the team had seen the picture of

Darren alongside the local chief constable. It was going to surface soon, putting a totally different angle on things.

'Okay Ray, what do you need to talk about?'

'As a result of the visit to the prison today, we now have a name to work with, though it is possibly going to cause an awkward situation.'

'I like to think it is a speciality of mine in dealing with awkward moments.'

'It is still a bit sketchy at the moment. PC Dan Carol is currently doing some research for me, as I feel I may have to visit this person. The name we have been given is Darren Plant; Dan has some knowledge already in that he is a local businessman.'

'He would not be the first business owner to work on both sides of the law. If you feel it is necessary to speak to this Darren or even reach the stage of inviting him in for an interview, then do it.'

Ray felt himself relax, and from the way the conversation was going, he could tell that Angela would be supportive of whatever action was needed.

'I hope that if Dan can find me enough information this evening, I will pay Mr Plant a visit at some stage tomorrow.'

'That all sounds fine. I have also spoken to the superintendent at Jenny's station; he has given her the go-ahead to allocate some time to work alongside a colleague to see if they can get any information to help us.'

'Thank you for that. I think she was struggling to adjust to a new team, along with having no major case to work on.'

'Maybe she needs to allow herself time to settle in. It could be a good thing not to be thrown straight in.'

Ray knew this was true, but he also understood Jenny's frustration. Basically, she had gone from being his number 2, to being 1 of a group. He knew she would deal with it all professionally; it would just take time.

'If you go to see this Darren tomorrow, tread carefully to start with. If he is involved in drugs and ultimately the murders, make sure any case is watertight, so we avoid him slipping away.'

Angela explained that at her last station, they had a case where a prominent businessman had expected contacts he had made in the force to protect him from the law. Even when he was charged with the brutal assault on a rival, he sat smugly, thinking friendship would allow him to walk free. Angela knew she had put herself in the firing line by ensuring a conviction; fortunately for her, the higher-ranking officer, who was in no way involved in any crime, distanced himself from the investigation. If any proof was needed, this was enough for Ray to know that he would have her full support. Having agreed on things for the morning, Ray left to make his way home, and in the evening, he discussed things further with Jenny.

While Ray had plans for the evening and several of his team were still out and about gathering information from various sources, The Red Eagle was a hive of activity. The saying that there was no such thing as bad publicity was certainly proving true for the pub, and landlord Jerry was determined to make the most of it. It had not taken long for the gossip to spread, and as news circulated that the 2 people found dead were regulars, lots of morbid sightseers were interested in a night out. With the thought in the back of their minds, would they hear something that the media would be interested in. Visiting the pub this evening for the first time since the discovery of Sergei, Maria and the others were shocked by how busy it was. They also saw it as an extra chance to possibly find out more. Jerry was pleased to see them all and greeted them as he would any regulars.

'Good evening, all of you. What can I get you?'

This greeting was a surprise to them. Jerry had always been polite, though they took this to be from his liking of the cash they spent over the work season.

'I was sorry to hear about your friend. Please, these drinks are on the house.'

At first, they were reluctant, then graciously accepted the drinks. After a few minutes of small talk with Jerry, they went and sat at a table in the corner. It was not possible to say it was a quiet corner, though it was away from the main bar. It was Maria who spoke first.

'Good to see someone is doing well despite the publicity of Sergei being murdered.'

The others glanced around, all with looks of disdain, adding comments along the lines of, we have to realise they will not feel the same as us. They had just about finished their drinks when 3 others approached the table; they were all men in their early twenties. One appeared to be the spokesperson.

'We were sorry to hear about Sergei; he was always good to us. He was always up for a laugh and some fun.'

This seemed to encourage one of the others to find their voice, 'He always liked Nick as well; he looked out for him, as well as the fact that they worked together.'

This was the first time they had heard anything like this, so were wondering were Sergei and Nick killed because of this connection. They were all aware of experiences from home and that people didn't always like to be questioned about things. This had made them decide before coming out that rather than ask direct questions, they would sit and listen to conversations to see if they heard anything interesting. It seemed as though the 3 lads had said their piece, seeming ready to leave. Andris could tell they knew more and didn't want to miss anything.

'What do you mean by they worked together?'

This comment was met with a slightly aggressive response.

'Who are you, the secret police?'

The other 2 laughed as though the joke was on them, due to their backgrounds. Maria was quick to speak up, as she realised the significance of the conversation, 'No of course not. You all know us; we worked with Sergei, and he was a close friend. It is just that the police don't seem to know what happened. We just want to understand why he was killed.'

This appeared to calm the matter down.

'Well, what can you expect from the coppers? Chances are they have moved onto something else by now.'

They all knew this comment wasn't true; they saw it as a way to keep the lads talking.

'You don't need to tell any of us how law enforcement favours themselves. If we can find out anything, then hopefully they will let us return Sergei to his family.'

It seemed as if this was the encouragement others needed, as their spokesperson decided it was worth talking.

'How about you buy us a drink, then we can tell you all about Nick and Sergei?'

Once drinks had been bought, everyone sat around the table. The farm workers heard a lot of things that the men accepted, as they already felt they knew some details of what Sergei had been up to. For Maria, it was different from her hearing about drugs; it was a total shock; she could not understand it at all. Why did Sergei get himself mixed up in any of it? She found it particularly difficult, in that, along with her, he had seen the fallout from drugs so many times at home. There was also the fact that a lot of the drug barons at home had been in league with the local police officers, meaning there was a legal system that was not even lawful. Of all of the workers, she had dealt with his murder the worst; now there was the possibility he had put them at risk as well. Questions continued to be asked, and the guys seemed happy to answer them.

It was Andris who had settled into the role of asking the questions; the others were happy for him to lead. After an hour of talking, they were more aware of Sergei's movements over the last few weeks of his life. A couple of the group decided they had told them enough, so they got up to leave. Andris said, 'Please, one more question. We keep hearing the name Jack in connection with Nick. Do any of you know him?'

'You mean apart from him being a bit of a psycho. He is someone you avoid.'

'We just need to know more, if he was involved with Sergei. Like his surname.'

The group of lads looked blankly at one another, 'Don't think I ever heard his full name.'

The youngest one of the groups then spoke for the first time since they had sat down, 'I know it.'

His mates looked at him in disbelief.

'Go on, then smartass. What was it?'

'It was Marshall. I remember it 'cause it reminded me of the cowboy films my mum used to watch.'

As they left the table, the 2 others were laughing at the expense of their mate about the cowboy films. One of them even adding.

'Are you quick on the draw then?'

For Maria and the others, it felt important that they had a name. The next thing for them to decide was what to do with this information. None of them were aware that the decision they would make would have a major impact on them all.

Chapter Seventeen

If there was one thing Ray enjoyed about the commute he now had to make to work, it was the early mornings. He encountered very little traffic, and the surrounding area meant he got to see and enjoy plenty of wildlife, whose home was the countryside. Due to the recent pandemic, he had seen on various news programmes that wildlife was venturing into towns like never before. Having been brought up on a farm, he was used to seeing animals in their own habitat. Once he moved into the town, on his walks through the park, he spotted the odd deer, usually from a distance. His journey now involved being aware in case a deer decided to cross the road and into the traffic.

The first time he spotted a small herd of deer wandering along the roadside, he was able to slow down and enjoy the spectacle. At the opposite end of the day, he would often see barn owls out hunting for food; it was amazing seeing them highlighted in the headlights of the car. It had taken a while, but he had to admit he was now used to the car to drive in and out of work. Even though he forced himself to concentrate, he did find parts of the journey he would do on autopilot. This gave him time to think through things; he had the feeling today was going to be important in starting to put things together, and he had an instinct that meeting Darren Plant would be key to it all.

Ray made his way into the office, as seemed to be normal nowadays; it never mattered how early it was, someone would already be at work. Today it was Dan Carol. He was sitting at a computer screen, as, Ray glanced at the screen, he could see several pictures from different events that all featured the same person.

'Morning Dan, our gentleman businessman, Mr Plant, I take it?'

'Good morning, Ray; yes, it is I would say he looks like a smiling assassin.'

'There is certainly something in the eyes; you would not fully trust him.'

A number of times over the years, when people were arrested, and pictures appeared in the media, it had been remarked on. The person arrested had a look about them; the classic one that they had all heard at some stage was, they must be guilty; their eyes are too close together.

'You will be able to have a closer look later, sir. I emailed the P.A. last night, arranging an appointment for 11 am today at the office he uses.'

Ray liked the fact that his team, including the newcomers, felt they could work using the initiative as a way of moving things forward.

'Do we know yet what sort of business he is involved in?'

'It appears to be the classic line; import and export. What, though, is in question.'

'That covers such a multitude of sins; see if you can find out more. Also, print off the main points so I can read up on them before I meet him.'

By now, others had started to arrive, only to find Ray standing by the incident board. He had organised a separate board placed alongside the other 2, this happened in each case, and was taken by the team as a sign that he felt they were heading towards a conclusion. The purpose of this board was to assign particular roles to people. They were all used to spending time working of their own backs. When it got down to it, Ray had found it worked well and avoided repeating things if he controlled it from a management level; this had taken him as long to accept as it had the team. He preferred being hands-on but knew it was not always possible.

On the board, as they came in, they saw he had been busy; at the top of the board was his meeting with Darren. As the list continued down, with Dan getting as much background on Darren as he could, Sheila was to coordinate things in the office while working with the 2 P.C.'s to gather more information about the white van. Tim and Jill were to revisit the farm to speak to the workers. The idea was to see if they had remembered anything, though currently they were all unaware that by the end of today, Tim would have a lot more information to link things together. Ray kept the morning meeting brief by telling everyone their roles for the day, then left them to get on, reminding them to update the boards as needed.

He went into his office knowing he had his paperwork mountain to attend to before going to see Darren. 1 letter that was of particular interest was the final report from the coroner's office and also the Crown Prosecution Service, showing that the death of Jimmy Hammer was accidental, and that Brenda Roebuck would not be facing any charges. It was very difficult for him, but he had to accept the result of the case for what it was. Despite not getting the criminal who murdered Steve Edwards into court, it was justice of a sort. He was about to start scanning his eyes over the emails when Dan knocked at the door, 'Here you go, sir; all I can find out so far about Darren Plant and his dealings.'

'Thanks Dan. Run me through it. Anything that might help us?'

'All a bit vague, I'm afraid. He was a bit of a rebel at college and was actually arrested for selling drugs, though according to reports, dad got him a good solicitor, so apart from being kicked off the course, nothing else came of it.'

'Maybe not at the time. It could be a scab worth picking at to see what happens.'

Dan carried on giving Ray as much detail as he could to show the type of person he would be meeting, and when the internal phone on his desk rang, he indicated for Dan to wait as he answered.

'D.I. Ray Keane speaking.'

'Good morning, Ray. I just thought I would ring to say, let me know if I can do anything regarding your meeting.'

'Thank you, Angela. Until I see this man, there is not a lot to do. I will report to you when I get back.'

Ray hung up, then looked at Dan.

'Anything else?'

'Only, really, his dad, after hoping he would follow him into the family business of builders, set Darren up in a flat and a nice office, which allowed him to start up his current business.'

'Do we know any more about what he deals in?'

'Unfortunately, again, very little. He might be more forthcoming if you ask him outright. There is a website that looks impressive, complete with glossy pictures, but honestly tells you very little. I did find out he deals with a container company that ships stuff out of the port in King's Lynn; the little I can see shows documentation but is very vague.'

'So, it could be a way for drugs to arrive?'

'It has to be a possibility; obviously there are checks carried out; it could be that he thinks that being a smaller port he can get away with things. If, as we think, the business is a front for drugs, the website and information suggest it is not his main income. Though proving that will take time.'

Ray realised he was going to have plenty of questions for Darren and was hoping to get the right answers; he just doubted it would be that simple. He still had some time left, so he spent it on paperwork. He was quite proud of the fact that before he left for his meeting, his in-tray was not empty, but certainly a smaller mountain was left. As he got himself ready to go, Dan came running through the door.

'Slow down, constable; you could injure someone.'

Dan was obviously flustered.

'Sorry, sir, I wanted to catch you before you left.'

'It must be important.'

'I was running some searches on the container firm Darren uses. It is owned by his dad, Joseph Plant.'

'Are you suggesting he is bringing drugs in via containers that his dad owns?'

'It has to be a possibility, doesn't it, and he would not be implicated if anything was found.'

'How easy would it be to bring something in not on the docket, along with a full container that is listed?'

'Surely not that easy; he must think it is worth the risk; these containers could be searched at any time.'

'Dan, a job for you. While I am out, visit the port to see who you can speak to. I want us all to have an idea of how these things work; at different times, we need to work alongside customs and let us know what we could be dealing with.'

Since being seconded to the CID, it was the first time Dan had been given a role of his own. Ray had no qualms at all about his ability, even thinking Angela would allow him to be another team member. Dan left the room with a spring in his step, while Ray went out to his car to go and see Darren. Small gatherings of press were back in place, hoping to get a little nugget of information before the others. This time, as he walked past near enough for them to speak to him, Ray adopted his usual attitude towards the press and, apart from a polite good morning, said nothing else. He had plenty to occupy his mind as to how he was going to approach the next few hours.

He drove out of King's Lynn; it had been a surprise when Dan had told him he was visiting a complex based at a local golf club. Obviously, as a way of increasing revenue, whereas in years past golf clubs were very much a members-only affair, this one he was visiting had a restaurant open to non-members, a local parcel collection point, and as Ray found when he arrived, a few glorified portacabins that served several businesses. His first thought was how clever it was to put some distance between an office you ran a business from and the area you lived in.

Also, it would be good if they were correct in their thinking that illegal activities were run from here as well. Keeping a low profile did not reach this place of business; it may have only been a cabin, one of which stood out from the others. Outside of each were signs detailing the name of the company within. The signs were sufficient, though insignificant, alongside the gold-coloured plague that announced Darren Plant Industries. Even this sign left no clue as to what business it was.

Ray walked up a few steps and pushed the door open; as it swung shut quietly behind him, he found it hard to believe what he was seeing. The outside was definitely a portacabin, while the inside could have been the boardroom of any big company. Facing him as he went in was a large desk behind which sat a secretary, who looked up from her computer, saying, 'Good morning, sir. How may I help you?'

'Detective Inspector Keane. I am here to see Mr Plant.'

'If you would like to take a seat, I'll let him know you are here.'

Ray thought this was totally unnecessary, as surely if he were in the cabin, he would have heard Ray enter. Ray sat in one of the two very plush leather chairs, waiting, and then through a partition wall, he heard a phone ring. He watched the secretary as she put on a practiced smile as she said, 'A policeman to see you, Mr Plant.'

It took a matter of seconds for Darren to open a door in the partition and invite Ray in; if appearance was everything in business, then Darren was doing alright. The cabin stretched back further than expected as Ray followed him through. He was startled to be in front of a boardroom table surrounded by chairs and a large desk with more leather chairs on either side.

'Pleasure to meet you, Detective Inspector. Can I offer you a coffee?'

Ray took one look at the very impressive coffee machine and saw no reason to refuse.

'That would be very nice; thank you.'

Once the coffee had been made and they were sitting opposite each other at the desk, Darren spoke again.

'So, how can I be of assistance to the local police?'

Though he was unaware of it, these few words and tone of voice showed some of his true nature, as it was basically how Ray and most other officers had been greeted by criminals over the years, as if by offering to help, they were hiding something at the same time. Ray had decided within moments of meeting Darren to be as direct as possible, though in his head he heard the warning from Angela to be careful with his questions.

'It is a bit awkward, Mr Plant. Your name has been mentioned to us in the course of an investigation.'

'I would not be surprised on 2 counts. First, I have several acquaintances in the police, along with many business associates. Then you have the jealous people who would all stick the knife in, given the chance.'

'Unfortunately, the way you have been connected by our sources is not anything to do with another business or high-powered friendships. We are currently investigating 2 murders that are linked by a drug connection; you have been named as a possible supplier.'

Ray was in no doubt that the shock portrayed was an act that had been well polished over several years; it was certainly a good act.

'I am shocked, D.I. Keane. Do I look like a drug supplier? I have nothing to do with drugs.'

Ray saw he was going to have to push harder for anything of benefit to come out of the meeting, 'Is this despite your arrest at college for supplying drugs at a party?'

Ray had to admit the facial expressions he was witnessing were very good, as again, Darren appeared totally shocked.

'Which were all fabricated rumours, and if you check your records, then you will see nothing was ever proven.'

Darren seemed to relax a bit, even adding with a laugh.

'We were all young once, weren't we?'

Ray could see how Darren was able to mix with all the people he did, as even if he did feel awkward at all by the conversation it was not allowed to show, he was happy to sit and chat.

'We were all young, sir, but I never used drugs at all.'

'Neither did I, inspector.'

Again, it was very much a case of Darren putting distance between himself and any wrongdoing.

'What sort of business do you deal in. Mr Plant?'

'Do we have to keep things so formal?'

'I find it works best that way; there is no possibility of any misunderstanding.'

This had always been his way of letting anyone who might be thinking differently know exactly where things stood.

Darren pulled himself upright in the chair, then put his body forward towards the desk. Ray knew enough from some of the others about body language, so he knew this was Darren trying to assert himself. Ray made a point of not moving at all.

'If that is how you want it, then fine. I basically supply a service. If anyone wants to ship stuff abroad or bring stuff in, they let me know, and I can then arrange for containers to carry it.'

'How does that work? Do you own the containers? I would imagine it is a costly business?'

'That is where my contacts help. You would have seen all the containers piled high on ships, so, I make sure they are all filled up to cover costs. I can offer any business a good price to ship a full container or 1 item in another. It is never a problem to find space or customers, and it works well for everyone.'

Ray was already visualising how things could be organised, and small amounts of drugs brought in across several containers could quite easily avoid detection. He was as aware as others how busy border checks were and, by having the advantage of pieces being spread around if one supply line got found, how many others got through. He could see a picture forming and wanted to keep things moving, though he decided on another angle, 'Just so we are clear on how things work; I understand that the container side of things is in the name of your dad's business. Is that correct?'

'Someone has been doing their homework. Yes, it is, due to it being convenient when I started up. Dad already had some containers that he used for supplies for his building business.'

Ray could not help but feel even more that there were a lot more questions for Darren to answer, though he felt it needed to be in a more official capacity. He also thought, I wonder if your dad knows what is in some of those loads with his name on all the paperwork.

'I think, just for the sake of elimination, I am going to need more details about your line of work.'

It was obvious now from Ray's body language that had placed Darren in an awkward situation; he had the choice of flat-out denial, which would lead to showing no cooperation. He was intelligent enough to know this would not be a good move. Again, how much did he reveal in order to protect things? Due to the speed at which he had shut down operations, there was currently only 1 container he had concerns over. He knew from his contacts that if you were to appear too awkward to the authorities, as if they decided to look into things, businesses could find themselves being watched very closely.

'I am sorry you feel the need to take things further. Inspector, all I want to do is help the police; so far, I think I have given satisfactory answers, while you seem intent on a witch hunt.'

'Not at all, sir. I am sure that with you being an understanding citizen as you are, you would want us to do everything we can to solve crimes.'

Ray was impressed with himself that he had managed to make this last sentence sound sincere. He continued.

'I just have a few more questions for you, regarding your knowledge of the people involved.'

He could see that Darren was shaken, and he saw his opportunity to push home his point.

'First, did you know a young lad, Nick Crowe?'

Ray watched closely for a reaction, but there was nothing.

'Sorry, Inspector, I understand and know the saying; if I have nothing to hide, then I should just answer your questions. For the sake of my own peace of mind, I'm going to tell you, I will not answer any more questions until I have spoken to my solicitor.'

'That is obviously your choice, sir. Do you want to contact him, and hopefully we can get things cleared up quickly?'

Ray wanted to keep things moving at a pace; he did not want Darren to have any chance to speak to too many others, with the possibility of getting stories organised. He was already expecting the answer he received.

'I'm sure you are aware that people can be very busy. I will ring him now and see when he is available.'

Ray felt himself bristling with annoyance as some of the earlier arrogance had returned to Darren; his hope was that the solicitor, whoever it was, would be proficient enough to want to sort things out on a relaxed level. Darren did not know that Ray was already building up to, if needed, arresting him to get the answers he required. Fortunately for them both, the solicitor on the other end of the phone was quick enough to foresee any problems and agreed to meet Darren and Ray at the police station within the next hour. Ray was pleased with the outcome and could see how uncomfortable Darren was becoming. Usually, to avoid any issues, Ray would suggest taking Darren to the police station. The decision was made for him by Darren, who reacted as if he had a point to prove.

'I take it, you will be my chauffeur to the station?'

'That is no problem, sir.'

Ray did have mixed feelings about this, which meant Darren could not speak to anyone, but Ray had calls he wanted to make. The opportunity to make at least 1 of these calls presented itself when they were on the way out. Darren stopped to give details of the rest of the day to his secretary. Ray stepped outside and left the door open so he could hear any conversation that took place; he made a call to speak to one of the team members. Not knowing if Dan had left for the port, he was able to keep the chat brief. Along with the work Dan had already done, it was Sheila who answered, 'Hi, Sheila. Following on from the stuff Dan found out for me this morning, I am on my way back with Darren Plant. I need as much information as possible on the family.'

'No problem, Ray; it has already been started, so I will get on it now.'

Ray hung up as Darren came out of the office and had a smug look on his face as he stood by the car and said, 'I take it I'm to open my own door?'

Ray kept his voice as light as possible, 'Yes, sir, you are correct.'

There were no other words exchanged on the journey back to King's Lynn. Neither Darren nor his solicitor had shown any surprise that they had been requested to be at King's Lynn rather than a local police station.

While their journey was in silence, Tim and Jill were trying to make sense of some heated conversations taking place between Maria and the 3 men currently sitting at the table in their caravan. Tim had been surprised at how nervous Maria had been when they first arrived. The last time he had spoken to her, she had been in a state of shock due to events but had seemed more than capable of looking after herself. Today, she was showing signs of partial relief to see them, along with concern as to why they were there. When they first got to the farm, the men had been busy cleaning some machinery that was ready to be stored for the winter. Tim and Jill had waited with Maria, who had busied herself making coffee, then they had all sat down in the living room area of the bigger caravan. The chat had started politely enough, even though Tim couldn't help but notice there was an atmosphere

220

that was distinctly cool towards him and Jill. Andris made this point verbally as well.

'So, what are you doing to allow us to return home? In my country, we would already have this dealt with.'

Tim was able to keep himself in check and just wanted to let them know things were progressing; he also had no desire to badmouth other countries' law enforcement.

'Perhaps you would have done things differently; surely you have travelled enough times now to realise while in our country, you have to respect how we do things. Obviously, things have changed as well with the discovery and link between the 2 bodies.'

For a brief moment, Jill was thinking that this was not the right thing to say as Andris slammed his hand on the table.

'We just want to know who killed our friend and when we can take his body home to his family.'

'I can assure you we are working as hard as we can to discover the facts of what happened.'

Tim had with him a picture from the traffic cameras of the white van; he placed it on the table so they could all see it.

'This van has been seen in the area where both bodies were found. Do you think any of you have seen it at all?'

They all glanced at the photo, and all indicated with shakes of their heads that they had not. Andris took it further.

'Is that the best you have managed so far? You certainly don't need any of us to tell you how many of those types of vans there are in this area, do you?'

Tim already knew this was a fair point, though he was having to control himself, as he had a nagging feeling they were holding something back. This was the side of his character that he felt he owed Ray thanks for. Early in his career, Tim had been a bit hot-headed. This led to a couple of incidents while in uniform that he was not proud of. One of these incidents had been during a protest march. Tim now could not even remember what the protest had been about; his memory was completely around the fact he had let 1 of the protesters goad him into losing his temper. This was something that during training school was pointed out time and time again; no matter what anyone said or did, you were no good to your colleagues if you lost your temper.

Ray had obviously read all his historical reports when considering Tim for CID and in his initial interview, Ray asked him if he was now at a mature enough stage in life and career to control himself better. It didn't take long for Ray to note that Tim was a very capable officer who showed signs of being able to progress through the ranks. He also mentioned that Tim was the type of person any of the team would like to back them up in awkward situations. Tim always credited his career moves to Ray, as he had shown him how to handle himself; it was these thoughts that were helping Tim deal with the current situation.

'We know how many vans there are in the area; in fact, if you give me a moment, I can give you the exact number.'

As usual, it was down to Maria to try and defuse the anger, 'I'm sure you are doing all you can.'

'We are all working very hard on this matter. The reason I'm asking about the van is because it has been seen on cameras at specific times, so that is why I wanted to know if you've seen it at all.'

Along with the fact, Maria was calming things down and Tim was not getting agitated, they all leant forward to look at the picture again.

'It is very difficult to see properly. I do recall seeing a similar van parked near the Red Eagle on several occasions.'

This was helpful, as again it showed a link to the pub, despite anything Jerry, the landlord, might have said. Tim now felt they were getting somewhere. The next comment from Maria was a bolt from the blue; the reaction from the others showed they had not expected any of them to say anything else.

'I can tell you officer; we think the surname of Jack that you are searching for is Marshall.'

Tim was taken aback, and as he processed how they had found this out, he also had to raise his voice to silence them as they had all started to talk at once.

'Please, quieten down. Do you mind telling me how you know this and when you found out?'

Maria, who had been visibly upset by the others, stood up as she continued, 'We found out last night; we were talking to some people in the pub who knew Sergei and Nick.'

'Did any of the people you spoke to know where you would find this Jack Marshall?'

Alekesji seemed to have collected himself quicker than the other men, so he replied.

'No, they didn't. Surely, if someone kept an eye on the pub, there has to be a good chance he would turn up. If he is supplying, then he will want to keep making money.'

Tim looked across at Jill, and between them, with a look, it was obvious they were not going to get anything else of use at the moment. It was left to Tim to issue a warning.

'I think that is all for now; we will need to speak to you again. Also, take note; do not start trying to investigate this yourselves. You must see that these people are dangerous.'

Jill was then impressed that it was obvious someone was going to speak out; just by raising his hand, Tim stopped them.

'I know some of what you are used to at home; just leave this to us.'

He knew there was going to be some heated conversations when they left. Not wanting to get involved, he indicated to Jill they were leaving.

With no idea how things were developing with Ray after his meeting with Darren, Tim felt it was important for them to return to the station as soon as possible to update everyone. To this end, he pulled out of the farmyard and engaged the blues and twos to make the journey rapidly. This journey was cut short. As he was concentrating on the road, Jill took a message from control to say there had been a report of a partially burnt-out white van, and it was thought they would like to take a look. Tim safely and efficiently made a U-turn to go back past where they had just been, following the address they now had for a neighbouring farm.

Chapter Eighteen

Over his many years in the force and recently in his personal life, there have been many occasions on which D.I. Ray Keane had been surprised. Nothing could have prepared him for being met by Superintendent Angela Johnson as he entered the police station and to ready himself to interview Darren in the presence of his solicitor. He knew there would be time before the solicitor arrived but did not want to get caught up with anything by the team, so on entering the custody suite, he gave details to the desk sergeant of the interview and to expect the solicitor.

As he looked and saw Angela, his expression obviously said a lot, 'Do not look so surprised, inspector; I do know my way around the station. I take it that you have no objection to me sitting in on the interview.'

Ray was not sure how to respond, so he kept it brief, 'No, that is not a problem.'

Throughout his time based at the station; he could not recall ever seeing Adam in the custody suite; he certainly would not want to sit in on an interview. Ray had always felt that Adam's attitude was that despite it being the reason they did what they did, why would he want to be around the criminals who were in this area of the station? In the few moments he had been standing there, Ray had composed himself; he addressed the sergeant.

'Can you escort Mr Plant to the interview room and arrange a coffee for him? Thank you.'

He waited for Darren to be removed, then spoke to Angela.

'Do you mind me asking, why do you want to sit in?'

'I know you would report everything back to me. I have had a call from the chief constable telling me you had asked Mr Plant to come in, so I thought it would be best for us all.'

Ray was saved from answering by the intercom buzzing and the agitated voice of the solicitor announcing his arrival. As the door released a man in a very smart suit strode in and started speaking immediately, 'Good afternoon; I am sure someone has a reasonable excuse for what is just a misunderstanding. If we can get on, then the quicker we can all get back to what we need to.'

Ray found he did not have time to reply before Angela stepped in, 'I am Superintendent Angela Johnson. We will deal with everything as quickly and correctly as normal, and we also appreciate your client coming in to help us.'

The change in the man was visible immediately; he had been subdued by Angela. Ray also felt he was thinking to himself, I can deal with a female officer easier. Angela had also noticed the solicitor relax, hoping that it would cause Darren to be forthcoming.

'If we go through to the interview room, we can get things moving.'

As they were about to enter the room, PC Dan Carol, who had returned from the port area, appeared on a run, explaining he needed to speak to Ray, who excused himself from stepping to one side.

'This had better be good, Dan.'

'I think you will be interested, sir. While I was out, I received a message on a follow-up for the white van. Partial plates we've had thrown up a few vans; interestingly, one such van is registered to Mr Joseph Plant as the owner of a building firm.'

'Thanks Dan; we will see what Darren has to say about that as well.'

Ray entered the room to find the others waiting for him, 'Can we please get on now?'

Ray presumed the solicitor was going to do most of the talking, as Darren had not uttered a word since they had arrived at the station.

'Sorry for the delay; I have just received some information that I think is helpful.'

As Ray was speaking, he carefully watched to see how Darren reacted. He knew that Darren was involved; it was just a matter of getting the evidence to place him where he was in the chain, which Ray felt was at the top. He knew he had to tread carefully this early in the interview to ensure that they did not lose him. In past cases like this one, it seemed that some people avoided prosecution, usually down to a technicality; he was very determined this would not happen this time.

'For the benefit of all involved, we will be recording this interview.'

Angela reached and pressed the buttons on the machine, and after a long bleep, Ray introduced the people at the table.

'Interview with Mr Darren Plant; present are Mr Plant, D.I. Ray Keane, and Superintendent Angela Johnson.'

Ray looked at the solicitor, who said, 'Mr Jeremy Taylor, solicitor.'

'Thank you. I will point out that this is a voluntary meeting, as Darren has offered to help with our inquiry.'

There were a few minutes of conversation replaying the questions Ray had asked Darren at his office. The solicitor seemed to think that it was a waste of time.

'Going on everything I have heard so far, inspector; do you have a genuine reason for asking my client here? Mr Plant, after following his father into business, is a respected member of the community, and along with some of your officers, does a lot of work to help local charities.'

Ray saw this as a chance to see if there was a chink in the persona Darren portrayed.

'He would not be the first person to hide behind a business to commit crime.'

The reaction was just as Ray hoped as Darren jumped up, knocking the chair over while shouting, 'I've had enough of this; I came to help. If you have evidence, then bloody arrest me. If not, I'm out of here.'

'Mr Plant, please sit down.'

Before Ray could continue, there was a knock at the door.

'Come in.'

The door opened, and PC Dan Carol entered, Ray added this to the interview tape.

'PC Dan Carol has entered the room.'

Dan apologised for the intrusion and passed a note to Ray.

'It is important, sir.'

Ray unfolded the paper to read a message from Tim Jarvis, he hardly broke stride in the conversation as he looked across the desk.

'Mr Plant, does the name Jack Marshall mean anything to you?'

For the briefest of seconds, it was as if Darren had been slapped, quickly but not quick enough for Ray not to notice; he recovered his composure, 'No, I never heard of him.'

'You might want to take a minute more to think carefully. I will just add that, as part of our inquiries, your name and his have been mentioned together.'

Ray had to admit that he had come across several very cold and calculated people in his career. Darren was showing signs of being one such person. He appeared to have gathered himself, and the arrogant attitude Ray had first encountered was coming to the surface again.

'I can assure you, inspector; I do not know this person. I would say that though his name is vaguely familiar, I may have heard it mentioned at some stage during my many discussions over work or at charity events.'

Ray found it was vague, that Darren kept on pointing out his charity work, and it was always mentioned with a certain smugness, almost as if he felt it was something to hide behind. Before anything else could be said, Jeremy Taylor spoke with an abrupt tone.

'Superintendent, I do feel this is a waste of everyone's time. It would appear that your officers are on a fishing expedition with no evidence of a crime. I think it is time for us to leave.'

Angela showed her support for Ray with her reply, 'I should explain; I am here as an observer. As for it being time for you to leave, I am not sure if the inspector is finished yet.'

If Jeremy had any thoughts on being able to influence Angela, this comment ended them. Ray looked at the faces sitting at the table he realised that no matter his instincts they did not have enough to detain Darren anymore. He decided to see how Darren reacted to a couple of final questions.

'Mr Plant, do you own or drive a white transit van?'

He did have more to say, but Darren interrupted, 'Really Inspector, you have seen my office and car; do I strike you as a white van man?'

'I am not sure how you would describe what such a person would look like. Finally, I would ask you to stay in the area in case we need to speak again.'

As Jeremy made to stand up, Ray added, 'Would you mind giving us a DNA sample, just for elimination purposes?'

It was now Jeremy's turn to react angrily; he stood up with enough force to cause his chair to fall over. He was so outraged that he hardly seemed to notice the noise.

'That really is a step too far, Inspector. There is no logical reason why you need my clients DNA.'

If Jeremy was upset by the request, he was totally shocked by Darren's response.

'That is no problem if it will help clear up this whole issue.'

Ray decided this was either arrogance or stupidity on Darren's part; he went with the former. This suggested to Ray that Darren never went anywhere near anything that might involve him getting his hands dirty; they had already made this assumption but knew that having the DNA sample could come in handy.

He was hoping that Darren had made a mistake at some stage and left something behind that would allow them to get a result. His main reason behind this thinking was the arrogant attitude he had picked up from the beginning. During the interview, he also witnessed the angry side of Darren. To Ray, this was all outweighed by the fact that everything Darren said was accompanied by a smirk.

'Thank you for agreeing to the request.'

Ray then acted out of character by taking a snipe at them both.

'As I am sure you are both aware, once everything is tidied up, any DNA sample, if you are innocent, will be destroyed.'

Their joint reaction of no acknowledgment to this remark suggested to Ray that he had gotten under their skin; he was happy to chalk this up as a small victory for now. He finished off the interview by telling them he would arrange for someone to take the samples. Angela switched off the machines, and they both left the room with Ray looking back from the door.

'Thank you, gentlemen. I will speak to you again soon.'

Neither had a chance to reply before he closed the door.

'You are convinced he is running things, aren't you?'

'Definitely, and I am working on the theory that, due to his attitude, he has already or will soon make a mistake; I will be waiting.'

'I agree with you; it was interesting to watch you in action, so to speak. I am going to call the chief constable and make him aware of how things stand. A word of caution as well, keep any information about Mr Plant on a need-to-know basis for the time being.'

Ray felt this did not need an answer, due to how they were already feeling things were not right regarding Jackson, the prison officer; he was totally aware of what Angela was thinking. Ray made his way back to CID. If his mood was already so good that things were moving in the right direction, the phone call he was about to answer would make him feel even better. As he went into his office, the phone started to ring. In the middle of a case, he always answered the phone, wondering if this would be the call to pull everything together. He could not help but have a small niggle of doubt, but it could also be the call that blew everything up in the air.

'D.I. Ray Keane; how may I help you?'

'Good afternoon, inspector. It is DS John Maxwell. Your partner Jenny works out of our station; she had a word with me this morning. I thought I would give you a call to see if I could be of help.'

'I hope you might be; possibly your intel on the county lines drug trade may be more current than ours.'

It was something Ray had always been thankful for in that drugs had been involved in crimes, but never on a grand scale, in the region. He was realistic enough to know that they were always just bubbling away below the surface; he also knew that there was a good, hard-working team of several community support officers who visited schools and youth establishments in the area to put their message across. John went on to explain his role, 'I have been working alongside the drug squads from various regions for the past 3 years. Jenny told me you had a couple of possible names to look into.'

'I now have more details on the names, so that could help. The seller on the street appears to be Jack Marshall; at present, the person I think is the main dealer is Darren Plant.'

'Do you know anything more?'

'Sorry, not yet. We only got full details on the names a couple of hours ago.'

'Leave it with me to look into; I will just say that the name Jack Marshall has been flagged up to us a few times in investigations, though so far never enough for a conviction. That means either he is extremely careful or he has someone watching out for him.'

'Thanks; anything you can find would be appreciated.'

Ray thought carefully before his next comment, though he felt it was important enough to mention.

'Another thing you could look at on your intel. This is purely my instinct at the moment; there could be a connection between the drug dealers and someone in authority.'

Ray felt this left it open, and if John found anything, he could give Ray the name rather than the other way round, this would then show John was on the level. Ray did not like to think about crooked officers but knew it went on.

'No problem; you would be surprised at how discreet I can be. It wouldn't be the first time a member of staff you would usually trust abuses their power. From what Jenny has told me, your instinct is normally good.'

Ray always found accepting praise awkward, 'Thank you, though I will add that my instinct is only good enough; once others have helped put things together, that show, I was right.'

Having said goodbye, Ray hung up just as his mobile vibrated from the pocket of his jacket. The custody suite was a notoriously blank spot to get a signal. When he looked at his phone, he saw 3 missed calls from Tim. He was just in the process of ringing him back when Sheila came to the door.

'Message from Tim; please ring him; he has some news on the white van.'

He held out his phone to indicate that was exactly what he was doing, just as Tim answered.

'Hello, Ray, we may have had some luck with the van. There is not a lot of information yet, though I will say it is now a white van with a touch of smokiness. We have just arrived; the fire brigade is finishing off extinguishing the flames.'

'Does not sound too hopeful if there was a fire?'

'Have faith, sir, a farmer spotted the blaze and was already on top of things before the brigade got here. From what I can see so far, we are going to be lucky. Let me speak to the brigade, and then I will call you back.'

While Ray had been busy interviewing Darren Plant, Tim and Jill had been getting the breakthrough of the name from the co-workers of Sergei. Tim's first response to the call about the discovery of the white van was that maybe things were falling into place, but his hopes were dashed as he heard the rest of the message regarding the fire. The hope that he would be able to report major help to the case was raised slightly as the car pulled into the yard of a farm not too far away from the disposal sites. He could see a fireman busy at the entrance of a lean-on shed. To his eye there was not too much damage to the van. Having been to similar scenes, Tim got out of the car and approached the shed cautiously; he had soon learned at the start of his career to always allow other emergency service workers to do their job. He was met by the Chief Fire

Officer, 'Hello sir, I'm DS Tim Jarvis from King's Lynn. Has anyone been hurt?'

'No. Luckily, this shed is not used very often. The farmer who called in had been able to use a nearby water standpipe to get the blaze under control before we arrived. If you think it is of interest to you, then it is down to him that you have something to work on.'

'Okay, thanks for that. When can I have a look round?'

'Just give us a bit longer to make sure it is all out; I also want to check that there is nothing hot lingering in any of the construction.'

While the fire brigade completed their task, it gave Tim and Jill a chance to talk to the farmer. Unfortunately, he could not tell them too much; as he explained, it was not a shed, he used very much due to the fact it was away from his main farm and was only the walls and a poor-condition roof, with no way to secure anything. The field he had been bringing the tractor over was not a proper access route; it was one he used as a shortcut to his house.

'I can tell you the van was not there 2 nights ago. I just happened to be coming back from my break today and saw the flames. I suppose whoever set light to it may have been thinking the flames would not be seen so readily in daylight.'

'Well, thank you for dealing with the situation so promptly; it is a possibility this van is involved in a crime currently being investigated, so you have been a big help. As soon as the fire brigade is satisfied, I will make an initial check and then get the van removed.'

It was Jill who spoke next, and her question prompted a reaction, which sometimes happened. This was that at a scene people could see something that their brain would not necessarily connect to events.

'If you remember anything else you may have noticed, please give us a call.'

She handed him a card with phone numbers that would take him directly to CID.

'Now you come to mention it. There was something; I certainly didn't take much notice at the time, as just a minute later I saw the flames. As I came along the road to the edge of the field, there was a motorbike, revving its engine. Another person came running around the field and jumped on; they were lucky as the driver roared off in such a hurry the passenger nearly fell off.'

'Any chance you got a look at either?'

'No, they were both wearing helmets. We do get youngsters on motorbikes going up and down, so it is not unusual. As I said it was just after this, I saw the flames.'

Tim knew it would be a long shot, but it was too much of a coincidence for the bikers not to be involved. This just meant that the luck of finding the van, if it was one, had now made more work of visiting the few houses in the area to see if anyone else had noticed the bike.

'Thank you; we will get the van moved quickly and can let you get on with your day.'

They made their way back to the shed as the fire brigade finished putting hoses away on the side of the engine. The fire chief was waiting for them.

'It is all yours now. Everything is safe. You have the majority of the van to work on. If any of your team members need to know, the fire was started in the back of the van; presumably they were hoping the petrol tank would go quickly. The remains are in the rear of rags that have been soaked in petrol. Tell them to ring me if they want more details.'

Tim proceeded to make a quick visual check on the van; he could see the damage caused by the fire; fortunately, the quick work of the farmer and then the brigade meant most of the damage was confined to the interior.

According to the fire chief, the evidence suggested one of the rear doors had been left slightly open; this meant that any breeze would have fanned the flames, though consequently, it allowed the farmer to get the water directly at the seat of the fire. He also told Tim that if the door had been shut, it would have allowed the fire to take hold easier, and the damage would have been a lot greater. Tim was just about able to make out the start of the rear number plate, which had started to melt due to the heat. He could see the first 2 letters of WA, which convinced him it was the van they were looking for. His next job was to make some calls and get the van back to forensics for a thorough check, though looking past the damage in the rear, if they were right about it being registered to Joseph Plant and his building company, it was the cleanest builders van he had ever seen. He looked at Jill, then said, 'If you shut those doors and look at the van from the front, it looks as if it has just come off the assembly line.'

'You are right, but you know what forensics is always telling us, it doesn't matter how hard people work to clean things; they have lots of tricks up their sleeves to find just the smallest speck of anything left behind.'

They would have to wait for the others to arrive to remove the van before they could make their way back for what was going to be a very busy briefing. Tim got started on his calls;

he felt they were lucky at King's Lynn to have their own recovery truck on call, so his first call was to arrange collection. He then let forensics know to expect a delivery for them to go over. Lastly, he rang Ray to give him the details and get him to organise some uniforms to carry out house-to-house enquiries, with the idea being if anyone had seen the motorbike the farmer had mentioned. He was not aware of it yet, but within 10 minutes, he was to get some of the luck that Ray always told him they needed during a case.

While they waited for the others, Tim carefully gave the van the once-over, making a point not to disturb anything. If he had been surprised by how clean the rear of the van was, the front seating area was even cleaner; to his untrained eye, it was spotless. Meanwhile, Jill was checking around the area outside the shed. At first glance, there were several sets of tyre marks, some of which were obviously from the beasts of farm machinery. Leading to the shed, she could see parallel sets that were from the van, and it was only on closer inspection that she noticed overlaid on one set of marks were the distinctive tyre marks of a motorbike. This suggested that the bike had carefully followed the van in, possibly then being lifted to turn it around, before driving away to wait for its passenger. She called for Tim to come out.

'Is anyone from forensics coming here?'

'Yes, I asked Lisa to attend, not that I think she will find much on site.'

'I agree, but she can take prints of these tyre marks.'

As she was pointing to the ground, there was a loud, booming voice carried across the field. As they both looked up, they heard.

'I don't know what you are up to; this is private property.'

Tim moved towards the man to stop him from encroaching on any possible crime scene. At the same time, he held out his warrant card for the man to see.

'Hello sir, I'm DS Tim Jarvis from King's Lynn police. We are here officially, so there's no need to worry.'

'I can't see you doing much; shame you are not here about those yobs on their bloody motorbikes.'

'We have had no reports that I am aware of about motorbikes; I would think it would be your local constables who would deal with that.'

For a moment, it was as if the man had lost interest, as he turned to walk away. Tim wanted to talk to him more, so he knew he had to get him on side.

'I will have a word with the local station, sir, and see if I can get any complaints chased up. Is it a big problem?'

'Yes, we have a nice area to live in; everybody accepts the noise of farm life. Then we have to put up with these morons racing bikes up and down the road; it is not just at night either.'

'You didn't happen to see a motorbike recently, did you?'

'As it happens, yes.'

'Did you get any details at all?'

'I can do better than that officer.'

Tim bit his tongue as he felt the man was helping but at the same time was trying to prove a point with his tone of voice.

'What can you tell us?'

'I can show you camera footage from outside my house.'

Tim felt his heart rate increase as he shouted across to Jill to wait for the others while he accompanied the man to his house to look at the footage. Again, silently, he thanked Ray for his advice to always control your emotions, especially while the man insisted on explaining about the cameras he had and their benefits for safety.

'If you can show me the footage, sir, it would be a big help.'

The man sat at his computer and first ran through things, showing Tim how much area, he had covered. Usually, this sort of thing would have interested Tim, though now he just wanted to see this morning's events. As the man started to rewind the tape, Tim saw a motorbike going at speed along the road.

'Can you stop it there, sir?'

The tone of the reply was aggrieved.

'Well, if you want, don't you want to see it when it, is first sighted?'

Tim made the decision that, as they were going to have to wait, he would humour this man, who obviously liked to chat. Within minutes, Tim was just happy that he did this. As the man stopped the film, the time stamp showed 1 hour earlier in the day. At first, Tim could not believe his luck; on the screen was the white van being followed by the motorbike in the direction of the farmers shed. The camera lost sight of both machines, and the man quickly forwarded the tape to 20 minutes previously, showing footage of the motorbike now with a passenger going much faster back past the house. Tim, being so interested in computers and how they helped in the job, always had pieces of equipment with him, so producing a USB stick, he said, 'Can you please save me a copy of all that footage?'

Without any knowledge of the help, he was being the man replied, 'If it helps you catch those idiots, no problem.'

Tim thanked the man and made his way back across the field to meet Jill, who could tell from the grin on his face that he had found something out.

'Come on, then, what did he know?'

Tim laughed.

'If you asked him that question, he would most probably say everything. Better than knowing anything, he had camera footage of both the motorbike and, I think, our white van.'

As they were speaking, the others had started to arrive. Tim wanting to get back to tell Ray everything, spoke quickly to Lisa.

'We will need the van assessed, then taken back to King's Lynn. We have been careful, so hopefully we have not contaminated the scene at all.'

Lisa smiled as she said.

'Trying to teach me my job, Tim. I will get it sorted; tell Ray, I will get my initial report to him later.'

Tim laughed, and Lisa noted how he was developing into a reliable officer to work with. As he looked over, he recognised the 2 P. C's from the discovery of Nick's body.

'Hello, how did you know about this?'

'Apparently your superintendent rang our station as you needed some house-to-house completing.'

Tim was impressed by how quickly Angela had reacted and that she was happy to get others to help out; it would prove helpful as PC Newby and Wilson would possibly know some of the people they would talk to. He explained the man he had already spoken to, then realised he had been so taken with the information he had forgotten to get a name. As soon as he mentioned the problem with the motorbikes, PC Wilson said, 'You met Mr Moaning.'

'Sorry, is that his name?'

'No, it is Mr Harper, but if you talk to anyone around here, he is known as a professional moaner.'

'It sounded as though he had a point regarding the bike situation.'

'Yes, I agree with you. But you know what it is like; they call us about the noise, and by the time we get here, the bikes have moved on.'

Tim understood the problem and explained the camera footage that he now had, finishing off by telling them to go house-to-house and make a point of visiting Mr Harper to tell him they would make a point of getting details to all patrols about the bikes. He then, along with Jill, made the journey back, feeling very pleased with the information he had to pass over.

Chapter Nineteen

The investigation was now reaching the point where there was so much going on that, along with the work the police were doing, there were outside influences that would eventually have a bearing on the outcome. To an outsider, it would appear that it was all a bit of a jumble, but for the team, it was all the pieces of the puzzle that they needed to get in place to gain a complete picture. As the team started to gather in the office for the briefing, the noise level was a lot higher than normal, with everyone interested in knowing what the others had achieved throughout the day. They all worked well as a team, though Ray liked to see there was a level of competitiveness to see who could find the important piece of information first.

The noise level also gave Ray a clue to the success of the day; if it was quiet, he knew there would not be a lot to add. As it was today, he guessed the briefing would be busy. Having left Darren and his solicitor in the interview room, waiting to give a DNA sample, and telling Angela she was welcome at the briefing, he had returned to his office and was working through the seemingly endless communications as they all came in from the day's work. He saw this as a good excuse to leave the paperwork and get on with things. He walked out and stood beside the incident boards, clearing his throat as he went. As always, silence fell immediately.

'Good evening, everyone, I take it from all the noise you are making; it has been a good day. Shall we start with your report, Tim?'

Having led a briefing recently, Tim was now comfortable not just standing at his desk talking but walking to the front of the room to pass on his news.

'First thing today, Jill and I saw the co-workers of Sergei. After some initial animosity, due to them thinking we were not doing enough, we found out from them that they have been doing some investigating of their own.'

This brought several groans from throughout the room. The one thing that could cause problems during a case was members of the public trying to do the job of the police. They relied heavily on getting information from the public, though on numerous occasions they had to point out that there is a fine line between asking a seemingly innocent question and putting yourself at risk. Especially if people got involved in a murder case. Ray had been in the position of having to explain to people that if someone was willing to kill another person, they would also be prepared to kill again to avoid capture. Ray spoke to get the room back on track.

'Okay, quiet; let Tim finish.'

'We did warn them to be careful and leave it to us, though they did have some information that could be useful. From what they told us, we think the dealer on the street is Jack Marshall. They came across this name while talking to some locals in the Red Eagle; also, the photo of the van, they think they have seen it or something similar near the pub.'

Ray would not normally interrupt a briefing but felt it was important, 'Right, now we have been to the pub several times; why have we not had this information sooner? Everybody needs to start asking more questions and get their ears to the ground.'

As he finished talking, he could see some of them were not used to seeing this side of him. Seeing Angela come into the room, Tim decided to move things along; at the same time showing how he had matured as an officer by pointing something out, which partly answered Ray.

'I think it is safe to say that the locals in the pub may talk more freely to other regulars rather than us. We were going to arrange another visit to see the landlord, who must have some idea of what happens in his pub. We then got a call about a van on fire at a neighbouring farm.'

Tim could sense the reaction this was going to bring, so he gave no one the chance to speak, 'It was not as bad as it sounds; the farmer had acted quickly and got the blaze under control, as well as calling the fire brigade. Due to his actions, we have a white van with the number plate we were looking for, on its way to forensics.'

Tim was now in full flow and could see he had the full attention of everyone in the room.

'Something for you all to look at.'

He went to his computer, pressing a few buttons with a speed that always impressed Ray, who was behind the others in the use of computers. Some images came up on the screen beside the incident boards.

'There is more of this I have to work through; basically, this is film from a security camera of a house near the farm where the van was spotted.'

Everyone watched silently as they saw the van and motorbike go across the screen, moments later they saw the bike roar past on the road going away from the area. At this moment, Tim froze the image of the bike with a pillion rider on the screen.

'Good work, Tim. Hopefully, with anything forensics gets as well, we could be getting somewhere. Unless you have anything else to add.'

At this point, Tim shook his head to show he was finished.

'I will leave you to update the board once we finish. Okay, my meeting with Darren Plant.'

Ray outlined both his meetings at the offices of Darren earlier and then the interview with both him and his solicitor.

'Obviously, we do need proof, though I am convinced he is involved.'

Angela coughed to get his attention, then spoke.

'Just to make everyone aware. I am in agreement with the D.I. on this matter. As we progress, tread carefully, so he does not slip away from us.'

They all acknowledged this comment, and Ray felt good that they knew the support was there as he continued.

'Now this next piece of conversation stays in this room. Sheila will explain and will initially follow things up. We may need to act more as we find things out.'

Sheila followed Tim's lead and moved to where they could all see her.

'First thing I will say is that at the moment, this line of inquiry is based on instinct alone. However, after making a few calls today, I think there is something for us to look at. Prison Officer Ian Jackson has been in his current position at HMP Sutton Wells for the past 2 years. He joined the prison service 9 years ago, having previously spent 15 years in the army. In those 9 years he has changed prisons 6 times.'

Tim raised his arm.

'That surely is not that unusual in that profession, is it?'

'Normally no; on checking records though, each time he has moved, the reasons in his work history is vague to say the least.'

Ray took over at this point, 'Anyway, the main thing is that we are suspicious enough to think something is going on. Take note, and if his name is mentioned at all, then we all need to know.'

Despite press coverage, whenever a rogue person in authority was exposed, it was not a regular occurrence. Though it always left a bad taste for the other officers, who then had to deal with any fallout, Ray continued, 'Just be careful on 2 accounts; we do not want to alert Jackson if we are correct. Also, heaven forbid if we are wrong, and prisoners get to hear about it; it would not do him any favours. You are all aware of your jobs for tomorrow, so finish up and get back here bright and early. Jill and Dan, my office, please.'

'What about the pub visit?'

'Good point, Tim. Join us now.'

Once the 4 of them plus Sheila were in Ray's office, he sat on the edge of his desk and looked at them all.

'Good to see you are getting on my wavelength, Tim. The pub visit was the reason I wanted to speak to Jill and Dan.'

Ray went on to explain.

'Jill and Dan, some overtime for you. I would like you both to go home and get changed. Then visit the Red Eagle this evening and act as a couple out for a drink. No questions need asking at the moment; just listen to the conversations.'

'Do you not think the landlord might recognise me, sir?'

'I was hoping that if they were busy, plus you are not going to be standing at the bar in a pristine uniform, that would help on that score.'

Dan laughed.

'So, I can dress rough and ready.'

'Whatever you are comfortable in will do.'

Jill spoke for the first time since the briefing.

'If we are supposed to be a couple, Dan, dress remembering I have standards.'

This made them all smile, 'You have been warned, Dan. Right off you 2 go, ears open with no heroics, and report tomorrow morning on anything you hear. Then we can decide how we continue to approach both the pub and the landlord.'

After they had left the office, Ray said to Sheila.

'Good work on the calls regarding Jackson today. I think, based on what you have heard so far, we are going to hear more about him and possible connections.'

'I think you are right on that. I have a couple more calls I want to make now; then I am heading home.'

'That sounds like a good idea; Tim, what are you on next?'

'I want to do a bit more on enhancing the video we got. Then start again tomorrow.'

'Okay, I will see you both in the morning.'

While everyone at the station in King's Lynn was getting themselves organised for whatever their evening would involve, 70 miles away, Jack Marshall was about to make his first mistake that would lead to everything falling down around him. It was also to be the moment Ray would start to see exactly what was going on.

The reason Jack made the mistake was purely down to panic; he had agreed with Darren that laying low for a few weeks was a good idea. He hadn't allowed his own demons to take this opportunity to reappear. He had suffered from PTSD after being discharged from the army. This had been helped with support from various charities, though he had been left with bouts of depression; if anyone had asked him, he would have replied that he was fine. Usually in everyday situations, with Darren there in the background, he was, but being alone away from normality was a different matter.

The first few days had been alright; he looked at it as a holiday; he kept in touch via the news, including reading reports online about the current police investigation, with the feeling they were not getting very far. Against his better judgement, after a couple of days, he decided to switch on his phone just to see if there had been any contact. He expected to see a text from Ian Jackson with a new number he was not expecting to see several missed calls and texts from this same new number; that they needed to speak to him.

He sat in the caravan for a time, thinking through various scenarios as to the reasons for the texts. He knew the safest thing to do was to ignore them and stay put; unfortunately, human nature doesn't work like that. He decided he needed to be back on home ground quickly. It only took a few moments to throw his clothes in the car and then ring the number on the phone. Ian answered almost before the first ring had finished.

'We need to meet immediately.'

'Bit difficult I'm 2 hours away. Why the hell are you ringing me?'

'I told you last time that the police had been to see a prisoner; it was Nick Crowe's old man. Since then, I have heard rumours from contacts that the police are doing some digging into my past.'

'If that is the case, stop being so stupid. Hang up and get rid of the phone.'

The next words Ian spoke stopped Jack in his tracks. He was used to being challenged; normally, it would be some young drug user who was trying to push his luck. Jack usually found a quick, hard slap would sort it out. Ian Jackson was a different kettle of fish, 'I can promise you that if I go down, I will make sure you are firmly tied to me and come with me.'

This comment certainly annoyed Jack, though he knew he had to control himself to allow him to deal with things. The person he needed to talk to was Darren. First, he had to try and keep Ian calm.

'Right, listen! Okay keep yourself together. Switch your phone off for now, and I will make my way back. Check your messages after 10pm; I'll sort out a meeting place.'

After hanging up, he called Darren, and for reasons he had no knowledge of, the call went to voicemail. He decided, for safety, not to leave a message and thought he would try again later as he drove home. The guy he had rented the van from was surprised to see Jack at the door of his house, handing back the keys. Though he was quite happy when Jack told him he could keep the rest of the money, just telling the guy that he had to return home due to an emergency.

'If anyone should ask, I trust you will tell them you never saw me.'

'No problem, Jack.'

As he got in the car for the journey home, there was a jumble of thoughts racing through his mind. He pulled over in a layby to collect himself after a near miss at a roundabout due to him not concentrating. His first job was to deal with the situation regarding Ian; it would be a shame to end their business dealings as it had worked well for a number of years, and it meant he had a good amount of money stashed away. The next problem was how to keep things running smoothly with Darren while not letting him find out about the sideline he had run. In as much as they got on, he knew that Darren wouldn't take it well if he found out; he was also aware that Darren knew enough unsavoury characters who would be happy to deal with Jack for him.

He always knew he was walking a fine line; he knew he could look after himself and Darren in a fight, though he was aware of what could happen if the odds were stacked against you. After time sitting in the layby, he collected himself and decided to call Darren again; this time the call was answered very quickly; once Darren realised who was calling him, the tone of voice became very abrupt.

'What the hell are you ringing me for?'

'I think we have some problems.'

'Would that be the royal we? I have spent most of the day in the company of a detective inspector who, as well as asking lots of questions, seems to have already gotten me in jail.'

Jack was not sure how to approach the subject of Ian with Darren. Hearing the news he just had made it even more difficult, he decided for now to keep it to himself.

'I had heard from someone that questions were being asked. We need to deal with it.'

'We don't need to deal with anything. You need to stay out of sight with no contact. They may well have asked lots of questions; so far, they have not got any answers.'

'Maybe not; I'm making my way back.'

'Don't do anything stupid, Jack; we can see this through. If you insist on coming back, don't ring again. This will blow over.'

Before Jack could say anything else, the call had ended. If Ray could have heard the tone of voices during the conversation, he would have been happy that things were playing into their hands. A falling out amongst thieves usually meant mistakes would be made. The police could then act on these errors. Jack realised as he sat in the car that he was on his own; his main issue was dealing with Ian. Deciding he was now calm enough to continue driving, he made the journey home at the same time as formulating a plan for when he met Ian later.

As Jack was driving home, Sergei's co-workers were thinking about what to do next. It was a bit as if the 3 men had heard the warning from Tim about the dangers they were getting involved in, then took it as a challenge. Whereas Maria just wanted it all sorted out so they could all return home. After Tim had left, they had finished up some work on the farm. By late afternoon, they had heard from one of the many visitors to the farm about the fire and that it was a white van. The information just appeared to fire the men up wanting to do more.

'We need to see what anyone knows about this fire.'

Maria was feeling less motivated, 'You heard what the policeman said about it being dangerous.'

For the men who had all known Maria for several years, this was a different side to her; it had always been accepted that you didn't upset Maria, as she was quite capable of looking after herself. When anyone first met her, most men saw a good-looking young girl who they could try to chat up.

This usually involved the locals around where they worked; the people she worked with knew the sort of things she had witnessed at home, as well as hearing stories of how she reacted when cornered. One of the locals had found out exactly what she was capable of on an early visit to work. They had had a busy day at work and were enjoying a relaxing evening at the Red Eagle when a local man who always enjoyed chatting up the women went a step too far making a grab for Maria's breasts.

Before he had time to react, Maria had a vice-like grip on his testicles. After a few moments where no one moved, the man cried out in agony, then was squatting on the floor, and apologising before she would let go. On their next visit to the pub, there were a few comments aimed at Maria, but all were said with respect.

'We heard what the copper said—we are all capable of looking after ourselves. We just need to ask the right questions.'

Andris was really starting to want to take things further. It was as if he were back at home and with the police again. The effect was that the other 2 were being carried along with the emotion of it all; there was the feeling that they could do more than the local police. Despite her reservations, Maria felt she had to go along with things, even if it was only to keep an eye on them all. What none of them were aware of was the danger they would end up putting Maria in. If they had known, it is possible it would have influenced what they did next.

While this group of farm workers were organising themselves to go out and visit the pub, hoping to hear something about the fire. Dan Carol and Jill Addy met up to also visit the pub, with instructions from Ray ringing in their ears to listen and hopefully get some information. Meanwhile, Jack was driving home, and planning to meet with Ian Jackson, Darren had finished up with his solicitor for now and was sitting in his study at home. He had been busy at home, making calls to distance himself from events. Ray was sitting in his living room, having finished a lovely meal. Himself and Jenny were looking through some of the reports, trying to piece things together. If Ray had had any idea of what was happening at present, he would have used the analogy of several car drivers heading towards one position, with none of them aware of the impending crash.

Dan and Jill made their way to the pub; if Jerry did recognise Dan, he showed no sign of doing so. They ordered drinks and sat at a table that was in a good position to hear any conversations at the bar while also allowing them to see anyone who entered. They were there for 30 minutes and Dan had been for a 2nd drink; having so far heard nothing more interesting than the man they gathered was a local farmer moaning about how little he was being paid for his produce, then telling anyone who was still listening about a large repair bill for a piece of machinery. Any sympathy he may have received was quickly dispelled by someone else asking how his new car was going. Jill looked up as the door opened and saw Maria along with the others. They had some luck in that by moving slightly, they were out of view but could still hear things. If Jill was surprised to see the workers in the pub after Tim's warning earlier, she was amazed after they sat down with another group when she heard Andris ask, 'So, what do you know about this van fire earlier today?'

She couldn't quite hear the muted response, catching odd words at random; *arranged, Darren, lad, and arson*. Without making it obvious, she made notes of these words to relay to Ray in the morning. The group of workers seemed uncomfortable with one another; after a couple of drinks and a brief chat with 2 other young lads, they made to leave as they went to move. Dan and Jill heard something that made the evening worthwhile. A woman sat at the bar, looked at Maria.

'I heard you were asking about Jack Marshall recently.'

Before Maria could answer, Andris stepped in.

'We could have been. Do you know him?'

The woman who Jill recognised as having the signs of being a user.

'Only professionally. I was supposed to meet him the other evening; he seems to have disappeared.'

There was a reply from a man further along the bar, 'I heard he has been away for a few days, though he is due back this evening.'

Dan and Jill got up and left the pub by the rear door, one reason being the need to ring Ray; this information couldn't wait till morning. They also hoped to be in a place behind the others to hear any further chat. Dan placed the call to Ray as soon as they left the table.

'Sorry to disturb your evening, sir.'

'As seems to be your way recently, Dan, I take it; it is important.'

'The conversation we just heard is that someone knows Jack Marshall is going to be in the area this evening.'

Jill nudged Dan hard in the ribs, hard enough for him to think I was going to have a bruise there later. Also, hard enough that he quickly said into the phone, 'I will ring you back, sir.'

He hung up before Ray could say anything. The reason for the nudge in the ribs was that as they had walked around the side of the pub, they nearly bumped into the group of farm workers, who were standing on a corner close to the road. They were able, more by luck than judgement, to stop and get themselves out of sight, but they were still close enough to hear a very animated conversation taking place. The only difficulty was making out who was saying what, as it seemed that all 4 were talking at once. Every now and then, a voice was raised; they then heard a sentence that caused them both to worry, 'If this Jack is going to be here tonight, maybe we should wait and see him.'

Very clearly, they heard Maria say, 'That is stupid; if what the police have already told us, along with things we have heard, he could be the man who killed Sergei.'

After hearing this, they moved further away to allow Dan to call Ray back and explain, 'Sorry about that, sir; I think we could use more bodies nearby soon.'

Dan went on to explain the conversation they had overheard. After Ray had finished a rant about members of the public taking things into their own hands, he said, 'Okay, you and Jill wait in your car; I will get Tim and Sheila to initially join up with you. I will be there as soon as I can. Be careful.'

Ray was out of the front door and in his car within minutes of the phone call. One thing he took very seriously was the safety of his team. Jenny, who was used to things happening like this, took it in stride. In the time it took Ray to make himself presentable and ready, she stood by the front door with his car keys and mobile in hand. He placed a fleeting kiss on her nose, saying, 'I will call you later.'

She had no need to reply, nor the time to, as he was already in the car. His feelings were running high with the thought that they were about to reach a defining moment in the case. Unfortunately, with no power to see into the future, things were going to develop in a way no one could have imagined. Simultaneously, as he started the engine, he pushed the call button on the phone to call Angela; it would need her permission to get extra bodies to the Red Eagle as quickly as possible. Having now gotten used to her support, it was no surprise to hear her reply, 'Leave it with me; I will get some uniforms over as patrols.'

'Thank you; please let them know it is as support for now, and no sirens.'

With both of them knowing the importance of time, they ended the call immediately; this would allow Angela to call the duty officers and Ray to ring Tim and Sheila. The time of night meant the roads were quiet, which meant Ray could make the journey quickly, and only at junctions did he employ his lights and siren. Both Sheila and Tim had asked the same question, 'How much did they know about what was happening?'

Ray's answer was simple, 'At the moment not a lot.'

As they were all now used to the area, they arranged to meet on a side street away from the pub. Ray had called Dan and arranged for him to stay and watch developments from a safe distance and for Jill to meet them at the rendezvous point, when they would decide on a course of action. It was a pure coincidence, but helpful that they all arrived at the same time. It would have been an understatement to say they were all surprised to see moments later, Angela arrived as well.

'Once you have all gotten over your obvious shock, can we possibly discuss what we are going to do?'

Ray had had some time on his journey to think ahead, 'For now, I think, we need to observe. As such, we have no proof that this person who may be arriving is the Jack we need to speak to. We also need to be careful that if we rush in with no evidence, he can just clam up, and we will be no further forward, apart from letting them all know about us.'

'What did you have in mind, sir?'

'We approach with as much caution as possible; we can appear to be a group out together for the evening. Jill, where was Dan when you left him?'

'He was in the car at the rear of the pub, at the far end of the car park there is a footpath that the farm workers could use.'

'Okay, we will walk there from here; we can meet up with Dan and split into groups to observe from a distance.'

If any of them were unsure if this was the right thing to do, they didn't feel the need to voice concerns, and they all set off in the direction of the pub.

Chapter Twenty

At any other time of day, if people had looked out of their window, they may well have been calling the police to report a group of people walking down their quiet street acting suspiciously. Due to both the time of evening and the year, most curtains in the houses were closed. This particular road ended with a footpath to the pub; it had been the subject of several community meetings where people left their cars here to walk to the pub, sometimes blocking householders' drives. Jill sent a text to Dan letting him know what was happening as they reached the edge of the car park, where working in their favour it was poorly lit. Dan came around the side of an outbuilding to join them. Ray spoke first.

'Any sign of them meeting anyone?'

'Not yet, sir. The group has now gone back to the pub, and the woman who spoke to them about Jack is still in there, as far as I know.'

There was not much time left before the pub would be getting ready to close, so they needed to act quickly.

'How many doors are there in and out of the pub?'

'Only the main entrance and a side door that we used earlier, though it didn't look as if it got much use. There is also a fire door that opens out onto the car park.'

'That could help us then, Dan and Jill. While you wait in your car, if any of us spot who we think is Jack, you may need to follow him. For now, I just want to know where he goes. Hopefully, if we do this right, we'll be having a proper conversation with him before the end of the night.'

'What about the rest of us?'

'Tim and Sheila, you go into the pub and see what you can see; try not to arouse too much suspicion, though even if anyone sees you, they should not be surprised that officers are there during an investigation. Angela and I will enjoy the night air, but hopefully not for too long. For now, phones are on silent, and I know you youngsters are quicker than me, text messages only to start with.'

Everyone moved swiftly to get into position, and within minutes of Tim and Sheila going into the pub and the others moving away, a car pulled into the car park. It took a moment as the driver appeared to be looking for someone or something, then he pulled into a parking space facing out towards the road. It worked out well that Dan and Jill were in their car a couple of spaces back, so they were ideally suited to follow if needed. Ray and Angela saw the man get out of the car and both made the same judgement; he was certainly big enough to have done exactly what they thought he had. Once he walked away towards the pub, Ray took a picture of the car, including the number plate, for identification.

Inside the pub, Tim had been served by a barmaid he had not seen before; she also appeared too busy to take much notice of him, as customers were busy getting their last orders in. They had sat without knowing it at the same table as Dan and Jill had used; they just thought it was ideal to see the doors of the pub and hear conversations. Within moments of them sitting down, the door opened, and a man entered, and any problem of identification was gone as the woman sitting at the bar threw her arms around him, 'Jack, where have you been?'

Tim did the same as Jill and recognised the signs of a regular drug addict who was getting desperate for her next fix; if the person they were all there to observe had hoped to be discreet, it had not worked.

'Leave me alone, I might help you later.'

Hearing these words as Jack pushed the woman away to get to the bar confirmed a lot for Tim.

'Jerry about tonight?'

Tim could see the pieces falling into place, so far, he had not seen Jerry though he didn't expect him to be far away. As Jack finished speaking, the door at the rear of the bar opened as Jerry came through. Tim, not wanting to risk being spotted, leant in towards Sheila; if she was taken back by his actions, she didn't show it as Tim kept his head away from the bar and nuzzled her cheek. For her part, Sheila went along with things and took his head in her hands; if she had been surprised, he was gobsmacked as she planted a kiss full on his lips. As she pulled away, she whispered, 'It is okay now. They have moved out of sight.'

Tim was not sure what to say. Sheila helped him out; 'Don't take any notice, Tim; I can act as well.'

Tim just replied with a smile, as he then saw Maria and the 3 men walk towards the bar, obviously having heard everything since Jack had come in. They both heard Maria speak with a certain amount of venom in her voice.

'Hello Jack, we think you know a friend of ours, Sergei Romanov.'

Before anything else could be said, Jerry, who had sussed what was happening, pulled Jack behind the bar and towards the door. Andris went to speak, but Jerry never gave him the chance, 'Not now; no one wants any trouble, do they?'

If any of them had thoughts of doing anything, they were quickly dispelled by Jerry picking up a baseball bat from under the bar. Tim sent a very brief message to Ray, asking what to do next. Ray's phone bleeped with the incoming text, just as he was wondering what was going on inside. As he read the message, his concern was if there was another way out; they didn't know that he had not gotten this close to Jack to lose him again. Angela was watching as he read, and he found it very easy to talk to her as an equal, 'Please stay here, keeping Dan and Jill in sight. I need to take a look around the outside of this place.'

Angela had no time to reply, apart from a nod of her head, as Ray made his way to the side of the pub. For them, everything started to move very quickly, and inside the pub, the noise levels had risen as the group all shouted questions at a stunned barmaid who had no idea what was happening. Given her stature and being in the dark about things, she did very well in standing her ground; the others soon realised they were not getting past her. Tim and Sheila kept a close eye on events, though they didn't want to make themselves known just yet. Suddenly, it was as though Maria and the others had an idea, all making for the exit.

As the door closed behind them, Jerry guided Jack through the door at the rear of the bar towards the exit. Both had looks on their faces that suggested they had not had a pleasant catch-up. Tim and Sheila followed into the car park, and seeing a scene of chaos. Angela, not being sure what Ray was up to, had moved herself closer to the car where Dan and Jill sat. The 4 farm workers had come out of the pub and were currently standing to one side. It looked to Dan as if they were waiting for someone. Without knowledge of what had just happened, he didn't realise who they were waiting for. In what was only a matter of minutes of them exiting, the pub door opened again as Jerry pushed Jack out into the street; as this happened, Ray came running around the side of the pub, very nearly knocking them both over.

For a few moments, there was nothing but total chaos, as there were lots of raised voices, with nothing being shouted making any sense. As quickly as it had all kicked off, everyone seemed to gather themselves; fortunately, Dan had kept his wits about him and started the engine as Jack made a run towards his car, screeching out of the car park without realising he was being followed.

Tim and Sheila came out to join the rest, who stood around wondering what to do next; Ray and Angela were beside Jerry, who was standing speechless, though with a look on his face that suggested he knew the amount of trouble he was in. Ray looked across at the 4 farm workers who made to walk away, 'If you know what is good for you, you will stay exactly where you are. Tim, can you escort our friendly landlord back to the station as I think we need a serious chat.'

'No problem, sir. Do you want Sheila to come with us or do you need her here?'

Ray wanted to talk to the farm workers, though he knew at a push it could wait until morning. Dan and Jill were following Jack, he expected to hear from them soon. He decided that a night in the cells would possibly help Jerry be more forthcoming; by now, the remaining occupants of the pub had spilt outside to watch the action. It was part of the job that Ray had always excelled at the ability to make decisions in a split second to allow things to work.

'Right Tim, handcuff Jerry and get him booked in at the custody suite; we can speak in the morning.'

Any protest that Jerry thought about making was cut off immediately.

'Be quiet, sir. You will have plenty of opportunity to talk tomorrow. Angela, as long as you are happy with things here, you may as well go home. I think you may have a busy morning with the press to sort out. Sheila, you can go into the pub and tell any staff that they are to close up, just to show our community spirit, and just help them check that everything is locked up properly. I, meanwhile, am going to have a word with our extra investigators over there, then tell them someone will see them in the morning.'

Tim led a sullen and downcast-looking Jerry away to his car. Sheila entered the pub; Angela spoke to Ray, 'What are you planning for Dan and Jill to actually do?'

'I am hopeful that possibly Jack is heading home. Once we know where he lives, I will get night patrol cars to keep an eye out, then pick him up in the morning. We need to plan things out so that we get everyone we need to talk to in at the same time.'

Jerry seemed to have gotten over the initial shock of being caught up in everything, including as Tim locked the handcuffs in place. He maybe even had the thought that just being one-on-one, he could talk to Tim easier; some of his confidence resurfaced, 'I'm sure we can sort this out without me being detained any longer; I can help you out.'

Everyone who knew Tim knew this approach would never work. Tim had learned from Ray that there was a time to be friendly and a time to be totally in work mode; this was now, 'Sir, you will have plenty of time to talk, and as you say, help us out. It is not just now.'

The tone of his voice was enough for Jerry not to respond; they continued to the car in silence; despite Jerry making one more attempt to talk, which was quickly shut down, nothing else was said until Jerry was facing the duty sergeant. Angela had placed a call to the custody sergeant, so he was prepared for whatever Jerry came out with, 'I want to point out that I feel badly treated and don't understand why I'm here.'

'I can tell you, sir; you are mainly here for your own protection. The understanding is that you could be at some risk from some very nasty people. Our officers want to speak to you in the morning and feel it is safer for you to be here rather than at the pub on your own. I can make it official if you would like; we can charge you with allowing drug dealing to take place on your premises, though if you are helpful tomorrow, it could just result in a warning.'

Tim had noticed the colour leave Jerry's face at the thought of being charged; he had stood quietly while the sergeant told him what was happening. It was still possible that Jerry didn't accept he was involved or was just bravado. Slowly, he seemed to know what was best and accepted what the next few hours would be like. Tim also thought he may well realise that his licence was in trouble; he allowed himself to be led to a cell, even being brash enough to say as the door closed, 'Breakfast at 8 please.'

'Not heard that one before.'

Tim smiled and decided to make a visit to the CID before hopefully heading home. He was to be disappointed in the latter.

While Tim had had the pleasure of escorting Jerry to King's Lynn, back at the pub, the chaotic scenes had taken some while to get under control.

Fortunately, before joining them that evening, Angela had been able to divert some evening patrols to the pub, which meant that Ray had 4 uniformed officers to help out. After Sheila had returned inside to announce they were too close, the uniforms had come in helpfully to clear the spectators from the car park. Any police incident was always made more difficult by sightseers, especially when a lot of them had been drinking. At first, there had been some banter as Jerry had been led away; comments were shouted out, 'So, they have finally caught up with you for charging extortionate prices.'

Slowly, calm had been restored, so Ray was able to speak to the farm workers, 'Have you still not realised how dangerous some of these people are?'

Several huffs and puffs were taken by the men before Maria answered sheepishly, 'We do know inspector; we just want to know what happened.'

'I know that is the case. I can tell you we are close to finding out. Though it would help if we could concentrate on our job without worrying about what you might all be up to.'

'We are sorry.'

'That is fine; now do me and yourselves a favour; go home, and I will get someone to come and speak to you in the morning. Please let us get on with our work.'

The 4 of them walked away. Ray could tell by the grumbling and moaning from the men that there could be more problems involving them if they could not get the case wrapped up. Any hope he might have had that the night had calmed down disappeared in an instant as his phone rang. It was Jill.

'Jill, has he led you to his home?'

'Not yet, sir; though there have been developments.'

'Okay, what are they?'

'We followed him to a house, just not the one we expected. He drove to Darren Plant's place; he went inside, so we waited; he reappeared after 5 minutes; we are currently following him, though I have to say it is as if he is just out for a drive around the county roads.'

'For now, stick with him; see where he goes; it would appear things are linking together.'

Ray was fully aware that everything seemed to be falling into place, though he knew at the moment that there was no real proof in the investigation. He also knew now that he would not be making the journey home and rang Jenny to give her the news. The nature of the phone call was not unexpected for either of them. Jenny did have some news for him, which was another piece of the puzzle.

'I spoke to DS Maxwell after you left. He has a name that might be useful, though he does have some concerns over who it is.'

'That sounds good and bad in equal measures. Who is it?'

'Ian Jackson, the prison officer. Apparently, at his last prison, he left after an investigation regarding him allowing drugs to be brought in by certain prisoners' visitors. There was a suggestion he was taking money to turn a blind eye; nothing was proven, but he transferred soon after.'

'I knew there was more going on with him.'

'Is he already part of your investigation then?'

'I was not really sure, but this seems to point to the fact that he does know something.'

'I'll see if I can find out anymore in the morning.'

'Thanks; I think we will be seeing him ourselves in the morning. I will ring you when I can.'

As Ray hung up, his phone rang immediately.

'You are not going to believe this, sir. Jack Marshall went from seeing Darren to meeting in a supermarket car park.'

'Odd time for a meeting, mind, given what we now know, it is most probably quite usual.'

'Not only was it an odd time, but even weirder was the person he met. He was wearing a security uniform, and given the description we had, we both agreed it was Ian Jackson.'

'Are they still together?'

'They are, but from Jackson's body language, not for long. He is very jumpy.'

'I am not surprised. You stick with Marshall, and if from here, he goes home report in, and I will get a couple of night shift officers to take over.'

'Do you want to talk to either tonight?'

'No, as long as we know where they are, we can get things properly organised and pick them all up in the morning. I will ring Tim and let him know before the morning that we need as much personal information on Jackson. Surely, if he is going to cover his own back, he will either be at home or work tomorrow.'

Ray ended the call wondering if the evening had any more surprises in store.

While Ray was trying to make sense of everything that had happened over the course of a few hours. Jack Marshall had discovered exactly what Darren Plant was like; he was already aware to a point, but he had always thought that he could count on him to cover his back, as Jack had done for him on numerous occasions. Within minutes of knocking on the front door, he fully understood the situation. The door was opened by a guy who looked very similar to how Jack looked until a few days ago; the main difference was that the person staring hard at Jack was younger.

'I need to speak to Darren.'

'If you wait there, I will see if he is free.'

The guy never had the chance to move or say anything else before Jack pushed him to one side and walked in. Jack smiled to himself as he thought you might be younger, but you are also inexperienced. He had just had time to process this thought. As he felt an arm grab him and attempt to turn him around, anything the guy may have thought of doing ended as Jack brought his elbow back into the face of the other one. Jack was pleased as he heard the satisfying crack as the man's nose broke. He fell backwards in agony, knocking a vase to the ground in the process. It was the sound of the vase disintegrating that brought Darren out of his study.

'What the hell is going on?'

He paused for a second as he took in the scene, 'I would like to say I'm getting acquainted with your new staff, though I'm not sure he would agree.'

'Jack, what are you doing here?'

'I need to speak to you.'

'Well, I don't want to speak to you. I have spent the day fending questions from the police.'

'Yeah, so you said. What did they want?'

'I don't believe for a moment you are that stupid, Jack. They were asking about the discovery of 2 bodies along with other things.'

'So, what did you tell them?'

'Stop worrying; I never told them anything; my solicitor soon had me out of there.'

This was not the full story; Darren just wanted to pacify Jack and then get him out of the house quickly.

'I need you to leave Jack; I don't know if the police are watching me or not. I never mentioned your name, so we just need to avoid each other.'

Jack felt better knowing his name had not been given to the police; he also realised it was a mistake coming to the house.

'Sorry, Darren. I'll get out of your way.'

Jack saw no reason to tell Darren about events at the pub; he certainly didn't think about the possibility of having been followed from the car park. He had no intention of mentioning where he was going next. Darren was just relieved to get Jack out of the house. He pulled a wad of notes from his pocket, passing them to Jack.

'No contact at all. I will find you once things are sorted.'

Darren had no idea that everything would be sorted, but not in the way he hoped for. Jack took the money, even though he didn't need it. He couldn't shake the feeling that he would not see Jack again in this type of environment. As he left, he had a few words for the guy currently sitting and mopping blood off his face, 'You need a bit more practice before you try to mix with the big boys.'

The only reply was a grunt, as the guy realised he had also lost a couple of teeth. Jack smiled as he heard Darren say, 'Get yourself cleaned up, you idiot.'

Without realising the extent of the situation, Jack had now made 2 mistakes that would help the police build their case. Due to not being totally happy with how Darren had treated him, he made another error as he drove out of the gates onto the road. When slightly further back, he saw a car pulled into the edge of the road, he never gave it any thought as to what it was doing there. As Jack was already thinking about the next meeting, he never took any notice as the car pulled out behind him. The idea of the meeting with Ian had been to pass over some more goods and get cash as a reserve.

The money Darren had just given him meant this was no longer necessary, and he decided to still meet Ian and warn him of what was going on. As with a lot of supermarkets nowadays, they are open 24 hours a day, so even though it was quieter than the day, there were still several cars in the car park. This meant it was easy for Dan to park at the edge of the car park, but he still had a good view of things. As with the previous meeting, it didn't take long.

'You got the stuff?'

Ian had always been confident about everything he did, though he knew his life could change very quickly if he was not careful with the people he dealt with. Jack looked at him with some disdain. He accepted what he did to earn money but found it nasty that Ian was happy to abuse his position to earn more cash but also to have a hold over the people he supplied.

'There is some here, but this will be the last for now.'

Ian tried to be blasé about things, though he was soon to realise this was a mistake.

'You don't understand, do you? If I want more, then you deliver. There will be no problems as long as you realise if you slip up and try to blame me, I'll take you down as well.'

'No one is talking about slip-ups, we just need to be careful for a bit. Look, just stay calm, give things some time to settle down, and then we can start up again.'

For whatever reason this seemed to pacify Ian, Jack continued, 'I will contact you as soon as I can safely.'

Before anything else could be said, Jack turned and walked back to his car. As he drove away again, he gave no thought to the car behind him. Within minutes of leaving the car park, Dan pulled over at the side of the road, watching as Jack walked into a tidy-looking house on the edge of a newish housing estate. They sat waiting as the lights were switched on, then off as Jack moved from room to room. Jill phoned Ray, gave him the address, and he asked them to stay put, saying he would speak to D.I. Dave Hulme to get them some relief. He finished by adding, 'You have both done a good job. See you at the morning briefing!'

Ray was making his way back to the station, feeling good about the evening. He had already spoken to Tim, and they had an address for Ian Jackson, whom they would pick up in the morning. He had decided that Ian, along with Jack and Darren, would all get early morning calls; he would himself pick up Darren. Ray had always emphasised to his team that you did not celebrate until everything was down on paper, though he could not help himself but feel they were on top of things. He drove towards King's Lynn, totally unaware that things were going to go wrong in a major way over the next 24 hours.

Chapter Twenty-One

The first thing that went wrong was that no one in the pub car park that evening had thought that the farm workers needed to be escorted home. The following problem occurred due to D.I. Dave Hulme doing as even Ray would have done; he gave 2 relatively new CID officers a chance to prove themselves.

After Ray had spoken to Maria and the others, no one had taken much notice as they walked away. It went unnoticed that they only walked as far as the end of the street, stepping to one side out of sight of everyone, still in position at the front of the pub. As they had walked away, they spoke quietly, so again, didn't attract any attention; it was Andris who spoke first, 'We need to talk to that woman from the pub, who seemed to know Jack. If we are to find out what happened to Sergei, she has to be the starting point.'

'Surely we need to leave it to the police.'

'Come on, Maria, you can see how they work. We could still be in this position in months; they don't seem bothered.'

As they went to move, they saw the woman who had spoken to them earlier. For whatever reason, Alekesji stepped forward and took the lead, 'Excuse me, miss.'

If he had been thinking he could sweet talk better than the others, he was right, 'No one has called me miss in a long while.'

A smile broke across her face as she spoke, and then it was as if reality kicked in and she saw who had spoken to her along with the rest of the group.

'Here you lot were in the pub, causing aggro. I ain't got anything to say to you.'

'Look, all we want to know is how can we contact Jack?'

Maria stepped in, 'We just think he can help us.'

'I don't know how to get hold of him; I just heard a rumour he would be back tonight. If I see him, I can tell him you are looking for him.'

Alekesji thought quickly before speaking, 'If you can tell him, we are looking to buy some stuff. Please, you can tell him where to find us; most people know us around here.'

He nodded at the others to follow him as he walked away, already knowing that the woman would pass the message on. What none of them knew was the fact that they had just started things rolling, and that would bring a lot of trouble for one of them in particular.

Dan and Jill sat by the roadside for about 40 minutes after the phone call to Ray. Slowly, a car pulled in behind them; a man got out and came and sat in the rear of Dan's car.

'Evening you 2, we have been given babysitting duty for the rest of the night.'

'Okay with us; I'm ready to call it a day.'

'From the little information we have been given, you could be back bright and early to pick him up.'

The man got out as Jill spoke, 'Look after him; if he moves at all, follow him and let the boss know.'

It could have been the tone of her voice or just surprise at a young PC speaking to him in that way; they didn't know, but there was no reply as he quickly shut the back door of the car. Dan and Jill made for home; the other car quietly slipped into the space they vacated. The house was now in darkness, and both of the officers settled in for a long night, as well as they both thought a boring night. There was always a major problem with working night shifts. It was okay while you had something to do, the issue was always if you didn't.

Over the years, there had been many studies carried out into how the mind and body deal with things like this. The overriding findings always reached a similar conclusion; the hours between 2–4 AM were the time when a person's body felt the most need for sleep. Any officer would always say there was nothing more mind-numbing than being sat in a car with another person, though with nothing to do but watch. As the early hours arrived, the problems started to mount up for Ray. The officer in the passenger seat commented as he stretched as best he could, 'I spotted a petrol station back at the junction. How about I take a stroll and get some coffee?'

'Sounds like a good idea to me.'

It turned out to be the worst thing they could have done, within minutes of having no one to talk to or listen to. The driver had closed his eyes only for a moment was his thought pattern.

Jack still had no idea that he had been followed throughout the evening or that there was currently a police car sitting outside the house. He had been unable to get to sleep properly, so he had plenty of time to think through the events of the evening. Going over everything that had happened, he felt the main problem that needed dealing with was the friends of Sergei. He had never been able to understand why people allowed greed to colour their thinking.

If Sergei had stuck to just selling a small amount of what he got from Darren via Jack, then no one would have gotten hurt. Suddenly, though, it was as if Sergei decided he could take over the area, which Darren would never allow to happen. Jack decided, from what he had seen this evening in the pub and had already heard, that the weak point had to be Maria.

Jack made a decision to act immediately, or he could only see things unravel. He was under no illusion that if push came to shove, both Darren and Ian would not hesitate to give his name to the police along with information to protect themselves and get him behind bars; he also knew there were prison officers who were a lot nastier than Ian and his threats. Having made the decision, he acted quickly; he was at ease moving around his house in the dark. He didn't make a deliberate attempt to not make any noise; it was just a natural instinct. He left the house and quietly shut the front door along with the car door. He didn't roar away in the car, so when asked afterwards, no neighbours mentioned hearing anything untoward. On the subject of hearing things, the next thing the officer at the wheel of the car would hear was his colleague exclaiming, 'Where the hell has he gone?'

After the initial shock and jumping in fright, there was a mumbled reply, 'I don't know. I only shut my eyes for a moment.'

His colleague, who had discarded the 2 coffee cups in the gutter, was now on the radio to the station with the thought that this could be the end of his career in CID as he explained things to the duty sergeant.

'Can you get a message to D.I. Keane? The suspect has left the house. Do we try to follow?'

At first, this was a cryptic type of message; he was playing for time by not revealing all the details.

Ray was shaken awake by Dave Hulme he had; similar to his early days as a D.I. fallen asleep at his desk, though as usual he was alert immediately. After listening to Dave, he said, 'Yes, they need to stay with him. I want to speak to them.'

Dave left him with a mobile number while he went to convey the message. Dave returned a few minutes later to witness something that rarely happened. This was Ray losing his temper; he heard a lot of swearing, and then just before the mobile was thrown onto the desk, Ray shouted, 'Drive round, see if you can stay alert enough to possibly spot his car, I will expect you to return with good news.'

Dave really didn't know what to say; he was spared any awkwardness by Ray, '1 went for coffee, while the other fell asleep. God knows where Jack Marshall is now.'

'Ray I am sorry; I thought they were ready to step up.'

Ray had a minute to gather himself, 'It is not your fault. Dave, if I am honest, it is not even their fault. The operation was set in motion quickly; I should have had more bodies covering the area.'

Dave looked at him.

'That is as, maybe they don't need to know that do they. Hopefully, it will show them what is expected. I will have a word with them when they get back.'

Ray showed his grasp of man-management skills with his answer, 'Just go easy; we all make mistakes at times in our careers.'

'Okay, duly noted. What is your next idea?'

'I think I need to wake the team up and get them all in to start making some early morning visits. We need to talk to the major players in all this. If it is as we expect, I would like to get some answers soon.'

Ray's mind raced with thoughts as he started the calls to the team. His first priority would be to get things organised for Darren Plant and Ian Jackson to be picked up and brought in for questioning, along with someone talking to Jerry. His next problem was where was Jack Marshall. Dave had told him that radio messages had gone out to all patrols to keep an eye out for his car. Through the systems they had in place, the message had been relayed to local authorities who controlled the traffic cameras; it wasn't always easy for them to spot something, particularly as they could be looking at a camera featuring a large amount of traffic. The hope, at present, was that the time meant the roads would still be quiet, so they might be lucky. There were no complaints from anyone as Ray disturbed sleep patterns, even when he called Angela to bring her up to date.

'I will come in as well; it sounds as though you can use as much help as is available.'

Ray was just about to tell her this would not be necessary; he never got a chance, as she continued, 'You must have a lot to organise.'

She ended the call before he could say anything. By now, some of the team were starting to filter in. Ray had made sure the coffee machine was on and ready to go. As they entered, they were all greeted with the same message, 'Help yourselves to coffee, you are going to need it.'

Once they were all sitting in the available seats, there was the unusual situation of having 2 shifts of officers in the office together; it was crowded. The fact that Ray had a very well-organised team was mirrored by the team Dave Hulme worked with; all of the night shifts knew that Ray's team was in the middle of an active case. They allowed these officers to congregate at the front while they filled in the gaps at the back. As Ray went to speak, he looked up and saw Angela by the door. He was pleased to note that there was not the feeling of dread he used to get when he saw Adam standing in the same position.

'Okay, settle down, everyone. Apologises for the early calls; things have moved on at a rapid rate. You all know the plan for later this morning; this needs bringing forward. Jack Marshall has moved; he gave the 2 officers the slip. We currently do not know his whereabouts.'

This brought the expected groans out of the room, which Ray moved quickly to stop.

'That will do. There are patrol cars out looking for him. We need to concentrate on continuing as planned, just a bit sooner than we thought. Tim, did you get an address for Ian Jackson?'

'Yes, sir, he lives close to the prison where he works.'

'Okay, you and Sheila make your way there to bring him in. Jill, you and I will go and get Darren Plant out of bed. Dan, can you proceed to interview Jerry? It seems obvious he knows more about what is going on than he has already told us.'

Ray looked around the room, 'Dave, can you sit in with Dan just so we can keep things correct? Dan, if you are not sure on something, then the D.I. will be there.'

Ray had faith in Dan, though he noticed the relieved look when he knew Dave would be alongside him. Angela coughed.

'Yes, superintendent. Do you have anything to add?'

'Thank you, Inspector. I am not here to tell anyone how to do their job; please be careful; none of us know how these people will react. We already have 2 bodies we do not want anymore. D.I. Hulme, if it is okay with you, then your officers can assist others visiting our suspects; I can stay here to coordinate things.'

Ray found it helpful that he knew while he was out at Darren's house that if anything happened or was radioed in, then Angela was there as another capable officer to deal with things. It would allow him to fully concentrate on what he was expecting to be a heated discussion with Darren. Everyone moved extremely quickly; Ray actually took a minute to take a picture of the office. He was immensely proud of how his team, along with the support of the night shift officers, gelled together. Working in permanent nights, when a lot of the time it was quieter, allowed working friendships to form. With very little direction from Dave Hulme, his officers paired up and joined the members of Ray's, then made their way out. Within a few moments, the office was empty except for Dan, Angela, and Dave Hulme. Angela spoke first, 'If you 2 want to go and give Jerry his alarm call, then get him into an interview room. I suppose before we hear anything about abusing his human rights, you better arrange a cup of tea for him.'

Dave replied with a smile, 'Not like the old days, when he might have gotten a glass of water and a slap.'

Any tension this comment could have caused was eased by Angela adding, with a laugh, 'Hopefully, just the tea will make him more cooperative.'

'Come on, Dan, your lead.'

The night spent in the cell didn't appear to have bothered Jerry, as when the door was opened by the custody sergeant, he was sleeping soundly and didn't seem to have been disturbed by the locks clanging. Dave had deliberately stayed by the desk while Dan had gone to the cell.

'Good morning, Jerry; we need to have a serious chat with you.'

All the bravado they had encountered previously had returned, and Jerry looked at Dan.

'Do I at least get breakfast and a wash first?'

Dan had already learned a lot from being around the others; he knew the key was to assert his authority while being as polite as possible.

'The best I can offer is a cup of tea, and we could even get you a biscuit. Before we start talking to you, you have the right to a solicitor being present; if you do not have a solicitor, we can arrange for a duty one to sit in with you.'

'I can see no reason why I would need a brief, so just get on so we can get this over with.'

The custody sergeant stepped in due to the fact that the area was his domain.

'On your feet, Mr Reed, my colleagues need some answers, and they would like to get on. As much as I have enjoyed your company, I have plenty of people to fill your room.'

Jerry got up from his bunk, and Dan noticed a look pass his eyes that showed he realised this may not be as straightforward as he had thought. They made their way to an interview room without saying a word. Dave Hulme joined them as the door opened, and if Dan was feeling any pressure from leading his first interview, he did not show it as he went through the formalities. Once they were all seated, he switched on the recording machines and then waited, himself, like a lot of people had wondered why there was a loud bleep at the start of the tape, as he soon found out it was to allow everyone involved to know the tape was running and recording. Dan started the introductions.

'This is a taped interview with Mr Jerry Reed. The people present are PC Dan Carol, D.I. Dave Hulme, and Mr Jerry Reed. For the benefit of the tape, Mr Reed was offered a solicitor, which he declined.'

Jerry leant back in his chair with a bored look on his face.

'Can we just get on with it? I have a pub to run.'

His expression and demeanour changed in a flash as Dan continued, 'Mr Reed, I need to inform you that, having spoken to my senior officer, you are being charged with allowing the use of your premises for the sale of illegal substances. As to how we proceed, will depend on your answers to our questions.'

For a brief moment, Jerry looked like a balloon someone had stuck a pin in, as he visibly seemed to deflate in the chair in front of them. Dan was not sure how things were going to go as quickly the bravado returned. Jerry pulled himself upright in the chair before speaking.

'I don't know where you are getting this bullshit from; I can't be held responsible for everything my customers get up to.'

Dan remained calm, 'I can assure you, sir, that yes, you can. As a licensee, you have a responsibility to not allow criminal activity on the premises.'

Still, Jerry seemed sure he could talk his way out of things.

'If this has happened, then if you have proof, I can be allowed to help in clearing up this mess. I don't want those sorts of people in my pub.'

Dave had been impressed so far with how Dan handled the interview, and he was even more so as Dan carried on with the questions, 'I do think, sir. It would be best all round if you stopped beating around the bush. If we just take a look at the facts during our investigation into the deaths of 2 people...'

He was stopped from saying more by Jerry coughing and spluttering, as well as being short of breath, possibly caused by a panic attack. Dan sat quietly, giving Jerry time to calm down and compose himself.

'Now just hang on a minute; I have had nothing to do with anyone being killed.'

'We do not think you are involved with the deaths of these people. Though last night in your pub you were observed by officers that as soon as a known drug dealer entered, you took him out of the bar area to what we presume are your living quarters; then shortly afterwards you accompanied said person out of the pub. It certainly looked as though you knew each other.'

'I have friends who visit me; sometimes we will meet in my accommodation rather than the pub.'

'Stop wasting everyone's time, please. The person you claim to be a friend is wanted in connection with our investigation. He was heard being addressed as Jack by one of your customers, though there is a good chance it was also one of his customers. So shall we start again? Exactly what goes on in your pub? Before you answer, I suggest you give it some thought, as I am sure you know all that happens.'

'Look, I will tell you all I know, though first I want to say in my defence that the person you saw me with last night is not someone I would describe as a friend, more that he is the reason I am sitting here now.'

'I can tell you; we have time to listen; so, start from the beginning and let us judge what you are involved in.'

Suddenly, it was as if a switch had been pushed, and Jerry finally seemed to realise the severity of the position he was in.

'I am willing to cooperate, though I do think it would be best if I had a solicitor present.'

Both Dan and Dave knew this would hold up proceedings, and at the same time, knowing if Jerry was to be of help, having a solicitor would leave no room for any complaints afterwards.

'That is entirely your right, Mr Reed; do you have a solicitor in mind, or do you require a duty solicitor?'

Dan ended things for the benefit of the tape, then escorted Jerry back to the custody sergeant. He would arrange to contact a solicitor and let them know once they arrived. They both made their way back to CID Dan knew there was background work he could do until the others returned.

While Dan was carrying out the interview, the others, along with the support teams of the night shift, made their way to the addresses of Ian and Darren. Along the way, Ray had kept his ears open to the radio conversations taking place as to whether Jack had been located. The only sighting so far to raise hope was from 2 officers who had been attending a disturbance at a house when they saw a car drive past at speed. 1 of the officers had recognised the number plate as the car sped away, though by the time they got back into their car, the other vehicle had disappeared. All they were able to report was that it was heading towards Sutton Bridge. Ray had quickly arranged for them to keep searching and for another car from King's Lynn to head towards Sutton Bridge.

Tim and Sheila had arrived at the house of Ian Jackson to find him getting ready for work.

'Mr Jackson, I'm sure you remember me, DS Sheila Carr. This is my colleague, DS Tim Jarvis.'

'You are about early; I only have a few minutes, then I need to get to work.'

Sheila was determined not to allow Ian time to think he had the better of her, 'We will have someone contact your work; you won't be going in today. Depending on the next few hours, you may not be returning at all.'

She took a breath and decided to give him a jolt, 'In actual fact, I would go as far as to say, the next time you are inside a prison, there is a good chance it will be as an inmate.'

The response was the usual one, when someone realises they have been caught doing something wrong. Especially if that person was the type of criminal who never saw themselves as doing wrong. Despite his attitude, Ian fell into this category; he had been regarded as a good soldier and, by his bosses, an excellent prison officer; it was the way he went about things that ultimately let him down. He stood in the doorway, and it looked as though all his energy had drained away, though due to his nature, he realised it would all now be about protecting himself. Like all officers in authority, he knew what his life would be like in prison, so he would do whatever he could to make the next few years as comfortable as possible.

'When you are ready, sir, we can get started back at the police station.'

All the bravado had deserted Ian, and it was a different sort of person that accompanied them to the car compared to the last time Sheila had seen him.

While Ian's pickup had gone relatively smoothly along with the start of the interview, with Jerry passing off as expected, Ray and Jill were to be met with the most resistance from Darren. This was no surprise to Ray and was the reason for him doing this part himself. They knocked on the front door, and despite the early hours, it was promptly opened by a man Ray would describe as a clone of Jack Marshall. The t-shirt and jeans being worn did nothing to hide the fact that apart from spending hours in the gym, there was also help from, at a guess, several illegal substances.

'Good morning; we would like to speak to Darren Plant.'

The guy standing in the doorway looked slowly across the 4 faces stood in front of him.

'You do realise the time I take it?'

'I am D.I. Ray Keane, this is DC Jill Addy; stop wasting my time and get Darren.'

The 4 officers made enter. 'You 2 can wait inside; the goons can stay here.'

Ray thought this was rich coming from this guy, though it also solved another issue that the 2 officers could keep an eye out for in case Darren thought of leaving via another exit. Ray walked in.

'Just get Darren now.'

As he spoke, a blearily eyed Darren appeared at the top of the stairs.

'What the hell is all the noise about?'

'Mr Plant, I did say I would need to speak to you again. If you can accompany us to the station.'

The sleepy look was quickly replaced by one of thunder, 'I don't know what you are playing at, inspector. This is a big mistake. I would like to speak to my solicitor.'

'We can arrange all that back at the station for you. Just to keep things official, Mr Darren Plant, I am arresting you on suspicion of arranging the murders of Sergei Romanov and Nick Crowe. You do not have to say anything, but anything you do say will be written down and may be used as evidence in a court of law. Do you understand?'

'This has got to be one of the biggest mistakes you are ever liable to make, inspector.'

'You are entitled to your opinion, Mr Plant; now get dressed and we can be on our way.'

As Ray finished, the guy who had opened the door went to step in front of him.

'Do not even think about it. Currently, I have no reason to arrest you, though unless you go and sit down like a good boy, I am sure I could find a reason.'

As the guy realised the situation and went and sat in a chair at the side of the hallway, Darren came stomping down the stairs. Ray smiled as he could imagine this as the behaviour of a petulant teenager. Jill stepped towards the door as Ray said, 'After you, sir.'

As Darren went out, he said to the guy in the chair, 'I won't be long; call Jeremy. Tell him to get his arse over to the police station; make sure he calls whoever he needs to, to get me back here.'

Ray had no intention of entering into any conversation until in an interview room, so keeping his voice polite, he said, 'Mr Plant, if you can just move, the 2 officers outside will escort you to the station.'

If Darren was surprised that Ray was not driving him, he hid it well. As he started out towards the waiting car, all his cheek and bravado were back as he waited for the door to open. Ray thought he noticed slightly more force than was necessary used by the officer as he pushed down on Darren's head, saying, 'Mind your head there, sir.'

Nothing was said, so Ray let it pass.

'Come on, Jill; we have a lot of work to get through this morning.'

On the way back, Ray checked in with control to see if there had been any sightings of Jack. He was not particularly happy to hear the reply.

'Nothing yet, sir.'

'Tell everyone on the road to start another search of the area, he has got to be somewhere.'

'The message had already been sent out to let you know Ian Jackson is on his way here. Jerry Reed has asked for a solicitor; we are waiting for the one on duty to arrive.'

'Okay, thanks for that. You can add Darren Plant to your list; he is on his way. Expect Jeremy Taylor, his solicitor, to stomp through the door soon as well.'

As Ray arrived at the reception area, it was a hive of activity. Darren was at the forefront, shouting all the odds and wanting to know, among other things, where his solicitor was. The duty solicitor was there, waiting for the chance to get a word in that he wanted to talk to the person in charge. The only person who didn't appear to be shouting the odds was Ian, who was flanked by Sheila and Tim. Ray walked over as Tim looked up.

'Morning again, sir. Mr Jackson has declined a solicitor, so we can get on now and interview him.'

'Good, I will leave you to get on with that.'

The feeling was that by not asking for legal representation, Ian could be the weakest link that would tie things together. Ray did not think for a moment that he was involved in either murder; he was hopeful the link with Jack would be of use. He could not help but think that Ian looked different from the last time he had seen him; the attitude was gone. Ray thought this had to be down to him not being in a position of authority. Suddenly, they all looked round at a loud banging on the door. Once the duty sergeant was happy with who it was, the click of the lock releasing was followed by the door being pushed open with force.

'Jeremy about bloody time.'

'Do not say another word, Darren. Who is in charge of this debacle?'

This was a pointless question, as he already knew the answer. Ray stepped forward, knowing the importance of the next few hours.

Chapter Twenty-Two

Jack left his house without knowing he had given the police the slip. He had sat indoors but just couldn't settle his thoughts were causing him to become agitated. They were mingling together. He recognised the signs that, if he didn't put all the thoughts into some order, a meltdown was a possibility. He calmed himself down with some gentle breathing and made the decision that the people he needed to deal with most were the farm workers. Working through the things he had heard fleetingly, they had been asking lots of questions about him and his involvement with Sergei.

It had stood him in good stead, that if he kept calm over the years, he had cleared up several problems, which avoided other issues from causing bigger problems. The first thing he had learned was to look for the weakest link, which could be used to apply pressure. As far as he was concerned, the weakest link had to be Maria. The only logic was good old-fashioned male chauvinism—that she was female, so she would give him more bargaining power. His decision was made with no idea of what he would encounter; already, he felt better. His main thought was to take her hostage, then deal with any fallout, as once all the others got involved, he had no inclination as to how big a problem it could be.

Jack knew enough from the information that Darren had gathered about Sergei, so he knew they all lived in accommodation on the farm, in 2 separate caravans. What was a total guess turned out to be correct, and they were still there. Still with no idea that all police patrols had instructions to look out for him, he drove comfortably through the quiet nighttime streets, and soon he pulled up at the edge of the farm. His obvious plan was to get into the area he needed as quickly and quietly as he could; he was aware enough to avoid the main entrance as he expected security lights to be in use.

For now, luck was on his side, in that as he skirted the edge of the fields, he spotted the 2 caravans used by the people he wanted to see. In fact, there was only 1 person he wanted, and he was hopeful that the early hour meant that no one else would be involved. The next decision involved some guesswork as to which of the caravans he needed to be outside of. The guesswork was aided by the fact he was looking for a female; usually the accommodation was only for a few months, but Maria still took more pride than the men. The outside of her van was neat and tidy, even with a couple of pots with flowers in them.

Jack moved swiftly into action, as he knew that once inside the van, his window of opportunity would be short. Anyone who has ever had a holiday in a caravan knows that the doors and windows are flimsy; once he had made his decision, it was relatively easy with a strong screwdriver for him to jemmy the door open. Inside was a basic layout, with the kitchen in front of him and the lounge area to his left; he ignored these and went right to what was the bedroom. Maria had heard something, but not enough noise to completely wake her. Jack moved to the head of the bed and had a hand across her mouth before she had any idea of what was happening.

The reaction of them both was that of 2 people who knew what they needed to do. Maria was instantly back at home, hearing stories of women being dragged from their beds and raped and beaten during the many atrocities in her country. Jack was just in the mode of survival; it all came down to speed and preparation. Even though things happened quickly that evening, he was still methodical in his actions and had brought things with him to restrain his target. The speed came from them both; despite being half asleep, Maria had automatically gone to bite the hand across her mouth. Jack expected something like this and pulled his hand away. In the moment Maria thought about screaming, he replaced his hand with a scarf he had and tied it expertly across her mouth.

In one quick movement, he gagged her and lifted her body over his shoulder to make his way outside. One thing he hadn't thought of was the lack of space in a caravan. As he turned to leave the bedroom, Maria's legs caught against the side of the van, causing Jack to lose his balance.

If it wasn't such a serious problem, it would have been funny for anyone to see 2 people grappling in the small space. As Jack fought to regain his balance, Maria saw her chance and pushed against the window with her feet. If Jack had known how luck had been on his side so far, he would have appreciated the fact that the bedroom window faced away from the other caravan. He regained control of himself first, then Maria, and got a better hold of her again. He made his way out slower to allow him to manoeuvre easier. Once outside, he spent very little time looking around as he quickly walked to the car, opening the rear door and throwing her roughly across the rear seats. He grinned as he watched her scramble across the door, only to realise as she tried to open it that there must have been a child lock in place, as nothing happened. He quickly reached in, then tied her hands behind her back.

Jack felt he was now fully in control of the matter; with a quick check around that no one had seen events, he got in and drove away. Maria was making as much noise as possible with the scarf around her mouth. It was the first time since he had entered the caravan that Jack spoke.

'You will soon realise you are just wasting time and energy. There is nobody around to hear anything; all you will achieve is to irritate me.'

For reasons Maria couldn't explain, these few words sounded very chilling, so she went silent. Jack drove away from the area, suddenly realising that he didn't really have a plan in mind. He knew that he wanted to send a message to the others to stop asking questions, hoping that by absconding with Maria, it would make them stop and think. His next thought was what to do with her. The brief conversations he had had with Darren and Ian suggested the police were piecing things together. The short conversation with Jerry had sown seeds of doubt in his mind.

Jerry had explained the visits from the police at the pub recently. Jerry had asked a particular question that made him realise the enormity of the situation. This question had been that despite knowing what Jack got up to in the pub, had he really been involved in the murder of Sergei and Nick? Jack had always felt protected by Darren, but Jerry talking as he did brought home to him exactly what was happening; he was on his own. Jack drove around with no destination in mind;

suddenly he found himself approaching the swing bridge at Sutton Bridge. It felt as though the decision was made for him; there was one place he could hide out for a short time.

Also, at this time of year, there would be very few visitors. As he crossed the bridge, he turned left. Now he was on familiar ground as this road led to the farm; he had left Sergei's body at. while alongside was the river he had planned to dump Nick into until he was disturbed. Having now made a plan, he felt a new energy and followed the road as though he was driving out to sea. At the end of the road was an old, disused lighthouse. Jack had always known it was there, though he had no idea who owned it, just that if he could get in, then keeping Maria there would hopefully help him out.

The lighthouse was actually owned by a gentleman who lived away; he had bought it at auction with the idea of turning it into a posh holiday accommodation. The process was a lot slower than he had envisaged, as well as more costly. The lighthouse, along with many others around the coastline, had been taken out of service as more satellite systems were used by shipping companies. This meant that apart from an occasional visit from a caretaker, nobody had a reason to be in the area. There was some space for parking nearby, and ramblers and dog walkers did use the area, though not as often at this time of year.

Jack pulled up at the rear of the building, which would mean his car was not easily visible. He locked the car, leaving Maria in the rear as he walked to the door; it was, as expected, locked with a padlock in place. Neither of these was a problem for Jack to force his way in. He returned to the car, dragging Maria out and carried her into the room at the base of the lighthouse. Having not had a proper plan in place, he initially thought of tying Maria up in the room before deciding on his next move.

Looking around, it didn't take long to realise that if he was going to stay here for a few days, it would be better to be higher up. The stairs in the lighthouse presented a similar problem to the caravan, this being that there wasn't a lot of room. This time, he felt better prepared and roughly pulled Maria up, throwing her easily over his shoulder. She struggled at first, then it was as though the fight left her as she took note of the situation. The climb up was slow as Jack moved cautiously, but once at the top, he knew it had been the right thing to do. He was able to see all around and at a good distance of anyone approaching. He knew there was no one around to hear, so he removed the scarf that had been gagging Maria; she took in several deep breaths then looked at him.

'What do you want with me?'

'I would think even you could answer that question.'

'I don't see why you needed to kidnap me.'

'I didn't bring you here to chat. Let's just say at the minute you are my insurance.'

If Maria had not already realised the seriousness of the situation, Jack's next comment confirmed things.

'Obviously, as you have been asking about me, you already know my capabilities. It is best if you just sit quietly.'

Jack had sat her in a chair; using things he found lying around, he tied her feet to the chair, leaving her wrists bound as they were. He left her there and went down to the next level as he tried to think about what to do next.

While Jack was sitting contemplating his next move, he was still not aware of the large-scale investigation revolving around looking for him. Ray and his team were beginning their next stage of things. The duty solicitor was ready, so Dan and Dave could continue questioning Jerry. Ian Jackson had decided that he didn't want legal representation; it would soon become clear as he talked to Tim and Sheila that he was willing to give over details in order to make things easier for himself. Their main problem was going to be getting enough information together to build the case against Darren, as Ray was convinced, he was behind everything. Darren was currently stomping around the custody suite, yelling at anyone who would listen.

'Will someone have the bloody decency to tell me what is going on?'

Ray stepped forward, so there was no confusion as to who was going to interview him.

'Mr Plant, please calm down. I think you know what is going on, so if you can give the sergeant your details, we can proceed.'

Darren's solicitor stepped in as well, 'Darren, let's just deal with this, then we can move on.'

Suddenly, a feeling of calm settled over the custody suite as various people and police officers made their way to interview rooms. It helped Ray that Angela had happily agreed to any overtime, which meant the night shift officers were happy to stay on. With Angela overseeing things, they would carry on collating evidence while the interviews took place. The interviews followed a pattern in which Jerry and Ian were willing to give over information; both asked the same question.

'What is in it for me to talk to you a lot?'

Unsurprisingly, they both received answers in a similar vein, this was that no deal would be forthcoming, though any help they gave would be noted. Jerry was accompanied by a duty solicitor, who, without any knowledge of the background of the case, could only give basic legal advice. He listened intently as his client told Dan and Dave that the pub had done well.

'Though having you around recently had caused takings to drop.'

'We are not taking the blame for that.'

It didn't take me long to suss out why Jack became a regular, always followed around by Nick. 'I know it was wrong, but as customer numbers increased, I turned a blind eye. Particularly when Jack started to pass envelopes of cash over to me, telling me it was a token of appreciation.'

This information gave them enough details to charge Jack with supplying, though it still did not tie into the murders. The conversation in the next room was with Ian and followed similar lines, except for Ian saying that, 'I had no idea what the packages contained. A guy approached me outside of work, saying he knew I was not averse to a backhander. He made it sound threatening by adding that, if necessary, he would use force against me.'

Ian soon realised he was getting no sympathy from Sheila or Tim, so he just talked them through how he delivered the parcels.

Ray was the only one who was not getting anything useful from his interviewee. Darren was still full of bravado, having taken his stomping around the custody suite to shout at everyone in the interview room. The problem was that with just 4 of them in the room, there was less notice taken of him. Ray knew he had to take charge, and he very quickly left no one in doubt as to why they were there.

'Mr Darren Plant, I am charging you with the supply of illegal substances and the arranging for the murder of Sergei Romanov and Nick Crowe; you do not have to say anything, but anything you do say will be written down and used as evidence against you.'

By now, Darren was at the point of screaming at his solicitor along with Ray and Jill; Ray ignored this and continued, 'Do you understand, Mr Plant?'

Jeremy, Darren's solicitor, had a look on his face as if to say he couldn't quite believe things. He gathered himself, 'Darren, sit down. Detective Inspector, I feel that with the seriousness of your allegations, I need a few moments alone with my client.'

Ray was in no mood to let things settle, though he knew he had to agree to this request.

'Take as long as you need. I can assure you, Mr Plant is not going anywhere for quite some time.'

Ray and Jill left the room, with shouting still in their ears as Darren started screaming again, 'Jeremy, I'm not sure what I bloody pay you for, but you better start earning it.'

When Ray and Jill came out, they were met by Dan along with Dave exiting the room where Jerry was sitting. Dan was grinning from ear to ear, 'You will want to hear this, sir.'

'Dan, you look like a dog who has been given an extra biscuit. What is it?'

Showing how well he had settled into his role in CID, Dan continued smiling as he spoke, 'Jerry has just told us that Jack Marshall gave him cash to allow him to keep working in the pub, obviously supplying.'

Ray, who had been expecting better news, was discouraged, as this just confirmed their thinking. Before he had a chance to say anything, Dan carried on.

'I know that is what we had already worked out was going on. He told Jerry that any problems with police or rival gangs, then Darren Plant would sort them out.'

This could be the breakthrough they were waiting for. Ray allowed a smile to build as he took in the news.

'Well done; let us see what Mr Plant has to say now.'

Before Ray could turn to go back in, Angela came running along the corridor, 'Good, you are out here; save me interrupting the interview. We just had a call upstairs. Maria Shon, the farm worker, is missing.'

It was a simple equation to put together, that they had lost sight of Jack, and now Maria was missing. It was not the news Ray wanted to hear; he reacted swiftly, 'Okay, we get these 3 back into cells. Then everyone's upstairs for a briefing.'

Everything swung into action quickly and efficiently, despite Darren shouting the odds as expected. The custody sergeant, along with 2 other officers, took over while the team made their way to CID. Tim moved directly to his computer, and within minutes of being at his keyboard, had various scenes from traffic cameras on his screen. Ray could see what he was doing, knowing he would also be listening as he carried on, 'Listen up, everyone; developments are that Maria Shon has been reported missing by her friends. We have very few details at present. As soon as I finish here, I will head over there to speak to them. The rest of you I want out and about in the area, it could be nothing; though having lost sight of Jack Marshall, we have to treat it as being connected.'

One of the night shifts spoke up, 'Anything of use from the other suspects, sir?'

'Plenty to be going on with. Ian Jackson is looking to save his own skin, though he can give us details about Jack, as is Jerry, who has also tied Darren Plant into things. They are all staying with us longer as visitors; we now need to concentrate.'

The room was a crescendo of noise as teams were formed to go out and search Ray could tell feelings were running high, so he knew it all had to be controlled, 'Remember, there are several things at play here; we need to find Maria and arrest Jack Marshall, who I am sure can give us the final pieces to nail Darren. Ultimately, be cautious; it is safe to say Jack will stop at nothing to avoid speaking to us.'

Ray looked around the room and could see why the whole CID team worked so well and everyone was ready to go. His next comment disappointed one member of the team.

'Tim, I need you to stay here for now as soon as traffic cameras give you any sightings of the car you let us know. Jill, if you start to transcript the interviews so far, then if needed, you can pair up with Tim.'

Any feelings of disappointment they felt soon passed as Angela spoke, 'I will stay here, though, if I am honest, I would rather be out with you lot. There is important stuff to do here.'

Tim acknowledged everyone as they left the room with a slight nod of his head. Since he had sat down, his eyes had been glued to his computer screen; he had even borrowed the screen from the next desk, so he had more than 1 traffic camera image to watch. Jill made her way downstairs to retrieve the recordings of the interviews, unable to stop feeling envious as she heard cars pulling away at speed from the car park; the windows were full of colour as lights reflected through them. When she got back, Angela had made coffee for the 3 of them, also giving them words of encouragement.

'It might feel boring, but it is all a necessary part of the job. Make a start; you never know what you might hear from the different interviews or what Tim might spot.'

Jill had only been typing for a few minutes when Tim broke the silence.

'Got you, you bastard. Come on, Jill.'

If Angela was put out, she covered it well.

'Ma'am, can you call the inspector? Jack Marshall's car was picked up leaving the A17 after the swing bridge. He turned towards the area where we found both bodies; there is no sight of him coming back to the main road; he must still be in the area.'

There was no time to reply, as Tim and Jill left the room at a run.

Chapter Twenty-Three

The radios in the cars made a non-stop noise as messages were relayed between everybody. Ray had just been about to pull into the farmyard, where the workers lived. He knew time was of the essence; the men were gathered outside of one of the caravans, and Ray could tell from the various expressions that they could cause some problems. He moved towards them and took command before any of them had a chance to speak.

'What can you tell us about events in the last few hours?'

Andris tried his best to intimidate them both, 'If you had done your job properly, none of this would have happened.'

Ray was not willing to get into a slanging match about looking to blame people, so he refrained from mentioning them having interfered in the case.

'All I want to deal with now is finding your friend before it is too late. Did any of you hear anything last night?'

Ray could see they were struggling to keep emotions in check; Andris appeared to have elected himself as spokesperson, 'We all had a drink in the pub, then some more when we got back here. We were all angry with things that had happened. Maria went straight to her van; the first we knew something was wrong was as we came out this morning and saw the door swinging open.'

'Sheila, can you do a once-over through the van and look for any clue as to what may have happened?'

Sheila made her way to the van, pulling on a pair of latex gloves; it had to be treated as a crime scene. Ray felt he knew the answer he would receive, though he still felt compelled to ask, 'Is it likely she has gone off somewhere on her own, forgetting to lock the door?'

'I don't want to be a rude inspector; that is a stupid question. The door has been forced; also, Maria is the least likely of us all to go off alone.'

Before Ray could speak again, 'You better come and look at this, sir.'

Ray left the men standing together and walked across, repeating Sheila's movement from a few moments ago, pulling on a pair of latex gloves. Inside the van, initially, he was not sure as to what he was looking at; the kitchen and living area were all neat and tidy.

'Through here, Ray.'

Sheila had stood to one side of the bedroom door; the covers on the bed were tangled together and hanging off the end of the bed. The window was swinging open from where Maria had kicked out; there was also damage to the wall beside the door; unknown to them, this was from Jack struggling to keep his balance with Maria over his shoulder.

'It looks as though she put up a fight.'

'It does, sir, but where is she?'

'Let's tell these 3 to stay put, then we can start searching for her.'

Tim had decided the best place to start was with some local knowledge, so he made the journey in record time and soon pulled up in the yard of Chris Small's farm. Chris was currently standing on top of the combined harvester while 2 others were busy around the wheels. They all stopped their work and looked at the 2 people running towards them.

'DS Tim Jarvis and DC Jill Addy. Quick question, if needed in this area, where would be a good place to hide?'

'You mean apart from all the farm outbuildings there are around?'

Tim had to admit he hadn't given it a lot of thought on the drive-over; now all he could think of was the expression needle in a haystack, which was very appropriate.

'Sorry, I realise now that this seems like a stupid question. Can you think of anywhere else someone who is desperate might try?'

The help Tim had hoped for came from a voice underneath the combine, 'This time of year, now it is quieter; try the old lighthouse.'

They were both moving back towards the car as he shouted over his shoulder, 'Thank you.'

They were on their way out of the yard in moments, and Jill was on the radio, sending a message.

'Everybody heads for the old lighthouse at the end of East Bank Road; it is on the right at the junction, King's Lynn side of Sutton Bridge. Approach with caution and avoid using sirens.'

Anyone living in the area would wonder at ongoing events as a cacophony of noise from sirens fell silent. Tim and Jill were nearest, so they were first on the scene. Initially, as they approached, Tim could see nothing out of place, so slowing down, he drove past as he did, Jill spotted the black car they had all been looking for.

'There, at the rear.'

Tim stopped the car, blocking the other vehicle in; they got out cautiously to take a look around. It worked in their favour where Tim had parked; along with the other car, they were below the housing of the lighthouse, so neither could be seen from above. Tim called Ray to let him know the latest and to alert all the others that they could be spotted on the approach. This led to several cars turning into side roads very quickly as they were nearing the lighthouse. Tim and Jill had made their way to the door. Seeing the door swinging and the broken padlock hanging uselessly, Jill went to walk in, 'Hold your horses, Jill.'

'If Maria is in there, we need to get in and help her.'

'Yes, you are right. Think first, what are we going to be faced with as we enter?'

Jill looked bemused as to what Tim was getting at. Tim quietly outlined his thoughts, 'The first thing we will see are stairs; if Jack has gotten here, we have to assume he would take her up as high as he could. This gives him an advantage, agreed?'

'Sorry, Tim, I'm just anxious to get her back.'

'No need to apologise, though try not to be anxious about it; it could lead to you making mistakes. It is easier said than done, so try to stay calm and focused.'

Jill nodded and stepped to one side, which allowed Tim to ease the door open. The building was obviously cared for, as the hinges were smooth and made no noise. Jill could see that Tim had been correct; as soon as the door was open, there was a staircase facing them.

'What do we do now?'

'Slowly, and I mean slowly, we go upwards. If my memory is right, there will be several landings between the stairs on the way. Stop at each one and listen.'

In their favour were the rubber soles of their shoes, which made no noise on the concrete steps. Tim looked to one side as he entered and saw signs of the vision the owner had; there were several pieces of furniture still wrapped up, ready to be used at a later date. He also noticed the layer of dust that suggested slow progress. They made it to the first landing and stopped, hearing nothing untoward as they continued upwards. Soon they reached a second landing, standing still to listen. Suddenly, they heard several sounds at once; first it was the approach of cars, and with no sirens or lights being used, they could only guess at it being back up. Next, they heard a muffled sound of something scraping the floor above, followed by confirmation of what they had feared. It was a voice they took to be Jack Marshall, 'I told you to stay still.'

They had one more staircase to negotiate, and from their viewpoint, they could see above them an open space that would take them into the space where the light would have been located. The main problem now was that as soon as they put their heads through the gap, they would be visible. Tim tapped Jill on the shoulder, mouthing the words, 'Stay here.'

As slowly as he could, he climbed the last few steps, then, without realising it was possible, even slower, he moved so his eyeline was above the floor level. Quickly coming back down, he indicated to Jill to move down a few stairs. Stepping in close, he whispered to her, 'Maria is tied up to the left of the hatch. Jack is stood to the far side of her.'

'Any sign of a weapon at all?'

'No, nothing visible, though a quick glance at his size suggests he doesn't need one.'

'What next?'

'I think you need to go back down; if that were the others arriving, we don't want too many bodies in here; we would just get in each other's way. Tell the D.I. to come up and get the rest by the door and his car.'

'What are you going to do?'

'I'm going to be reckless. Hopefully to flush him out.'

The conversation, which seemed to have taken time, had passed in a moment when Tim left no time for an argument and turned to make his way back up the few remaining stairs. Jill knowing, she needed to act quickly, ran down the stairs, getting to the bottom as Ray was coming in the door.

'Sir, you need to get up there. Tim is going to try and flush Jack out.'

'Okay, bullet points only; tell me the situation.'

'There is not a lot of room; you have 3 flights of stairs that lead to an open hatch.'

Ray made the decision to move towards the stairs, 'Jill, brief Sheila as you did me. Sheila can then make the decisions here on how to react.'

As everyone turned away to start, Ray added over his shoulder, 'Jill, well done.'

Jill couldn't help but smile to herself at this praise, though she quickly reverted to work mode; she gave all the details she had passed to Ray onto Sheila. Sheila took in everything she was told and assessing the situation, organised the teams to be ready. First, she left 4 men outside the door of the lighthouse. She sent 2 to wait by the car that was at the rear; this left 4 of them in the small hallway at the base of the stairs.

Tim, unaware of all the activity going on below him, had made his way back to just below the opening. For a brief moment, he wondered if his next action was the right thing to do. He acted swiftly before he changed his mind, knowing his aim was to rescue Maria. He jumped up through the hatch, knowing where Maria was. He went to his left and put himself between Maria and Jack. Without knowing if they had been heard at all, he was pleased to see surprise on Jack's face.

'Right, come on, Mr Marshall, this is over.'

Glancing quickly at Maria, 'You will be okay, Maria.'

Speaking afterwards, Tim couldn't explain why, except to say it was as if Jack accepted he was beaten, though he was not going to make things easy. In the split seconds of Tim entering, Jack took a step back, then launching himself, he pushed Tim to one side and made for the hatch. Before Tim could react, he could hear footsteps running downwards. He shouted through the gap without knowing who would hear, 'Jack is on his way down.'

Ray heard this as a figure pushed past him on the landing nearest the top, and he turned to give chase. Jill had also heard a shout from Tim and automatically started to run upwards. She met Jack head-on as he came down the 2nd staircase; due to the difference in size, Jack ran through her as if she wasn't there. Jill felt herself falling backwards, then nothing, as her skull smashed against the concrete landing. Tim, who had heard the noises as he was untying Maria, looked at her, 'Stay here.'

He went down to see Ray picking himself up; they both carried on down, then froze as they saw Jill. There were 2 shouts together that mingled as 1, 'We got him, sir.'

'Get an ambulance now!'

Tim knelt by Jill and moved to cradle her head; he could see but couldn't believe the amount of blood that was seeping across the floor. He already knew it was of no use but still said, 'Stay with us, Jill; help is on its way.'

Ray moved forward as Sheila came up the stairs, 'Tim, come on, we need to get you outside.'

Even though he was still holding Jill, all the colour had drained out of Tim. Ray put his hand on Tim's shoulder, 'Sheila, get them to take Marshall out of here and back to the station. Then you need to go up and check on Maria. Stay with her until the ambulance gets here; I do not want her to see this.'

Ray was able to prise Tim away from the body as the ambulance crew arrived. He could feel Tim's whole frame shaking; he knew it was the first time Tim had seen a dead colleague, and he was aware procedure had to be followed. Though he could not keep the sharpness out of his tone in replying to one of the ambulance crew, 'Should we wait for a doctor?'

'No! We know what has happened. Just be respectful.'

He apologised immediately, 'Sorry. We just need her moved.'

For his part, the paramedic knew his role, saying no more as himself and a colleague moved Jill's body onto a waiting stretcher, then into the ambulance. Fortunately, Dan and Dave Hulme had left to transport Jack to the station. As they slowly put Jill into the ambulance, everybody stood and bowed their heads. The real feelings surged to the surface as the ambulance drove away. It was a uniformed officer who spoke for them all, 'You better sort him, sir. Make sure he is locked away for life.'

Ray could fully understand the feelings, though he knew there was still work to do. He needed to assert authority while also being compassionate, 'That will do constable, I understand. We still have a job to do.'

Before any other conversation could start, Sheila came down with a frightened looking Maria clinging to her for support. Ray went over, 'Maria, you are safe now. DS Carr will take you home; we will need a statement from you. The officer can stay with you as long as you need her to.'

'I don't know what to say; where is all the blood from?'

'You do not need to concern yourself about that. I can let you know we are sure we have found the man who killed Sergei.'

Maria managed a weak smile, though she looked relieved at the news.

'Go with DS Carr now and rest as best you can.'

Ray made a call to Lisa at forensics and arranged to wait for her to arrive; then he called Graham. Graham informed him the ambulance had just arrived and he would look after Jill.

'I do not think you will need to do a postmortem. Though I would like to be able to tell her family she did not suffer.'

'I can already answer that for you; looking briefly at the wound on her head, she would have died instantly.'

Finally, Ray rang Angela, 'Sorry to hear the news, Ray.'

'Thank you. I will be there as soon as I can; before I get back, can you possibly have a solicitor arrive? I want Jack Marshall charged with the murder of Jill and the abduction of Maria. I will speak to him about the others later. I have organised for Tim to come back with uniform; he will need someone to keep an eye on him.'

'Don't worry, I will see to it.'

Ray stood by the door of the lighthouse. He could see that everyone left was going about their work methodically. A constable came over.

'We have arranged a recovery vehicle to take the car away for any testing you want, sir.'

Ray nodded, then left them all to get on. He first put some shoe covers on so as not to disturb the crime scene, then went up to see if anything had been left behind by Jack. He stopped as he reached the landing without looking at the blood stain. He stood quietly with his thoughts about the waste of life, and at the same time, he felt immense pride in working with a young officer who gave her best. He turned away and carried on to the top of the lighthouse. He was disappointed that, apart from the remains of the ties Jack had used on Maria, there appeared to be nothing else left to suggest what had occurred over the last few hours. He knew if there was the smallest item left, Lisa would find it. As he turned to go back down, he heard a call from below. He recognised Lisa's voice, 'Ray, are you up there?'

'Yes. I will wait here.'

It explained to him how Tim had caught Jack out, as due to the soles on her shoes, Ray had no idea where Lisa was until she came through the hatch. Lisa looked across at him, 'I heard what happened—terrible news.'

'Yes, it is. Fortunately, we have everyone we think is responsible, I am hopeful that by the end of the day, we should have everybody who has been involved off the streets and where they should be.'

'What are you hoping I might find here?'

'Really just confirmation of the fact who was here. Also, anything that can tell us what happened. I am determined that there will not be any technicalities that any of our suspects can use to their advantage.'

'Right, I'll get on. Will give you a call as soon as I have anything.'

'Thanks; I need to get back and see the team.'

'Ray, I know you will want to get everything cleared up; just make sure everyone, including yourself, are ok.'

Ray acknowledged the concern as he left, saying he had to admit that suddenly his energy levels had fallen, and he walked slowly down the stairs, then out to his car. Despite the need to get back to tidying things up, he made the car journey with very little urgency. As he reached the edge of the town, his phone rang. It was Jenny.

'Ray, I have just heard. Are you okay?'

'Put it this way; I feel better hearing your voice. I am as good as I can be.'

'Will you get things tidied up today?'

'I really do hope so. First, I have to check on the team and pass on my thanks to John for his help on the drug angle. You can also tell him I might be able to push a couple of names his way later.'

'He will appreciate that. I should be able to finish at a reasonable time, so I will be waiting at home for you.'

'That sounds lovely. I will ring you when I am on my way.'

Ray parked his car as close to the entrance at the rear of the police station as he could; he had no desire to listen to or talk to the press, whom he knew would be hanging around. He made his way in and immediately could feel the sombre feeling in the air. As he approached and entered, he had never been in such a quiet CID office. The entire team sat at their desks, though no one was quite sure what to do. Ray moved to the centre of the room, ensuring everyone could see him. He noticed Angela was standing by the door to his office.

'There are no words I can say to make this better; all of us know the risks. We need to remember that Jill, along with the rest of you, did some great work today. I know you may not feel like it; but we need to put this investigation to bed quickly. I want you all to go to the canteen and get a coffee; give yourselves 30 minutes, then gather yourselves together. When I am ready, I will interview Jack Marshall; hopefully, he will see sense and give me some names. Then we can speak to the others and see where we are at. It sounds empty to say, but well done this morning.'

Angela took over, 'I totally agree with everything Inspector Keane has said. I will just add that there will be a time and place for us to remember DC Addy. If any of you at any time need to talk to someone, you must let us know. It does no one any good to bottle things up, and it is not a sign of weakness to talk. Now go and get those coffees.'

As they all left to follow orders, Ray went into his office, pressing the buttons of the coffee machine. He sat in his chair, taking some deep breaths. After a moment, he heard the coffee cup being placed in front of him. When he looked up to see Angela, he found it strange to think she had been in his office more in the short time she had been at the station than Adam had managed in all his years. Normally, he would receive instructions to be in Adam's office.

'I know the next few days and weeks will be difficult. As soon as you feel ready, I will join you so we can make the case against Jack Marshall and subsequently Darren Plant.'

Ray had to admit that this made him feel better. His phone rang; it was the custody sergeant.

'Ray, the solicitor to represent Marshall has just arrived.'

Ray finished his coffee, then said, 'Come on then. Let us sort this.'

The first thing they heard as they entered the custody suite was Darren yelling from his cell.

'Is he still complaining?'

'He has not stopped since we put him in there. I was hopeful he would shout himself hoarse; no luck so far.'

Ray could do nothing to stop the smile on his face, 'Hopefully, within the next hour, I will have some news that should quieten him down. Can we get Jack Marshall out for his interview?'

Ray could not be sure; looking at Jack, it was as if his energy had left him; there was none of the bravado Ray had expected from someone connected to Darren. Jack was still handcuffed as he was led to an interview room. There was a look of shock on the solicitor's face when he saw the handcuffs.

'Can we at least get rid of the cuffs?'

'We will deal with that in a moment. I personally need to make sure everything is done correctly.'

Ray held the door open as Jack was led in; the others followed. Angela inserted the tapes into the machine, and after a moment, when the long beeps finished, Ray took the lead, 'Mr Jack Marshall, you are charged with the murders of Sergei Romanov, Nick Crowe, and DC Jill Addy…'

For a brief second, it looked as though the solicitor was about to interrupt; a look from Ray stopped this from happening, 'You are also charged with supplying illegal drugs. Anything you do say will be taken down and used as evidence against you. Do you understand?'

Jack slowly nodded his head, 'For the benefit of the tape, please answer.'

'Yes.'

'Please sit down, officer; can you remove the handcuffs?'

Jack sat, massaging his wrists from where the cuffs had been. Ray started the proceedings with an introduction of who was in the room, 'Interview with Mr Jack Marshall. Those present are DI Ray Keane and Superintendent Angela Johnson.'

He looked at the solicitor for confirmation, 'I am Sean Taylor solicitor for Mr Marshall.'

Ray noted the name, 'Any relation to Jeremy Taylor?'

'Yes, he is my father; it is a family firm.'

'I suppose it could help us tidy things up quicker.'

'The first issue my client has is that it cannot be the murder of the police officer; it was accidental that he knocked her on the stairs.'

'I would concede that possibly it could be changed to a charge of manslaughter on that one, but before you say anything else, just remember that if your client had not abducted Maria Shon, himself and my officer would not have been at the lighthouse.'

'In the brief time I have had with my client, he is prepared to discuss his situation in relation to information he could supply you with.'

'Let us get it straight, Mr Taylor; I am never interested in doing deals over charges. If your client has something to say, I will listen. I'll leave it to the Crown Prosecution Service to go from there. They will get to hear everything he now tells us; so, what has he got to say?'

Ray soon knew he was listening to a man who, even though he realised the extent of the trouble he was in, would say whatever was needed to ensure he wasn't the only one in court answering the offences. Once Jack started to talk, it was like someone turning on a tap; there were a couple of times Sean went to interrupt. Jack just placed his hand on the man's arm, and he stayed silent. Over the next 45 minutes, Jack explained his business relationship with Darren. This made Ray very content, as he listened to enough information to put Darren in front of a judge. It was as though Jack didn't want to stop. Ray could not know for sure, but he had the feeling that Jack had been cast aside, especially by Darren, so this was his revenge. As he finished up, having given more than enough for all the others to be charged with various forms of drug-dealing activities, he then spoke quietly, taking Ray and Angela by surprise.

'I am sorry about your colleague; it was a genuine accident.'

Ray found it hard to respond, though after a deep breath, he was able to speak, 'Thank you for that, Mr Marshall. You will be held here until tomorrow, when there will be an initial court hearing.'

Angela switched off the tapes as they both left the room, with Ray noticing that Jack was now slumped low in his chair. Outside, Angela spoke, 'Not an easy listen, but very informative. I would say he expected Darren to look after him, then he realised it wouldn't be like that.'

'I am just glad it is over.'

'Are you okay with getting your team working on the other interviews? I will go and talk to Susan, so we can let the press know the latest.'

As Ray went back to the office, even though he felt exhausted, the smile he managed was enough to let the others know it was all over.

'I need some of you to continue interviews; you can tell Ian Jackson and Jerry Reed they are to be charged over several drug offences. Dan, can you visit the farm workers to check on Maria, as well as tell them the news? Meanwhile, I am going to have the pleasure of charging Darren Plant with drug dealing and being an accessory to 2 murders.'

Ray went into his office and saw Dave Hulme sitting at the desk with a coffee in his hand.

'There is one there for you as well, Ray.'

'Thank you for all your help today, Dave.'

'It is fine; it gave the night shift some excitement.'

'One last job if you do not mind before you go home to bed. While I go and break the good news to Darren. Can you ring DS John Maxwell? Jenny works with him.'

He passed a piece of paper over, 'These are some names that Jack gave us; they are drug-dealing friends of Mr Plant. I think John will be pleased.'

Chapter Twenty-Four

2 weeks had passed since the investigation into the murders wrapped up. The work was now in the hands of the C.P.S. who would be trawling through all the evidence and charges to put things in place for court appearances? Ray recently heard that the main charge against Darren Plant was the handling and supply of illegal substances. This was disappointing, as Ray had wanted him tied into the murders, and he was convinced that the instructions had come from him. Unfortunately, the information all the others had been willing to give up stopped short of any of them being willing to name Darren in connection with the murder.

The previous day had been spent talking to the other farm workers; the process had started to allow them to travel home and transport Sergei's body back for burial. He was amazed that despite everything that, had happened to them, they had already spoken to the farmer about returning the following year.

The police station carried on with work as normal, though everything was tinged with sadness over the loss of Jill Addy. It did not feel right at the time for the team to go out and celebrate their success. Ray had acknowledged the feelings, so it was left that they would all know what a good job had been done; they could raise a glass to both the success and the memory of Jill after the funeral. Ray had attended several funerals in his years on the force; this day was the closest he felt to a personal moment after his parents and wife. He had gotten to know Jill a few years previously when she was seconded to help in CID during a case involving children being abducted and killed. He was impressed by her work, as well as admiring how well, she had coped when, alongside him she attended her first postmortem.

He now stood solemnly a few rows back in the church, which was full. The rows of seats in front of him were all Jill's family; the rest of the mourners were friends with many colleagues who had met her through work. The service was in 2 parts, the church was the ceremonial side for her to be given full honours as an emergency worker, and then this was to be followed by a private family service at the crematorium. The service went as well as expected, with several people giving speeches about their memories of Jill. Once it ended, Ray was surprised. As they milled around the churchyard, a man who Ray recognised as Jill's father approached him. The man, whose eyes were red from the tears he had shed, took Ray's hand, and shook it, it said.

'Thank you for all you did during Jill's career. She's always spoken very highly of you.'

'Mr Addy, there are no words I can say that you will not already have heard. Your daughter was a very fine officer, and I, along with my team, will miss her.'

Mr Addy turned away, but not before Ray saw more tears start to fall; he was joined by his wife, who walked with him to an awaiting car. Soon after the cars carrying Jill's coffin and family following pulled away, several members of the public had gathered at the roadside to pay their respects. This gave Ray a good feeling that, despite several pieces of bad press regarding the police, some of which he accepted was deserved. People still gave a level of support; for others, they did not know, but they realised, along with many others, they did a difficult job.

Ray looked at Jenny as she linked her arm through his, and he managed a smile.

'A few of the others have invited me to join you all for a drink to celebrate Jill's life.'

'That is decent of them; you did play a part in helping with the case.'

'Come on, then, let's go and try to relax for a bit.'

'You make the idea of relaxing very appealing.'

As they went to follow the others, Angela fell into step beside them.

'I thought it was a lovely service. I never had much chance to get to know Jill; everyone seemed to have respect for her.'

'It was what she deserved.'

'How is the team doing, in particular, Tim Jarvis?'

'We are all getting there; it will take time. Tim is doing okay; give me a couple of days; I will find him some traffic camera footage to sit in front of; he will be in his element.'

'I do not want to keep you away from others for too long. I just wanted to have a quick word about moving forward.'

Ray found this disconcerting at first, but surely now that he had gotten used to working with Angela, there was not going to be another change.

'You are not going to tell me you have had enough of us already, are you?'

'No, nothing like that. In fact, I have already spoken to those on high to let them know how much I have enjoyed my short time here. I see no reason for that to change. I wanted to discuss concerns your team.'

'Okay, is it good news?'

'Hopefully, you will think so. Sheila has spoken to me, telling me that once all this is settled. She would like to study for her inspector's exams.'

'She will make a fine D.I.'

'I totally agree. Now, if it is okay with you, I have spoken to Jenny's superintendent and he is in agreement with me. I would like Jenny to transfer back to join your team. This will fill the unfortunate gap left by Jill. It would also allow Sheila, who would still be your number 2, time to complete her studies.'

Ray's grin could certainly be described as that of the cat that got the cream.

'You have no problem with us working together?'

'Not at all; as long as nothing affects the work, there is no problem.'

It was Jenny who spoke next.

'Thank you, Superintendent Johnson. It is a good idea.'

'Ray, I will leave it to you to explain how I would like to be addressed. Now I think people will be getting restless for me to buy a round of drinks.'

As they walked across the road to the pub, Ray made some decisions, ready to make an announcement. They were greeted by noisy chatter as they walked in, a sign of the respect they all held for Ray. As soon as he moved to the middle of the tables that had been set out by the landlord, silence fell.

'Thank you; I will not speak for long.'

Tim's response showed how settled he felt.

'That will make a change.'

Ray waited while the laughter subsided, 'I just wanted to say thank you to each and every one of you for the outstanding work you did and also for how well you have all done over the past 2 weeks. Secondly, a piece of good news, Jenny is returning to our team.'

This brought a round of applause.

'Lastly, DS Sheila Carr is going to show you what you could achieve by sitting her Inspectors exam. If the superintendent is happy to clarify things, Sheila can start her studies by taking on the role of acting D.I. while Jenny and I take a holiday.'

Again, after a silence as Ray never mentioned taking holidays in the past, there was another round of applause. This gathering gave Angela a clear idea of what a good station she was in charge of.

The fact, Ray wanted to take a holiday was another side of his relationship with Jenny; work had always been a priority. Though, if he had hindsight, he may have decided it would be better to stay at work.